MW00529614

GEMMA

Also by Lauren A. Forry

Abigale Hall
They Did Bad Things
The Launch Party

GEMMA

A NOVEL

LAUREN A. FORRY

ARCADE
CRIMEWISE

An Arcade CrimeWise Book

First Edition

This is a work of fiction. Names, places, characters, and incidents are either the products of the author's imagination or are used fictitiously.

Arcade Publishing books may be purchased in bulk at special discounts for sales promotion, corporate gifts, fund-raising, or educational purposes. Special editions can also be created to specifications. For details, contact the Special Sales Department, Arcade Publishing, 307 West 36th Street, 11th Floor, New York, NY 10018 or arcade@skyhorsepublishing.com.

Arcade Publishing® and CrimeWise® are registered trademarks of Skyhorse Publishing, Inc.®, a Delaware corporation.

Visit our website at www.arcadepub.com.
Visit the author's site at laurenforryauthor.com.

10 9 8 7 6 5 4 3 2 1

Library of Congress Control Number: 202493776

Cover design by Erin Seaward-Hiatt
Cover photography: © Bruno Guerreiro/Getty Images (silhouette of woman); © Jae Fogel/500px/Getty Images (cityscape); © David Wall/Getty Images (car scene)

ISBN: 978-1-64821-028-0
Ebook ISBN: 978-1-64821-030-3

Printed in the United States of America

For Jannicke—
If you hadn't found the right pasty shop, I don't know if this book would exist. Fingers crossed.

VERSION 1

No, that's not right. It's Sarah who wants to go to the Redner's Quick Stop. She really wanted Cherry Coke and we only have regular. *That's* how it starts.

I'm like, "Seriously? It's midnight."

And she's like, "I'm having a craving, okay? And you're on your third Coke Zero today, so don't judge me."

So I'm like, "Fine, go get a Cherry Coke if it's so important to you."

And that's when she leaves the apartment.

FYI, the whole "having a craving" thing is a lie because even though her doctor said a little caffeine during pregnancy was okay, she's been avoiding it for seven months—or I guess five months, since that's how long she's known she's pregnant—because one of those online mommy-to-be groups was saying how any caffeine at all during pregnancy would give the baby ADHD or Down syndrome or something. I remember the conversation because I had told her that's not how Down syndrome works and if those women thought you could give a baby Down syndrome by drinking Cherry Coke then she probably shouldn't listen to anything they have to say.

So last night when she heads out, she doesn't really have a craving for Cherry Coke. She just wants an excuse to visit the Quick Stop because she has a crush on the guy who works the night shift. I mean, I guess he's sort of okay-looking? Like, he has acne scars but good teeth, and I know he doesn't smoke because Sarah says he complains that the employees who smoke get extra cigarette breaks and she tells him that she totally agrees with how unfair that is, even though, like me, she smoked almost a pack a day until she peed on that stick.

Anyway, she leaves, and of course I'm nervous about her being out that late. The Quick Stop guy isn't a creep or anything, so it's not that, but the walk to and from our apartment? I mean, you know what that's like, right? So even though I'm seriously tired, I wait up and watch TV because I want to make sure she gets home okay. I mean, if your pregnant little sister goes missing or gets hit by a car or something, it's up to you to report it, isn't it? Or if, like, the police need to notify someone, they'll come to you first, won't they, since your parents don't even live in the state anymore?

So she's been gone about fifteen minutes and I'm sitting there, wrapped up in a blanket with my feet on the coffee table watching replays of Castellanos and Turner's home runs from the Phillies game last night—suck it, Braves, they can win the division all they want, but they'll never beat us in the postseason—and anyway I'm humming "Dancing on My Own" and thinking about maybe cleaning up some of the empty Coke bottles lying around because the apartment's starting to smell, when Sarah runs through the door all out of breath, super pale—no Cherry Coke in sight. And before I can ask her what happened, she says, "I saw her."

No, hang on, before I talk about that, what you need to know about Sarah is that she's a scaredy-cat. Thunderstorms, the dark, clowns, porcelain dolls with those eyes that follow you around the room—all of it. She's scared of so many things, I've even come up with this alert-level system to rank how scared she is. A one is your low-level standard barking dog, strange noise, home alone at night-type fears. Five is the highest. These are the code-red situations. A man following her home from work, potential death in the family, ghosts. I'm serious. Ghosts are, like, a huge phobia of hers. Phasmophobia, that's what it's called. I looked it up. I like looking things up, and one of the things I like looking up the most is stuff about the supernatural. Sarah and I are total opposites that way. Ouija boards, haunted houses, horror movies, true-life ghost stories—I love all of it. I even wrote a paper in college about the witch trials in Scotland and all the women who were burned to death. I can't remember what the paper was supposed to be about, but that's what I wrote. Anyway, I'm not saying I believe in any of it. I just find it cool. Interesting. I mean, getting burned alive isn't interesting or cool. Poor choice of words. Fascinating, maybe?

But Sarah's not into that stuff, especially ghosts. I mean, she once locked herself in her bedroom for an hour blaring Taylor Swift on repeat after trying to watch *The Woman in Black* because she thought her crush on Daniel Radcliffe would trump her fear of ghosts. It didn't.

Anyway, she's been like this ever since this one summer we spent at our grandma and grandpa's house—our mom's parents. They live in this old farmhouse in New York state near Binghamton. It's seriously old and seriously run-down. Plus it's in the middle of nowhere, so there's, like, nothing out there except fields and trees and a bunch of rusting pickup trucks that we weren't allowed to go near. No Wi-Fi, the TV reception was awful, and Grandma and Grandpa didn't even have a DVD player. So when we stayed with them, all there was to do was run around with their border collie or play some dusty board games that had been our mom's when she was little. If you couldn't guess, it was really fucking boring. So once, as a joke, I locked Sarah in the cellar.

I wasn't trying to be mean. We'd been playing hide-and-seek a lot, and she'd hid down there tons of times before. So it wasn't like I was trying to terrify her or anything. I just thought it would make her angry. So we started playing and I counted to ten, waited a bit, then crept over and locked the cellar door. I made this big fuss of checking the rest of the house and making a lot of noise so she'd think I couldn't find her. Then I went back to the kitchen and waited.

And waited.

And waited.

It had never taken me that long to find her before, so I figured she would get bored and give up. I waited for her to rattle the door, shout for help, call me names.

Nothing.

I can't remember how much time passed. An hour? Maybe two? I was super bored by then, but I didn't want to give in because I thought, *Okay, she's figured out my plan*, and she didn't want to give me the satisfaction of getting upset.

So more time passed, and Grandma and Grandpa got back from the store or came in from gardening or whatever it was they were doing and told me to get Sarah.

I sighed—very dramatically—then unbolted the door and called down to her. Told her I gave up, she won, it was time for dinner.

Nothing.

I called her some names, told her I wasn't playing anymore. The game was over, yada yada.

Still nothing.

So I stomped down the stairs and switched on the light.

At first I didn't see her.

I thought maybe I'd got it wrong. Maybe she'd been hiding somewhere else in the house after all. And I was about to go back upstairs when I saw something in the far corner. This little splash of pink in all the brown and rust. It was Sarah, huddled in this tiny, tiny ball, knees tucked to her chest, back pressed so hard against the wall, it was like she was trying to sink into it. She was super pale and her body was trembling and her eyes were glued to this empty spot across the cellar.

I swear I said her name fifty times before I could get her to look at me and another fifty before I could get her to move. Once I did finally get her upstairs, Grandma and Grandpa could tell something was wrong and yelled at me for tormenting her, said it was an unkind thing to do, especially after what just happened to our Uncle Mitchell, and sent me to bed without anything to eat. But I wasn't angry about it. I was actually really worried 'cause I'd never ever seen Sarah like that and I didn't know what was wrong. I had no idea what had happened. I just knew it felt like it was my fault.

Sarah and I were sharing a room, and when she came to bed, I apologized like crazy. I told her I never meant to hurt her, I would never hurt her, and whatever happened, I would fix it. I would always fix it. I was her big sister. It was my job to always take care of her.

But she wouldn't talk to me. Not for, like, another week. It wasn't until the night after we came home that she came into my room and told me she'd seen a ghost. But that was all she'd say. I couldn't get her to tell me what it looked like, what it did, how long it was there, anything. And I didn't even realize how big a problem it was until that Halloween when she wet herself after she saw a little girl dressed up as a ghost.

I wanted to check it out for myself. Research, you know. But Grandma and Grandpa never had us over for a summer again, and when we do visit, they've never let us back in the cellar.

To this day, whatever happened down there is, like, only one of two secrets Sarah's ever kept from me.

No, I know this isn't a game. I know she's not playing hide-and-seek or something. I'm not stupid. That's not what I think she's doing. I mean, I don't know what she's doing. All I know is what I already told you: the last time I saw Sarah was at the river. I haven't seen her or heard from her since. That's why I'm here.

No, it wasn't her idea to go there. It was mine, sort of. Well, actually it was our Aunt Joanie's. But it wasn't my idea to leave the apartment. I only agreed to go because I didn't think we'd be gone that long. I thought we'd do a quick circle around the city, not find anything, come home, go to bed.

Yes, the river was supposed to be our last stop.

No, *I* didn't run away. That's wrong. No, what happened was that when we got there, Sarah and Jeremy ran off ahead of me like they were possessed or something. They left *me* behind. Not the other way around.

Yes, I did try looking for them. It was only after I couldn't find them that I left.

Yes, I took Jeremy's car. But I didn't steal it. I took it so I could go get help. I'd lost my phone and I couldn't find either of them, and the car was all I had. What else should I have done?

No, I didn't go home first. I told you I drove straight from the river to Zadie's. And then the two of us went together to look for them and, when we still couldn't find them, that's when we decided we should come here.

No, I have no idea where Sarah could be. I know she's not home 'cause Zadie and I checked. And that was the first time I returned home since Sarah, Jeremy, and I left together late Friday night. Or, I guess it was early this morning by then. Zadie's tried texting and calling Sarah, but Sarah hasn't answered and her phone goes straight to voicemail. If Sarah's tried to text me, I wouldn't know 'cause I don't have my phone, like I said. But if Sarah still has her phone, I don't know why she wouldn't respond to Zadie.

So no, I don't know where Sarah is and I don't know what's happened to her. All I know is that the last time I saw her, it was at the river. And she was with Jeremy. So why don't you find Jeremy and ask him? And once you do, why don't you ask him about the last six months, or the last year? See if he can keep his story straight? Because I bet you he can't. He is such a liar. You can't believe anything he says. So when you do get the chance to ask him about last night, he'll make something up, I know it. He'll say something like, it all started when *he* came over because he always thinks the story begins and ends with him. But last night? He can't know how it all started because he wasn't even there. He didn't show up until *after* Sarah got back from the Quick Stop and told me what she saw.

So, yeah, like I was saying, Sarah bursts through the door and goes, "I saw her."

Now, it's just after midnight and I haven't slept much lately, so my brain is all over the place. Which is why, when Sarah says that, I'm like, "Who?"

It's a stupid question because there's only one person Sarah could be talking about, and Sarah knows it's a stupid question so she doesn't answer. Just stands with her back pressed to the door like some monster is going to bust its way in.

So I say, "What do you mean you saw her?"

It takes her time to answer, and it's the quiet that bothers me most. Sarah's such a chatterbox, it doesn't mean anything good when she goes quiet. Like with the cellar, you know? I'm afraid, when she does answer, she's going to say something, like *downstairs* or *outside the gate*. So I get up and go to the window. I look down at the gate to our building, bracing myself, but there's no one.

Finally, Sarah says, "Near the Quick Stop."

And I say, "What was she doing?"

And Sarah says, "Standing there."

And I'm like, "Standing there?"

And Sarah's like, "Yeah. Facing away from me. Facing the brick wall of the parking garage."

And I say, "Did you see her face?"

And Sarah says, "No."

And I'm like, "So how'd you know it was her?"

And Sarah shouts, "Because she was wearing the same fucking clothes!"

So I close my laptop. Now Sarah can see I'm taking this seriously 'cause I only stop watching Phillies videos if it's something important, but she still won't move away from the door or say more about what she saw. She just keeps looking down the hall toward our bedrooms, like she's suddenly going to see something else. I go back and look out the window again, but nothing's there. Nothing I can see.

So I say, "She's come back. That's all. She's finally back."

Sarah doesn't respond, so I say, "I guess Jeremy wasn't lying. I guess he really did drop her off at the bus station."

Then Sarah starts sobbing.

She's never been much of a crier, but she's cried a lot these past seven months. It's the pregnancy, I guess. It's changed her a lot.

So I go to her and tuck her hair behind her ear and rub her back and I'm about to tell her let's both just go to bed and figure this out in the morning.

But before I can get the words out, she starts saying, "She can't be back. It's impossible. She can't be back. She can't." And she sinks to the floor and tries to tuck her knees to her chest like she did in Grandma and Grandpa's cellar, but she can't because of her belly. So she lets her legs drop and hides her face in her hands instead. All the while, she keeps talking but not making much sense.

"All I did was cross the road," she says. "I crossed the road and I glimpsed this woman, but her back was to me. I looked away and when I looked back she was still there. Just farther away. But I never saw her move. It was like . . . it was like she was a piece on a board game that had been picked up and put somewhere else. So I got closer, and that's when I saw what she was wearing. Jeans and a T-shirt. A T-shirt with tour dates on the back. And I was thinking how I have that same shirt. How I used to have that same shirt. And then I realized . . . And then I saw . . ."

Sarah lowers her hands and says, "It was the same shirt. My shirt. With the bleach stain at the bottom and everything. And when I noticed the bleach stain, I noticed her hand. It was down at her side, and there was blood on it. And on her wrist. And it was dripping onto the sidewalk. Then she raised her hand to the wall and started scratching at the bricks with her fingers. The rest of her body was completely still. But she kept scratching and scratching, like she was trying to dig one of the bricks out of the wall, and she tore off one of her fingernails and it stuck to the brick in blood, but she kept scratching and that was all I could hear. Her scratching. And I ran. But I can still hear it. This *scritch-scritch-scritch*. And it won't stop until she gets a brick out, and once she gets one out, once she has a brick in her hand, she'll . . . she'll . . ."

At this point, Sarah breaks down again, and I cradle her head in my lap while she cries.

I want to tell her she was imagining things. That she didn't see what she thought she saw. That everything is fine. But I don't say any of that because all I can think is, *Fuck, it's not over, is it?*

While Sarah's crying, I look up at the fridge, and stuck on the door is the business card you left us back in May. I'm surprised it's still there. That it hasn't slipped down in the crack between the fridge and the counter, with all the Chinese takeout menus.

But I don't call you then because that's the moment Jeremy decides to show up. And I should've told him to fuck off home and leave us alone but I didn't, and now I'm sitting here in this tiny room picking pieces off a Styrofoam cup, trying to explain the last six hours of my life.

Have I seen who? This girl? No, I don't know her. Who is she? Does she have something to do with Sarah?

No, I honestly don't know who she is.

No, I don't know if Sarah knows her, but I don't know all Sarah's friends.

Gemma?

This isn't Gemma.

Because Gemma didn't have red hair. And this girl looks shorter and her face is a lot rounder. No, this girl looks nothing like Gemma. At least not the Gemma I knew.

Yes, when Sarah said she saw *her* last night, she was talking about Gemma, but she didn't mean whoever this is. She meant *our* Gemma.

"Gemma" is what she told us to call her, but no, I never actually saw anything official with her name on it—no ID, no credit cards. When she showed up that day, she just said, "You can call me Gemma." I guess that's not how people usually introduce themselves, is it? You say, "I'm so-and-so." Then maybe if you have a nickname or something you might add, "But you can call me . . ." Like, I had this friend in college, and she always said, "Hi, I'm Francesca, but you can call me Frankie." But that didn't happen with Gemma. It was more like she wanted to try the name on for size.

Or maybe I'm reading too much into it.

Anyway, she was the last person to stop by the apartment that day, so it was already five, maybe six? I just remember it was the last day of the MLB Winter Meetings in San Diego and the Phillies hadn't signed Trea Turner yet, but I wanted to hear all the updates on MLB Network. They would end up signing him the next day, but I didn't know that then, so I wanted to listen to Harold Reynolds talk about everything that was going on instead of listening to any more idiots talk about why they would be the perfect roommate. Sarah actually likes people, so for her the interviews weren't a big deal. But for an introvert like me? God, it was hell. It didn't help that every single person we'd interviewed was so fucking weird.

Like, there was this one hippie girl who didn't use deodorant and looked like she hadn't brushed her hair this millennium. I actually sprayed some air freshener around after she left. And then there was this other girl who only knew, like, two words in English. And I'm not a racist or anything but how are you supposed to live with someone when you can't even talk to them, you know? At least she didn't smell. Then this guy showed up even though our ad clearly stated "Women only." His name was Taylor so I thought it was a girl, which was why I invited him. It took him, like, twenty minutes to accept that we weren't making any exceptions no matter "what a great guy" he was. Then there was this other girl who wouldn't shut up about cats. I mean, literally every other word out of her mouth was *cat*. *Cat* this and *cat* that and how she used to rescue and foster cats and weren't cats great and didn't we love cats and wouldn't our apartment be perfect for cats and we could install a cat tree there by the window.

And, okay, so I admit this wasn't the most mature thing to do, but I looked her dead in the eye and I barked. I did. No words. Just barking. In her face.

So anyway, by the end of the afternoon my patience was super thin. I was like, "I hate our parents."

And Sarah said, "Maybe we should ask Jeremy if *he* wants to move into the spare room? You know how hard it is for him at the house."

And I said, "God no! He hangs out enough as it is."

Catwoman was the last person we were expecting, so once she left, I changed out of my nice jeans and put on my comfy sweatpants and went to the kitchen to grab my snacks, and I was just pulling a bag of Doritos out of the pantry when there was this knock at the door. I looked at Sarah, but she just shrugged.

So I went to the door to see who it was, and as soon as I opened it, this voice said, "I'm here about the ad."

It was a girl around my or Sarah's age. Hard to pinpoint exactly 'cause she looked young but had dark circles under her eyes and she wasn't wearing any makeup. Her face was longer than this girl's here, though, and more pointed. Pointed chin. Pointed cheekbones. And she had darkish brown hair. Looked like her natural color, or at least I couldn't see any roots, and it was a bit greasy, like she'd gone a few days without washing it. She didn't smell, though, and her clothes were clean—a pair of jeans and this plain dark blue T-shirt. She wasn't wearing a coat, which I thought was weird considering it was December, but temperatures were pretty mild that week, like in the fifties, and some people are always warm anyway. She did have an old Adidas gym bag with her, a massive black-and-white one, the kind big enough to hold a body.

Anyway, she stood there waiting, and I didn't say anything 'cause my first thought was, "You don't have an appointment." But I knew that would've sounded rude and because of the barking incident, I was trying really hard not to be rude to anyone else that day, so instead I stood there like an idiot until Sarah finally said, "Oh! We weren't expecting anyone else."

Which was exactly what I was thinking, but the way Sarah said it, it came out all nice and sweet.

And this girl said, "Sorry I didn't email," and "I can go if you want," and she might've said, "Is the room taken?"

Honestly, I wasn't paying much attention at this point because my stomach was growling and my Doritos were right there on the counter, but if I opened them I would've had to offer some since that would've been the polite thing to do, and I didn't feel like being polite.

But Sarah said, "No, it's all right. Come on in." And she went to shake the girl's hand but the girl didn't offer hers, so Sarah pulled hers back sort of awkwardly, then offered the girl a seat. Sarah and I sat on the sofa and this girl took the armchair, and Sarah introduced the two of us and that was when the girl said, "You can call me Gemma."

I let Sarah take the lead on the questions 'cause I was still afraid I might say something rude. So Sarah asked the usual: "Where are you from? What brings you to Reading? How long are you looking to stay?"

I can't remember exactly what Gemma said. I mean, it's been almost a year—ten months, I guess—since then and I never thought . . . but anyway,

I do remember how she answered the questions. I mean, like, her body language. If you would've been there, you'd probably have a better understanding of what it all meant. You probably would've decided not to have her as a roommate. That's a big part of your job, isn't it? Interviewing people. Understanding them. But me and Sarah, we'd never had to do anything like that before, right? So I just chalked it up to Gemma being nervous around a bunch of strangers.

Anyway, there were, like, two ways she'd answer a question. She'd either look down at her hands like she was holding something that wasn't there, or she'd glance over her shoulder, like she thought someone was standing behind her. There wasn't. That armchair's against the wall. And she never once looked us in the eye. It was the way she spoke, too. Like, sometimes she'd speak really fast, like she couldn't get the words out quick enough, and other times she'd speak so slowly I couldn't tell if she was finished with her answer or not.

We eventually got the basics out of her—she was originally from New Jersey, had spent a few years in New York and Philly, wanted a change of scenery. Said something about working in hospitality and tourism, so I figured she meant she was a waitress or a hotel receptionist, something like that. She didn't know how long she'd be in Reading but could commit to at least six months if we needed her to. And it took maybe fifteen, twenty minutes just to get that out of her, and my stomach was audibly groaning at that point. Sarah even shot me a look, but what was I supposed to do? I just wanted this girl to leave. I wanted to tell her that Sarah and I would talk it over and get back to her tomorrow and then, after I stuffed my face with Doritos, figure out a way to get our parents to change their minds.

Gemma didn't even seem all that interested, like she didn't think this would be a good fit for her, either. But then she asked, "You two are sisters, aren't you?"

And we said yeah.

And she said, "I love sisters."

Then she put the Adidas bag on the coffee table, unzipped it, and pulled out a wad of cash. Wrapped bills—tens, twenties—like you'd see in a movie about a bank robbery. That gym bag was full of them.

And she said, "I can pay you a security deposit plus three months up front in cash."

Sarah and I looked at each other. We didn't even have a conversation about it. I just took the money and said, "Welcome home."

I mean, what would you have done?

Did you see the game on Thursday? My nerves are shot already, and we still have two more rounds. I mean I know we're going to beat the Diamondbacks. But I'm still super nervous about it. Look at how my hands are shaking just thinking about it. Crazy, right? But we're on a mission this year, and we're not stopping until we win the World Series. Texas or Houston—it won't matter who. The Phillies are winning it all. I have good intuition about things like this. But look, if this is going to take a while, could I get a more comfortable chair, please? This plastic's, like, digging into my back. And, sorry, but what's that smell? Did someone microwave fish in the lunchroom or something? I mean, my sense of smell's not as good since I started smoking, but I have cut back since Sarah got pregnant. You know, I don't smoke in the apartment at all anymore? And my plan is to give it up completely once the baby's born. Although, I could use a cigarette right now. It'd probably help me relax. Think more clearly. I mean, I don't know where my sister is or what's happened to her, and that's freaking me out, you know? Like, how can someone just vanish like that? Not that she's vanished. I mean, she must be somewhere. She *is* somewhere. But something must have happened to her, right? Because otherwise she would've been at home or she would've texted Zadie or something. And don't you think it's cold in here? Is there any way to turn the heating up? Maybe it's just me. I've been cold all night. I guess my body still hasn't warmed up. Or maybe I'm getting sick. My mom always gets really cold before she gets sick. Like her body temperature drops for a day or two, and by the third she's huddled in bed with a fever and tissues and Dad's bringing her chicken noodle soup every other hour. Her "scuzzy" days, she calls them. Fitting because she's a pain in the ass when she's sick.

It's sort of funny, but in a way, everything that's happened this past year is all our parents' fault. I mean, I never wanted a roommate. I never even wanted to live with Sarah. Sure, there can be benefits to having a roommate—companionship, split expenses, all that. And getting through COVID on my own would've been hard. I mean I couldn't even see Zadie in person for over a year, especially 'cause she works at a hospital.

But when you live with someone, you're always compromising. You have to. Or you'll end up killing each other. And when you live alone, you don't have to compromise. You want to watch TV, you watch TV. You don't feel like doing the dishes, you spray them with Febreze and let them sit there for a week. You want to leave your snacks out on the coffee table or forget to empty the ashtray—none of it matters because it's not like you're bothering anyone. Which is what I prefer. So I never would have taken a roommate if I didn't have to.

It was a bit of an adjustment when Sarah came to live with me, even though she's my sister. I mean, I'd had the apartment to myself since I left college. But I didn't have a choice. Mom and Dad said she was coming to live with me, so that's what happened. Our parents thought I could be a "stabilizing influence." Right, like a person who dropped out of college over five years ago and hasn't held a steady job since was a stabilizing influence. Don't get me wrong. Back then, I was always employed. I just couldn't find anything I wanted to stick with. A McDonald's here. A retail store there. An office job now and then. Surprised anyone kept hiring me with a resume like that, but I only went for entry-level jobs and told them stories about needing to find myself after leaving college, and they ate that right up. I once told Gemma how I'd pepper my interviews with stories of how I was still searching for something I could dedicate my life to the way I'd dedicated it to field hockey. Used to say I quit playing 'cause of a knee injury. Oh yes, fully recovered. No, doesn't get in the way of working, but I can't play anymore. You know, stuff like that. No one questions an old sports injury.

So getting a job was easy. But I'd put three months into a place, maybe four, and I'd start itching to do something else and feel like people didn't want me there, even if all they ever did was smile at me and ask how my day was. So I'd start coming in late, start slacking off enough that I'd get called into the manager's office once or twice. No real discipline, just a warning, a motivational speech. Soon after that I'd call in sick. Later I'd quit over the phone. Sometimes I'd blame a dead grandmother or something, even though both of mine are still alive. Sometimes I wouldn't give any excuse at all. Gemma told me she was the same way.

But see, at the time Mom and Dad made Sarah move in, I'd been working at the Santander Arena for about six months. I was as surprised as anyone that I still hadn't got the urge to leave. I even started to think I actually *liked* working there. I mean, I didn't do much. Took tickets, helped people find their seats. Sometimes worked the box office. But maybe that was why I liked it. 'Cause management was always changing the schedule and putting us on different duties. And every night was different—different job, different spectators. A few weeks later and it'd be a different show or a different sports team. I just . . . dunno. I really liked it there. And maybe our parents knew I'd found something I liked and thought I could be an example for Sarah.

Or they just didn't want her moving to Florida with them.

Honestly, I don't think they knew what to do with her. Unlike me, Sarah didn't even try to go to college. After high school, she did a year at RACC, then decided she hated community college and school in general. Which I think is so weird 'cause she's really naturally smart whereas I have to work for everything.

Anyway, I told Gemma once that Mom and Dad must've realized they'd fucked us up enough because they decided to run off to Florida as soon as they retired.

"Don't worry," they said. "We'll only be a phone call away." And they said they'd keep paying the rent on the apartment. But the deal was Sarah had to live with me.

The day she moved in was the same day they left.

It was all right at first, them being gone. Sarah and I always got along. And I don't mind looking out for her. I always have. Plus I had my job at the arena and they were starting this management training thing, and my supervisor told me I should try for it. That she'd give me an excellent reference for my application, even. So, things were looking really good, you know? For the first time in a long time.

Then the pandemic happened.

The entire entertainment industry just went dark, like, overnight. Everything was canceled—all the shows, all the games. So, the arena started laying people off. And even though I'd done really good work for those six months, it was still only six months. Last one in, first one out, basically. My supervisor warned me that even when the arena reopened, I shouldn't count on them hiring back all the former staff, and she was right.

I thought I could find something else. But the only jobs were, like, shelf-stockers or cleaning ladies and boring as fuck things like that. And I'd had enough of being on my feet all the time, of cleaning up other people's shit. I wasn't going to do a job like that. But part of the deal with Mom and Dad paying the rent was that I—that both me and Sarah—had to be working. So when enough time had gone by—according to them—and I still didn't have a job, they told us they weren't going to pay the rent anymore. And every time I tried to explain what job hunting was like, they'd shrug me off with "You'll have to figure it out for yourself, like we did."

So, yeah, how's that for parenting? I mean, I shouldn't have been surprised. I told Gemma, once I quit field hockey and college, they never gave a shit about me. Never even cared why I quit. Never even asked.

And they never really cared about Sarah, either. Basically, I was the one that raised her while they ran the business. It was me that kept her going to school. Me that got her to stop working at Garters and Lace.

But Sarah's always been there for me, too. She's never made fun of me for quitting a job or gaining weight or not wanting a boyfriend or girlfriend. She loves me no matter what. And I love her the same. We're all the other has. So I may never have wanted Sarah to move in, but she's honestly not that bad.

Anyway, it had been two years since the pandemic and Mom and Dad were fed up with me, so they said I either had to find a job or find a roommate to help cover expenses. Sarah suggested moving to a smaller place, but I didn't want to move to a smaller place. I like my place. You've been there. It's nice. It's on a quiet street, and it's got those big windows that let in lots of natural light, and the living room is painted that nice pale green color that makes it feel a bit like a forest, especially with all my potted plants. And all three bedrooms are a decent size with soft carpets, and the bathroom has that waterfall showerhead. Plus, it's one of these newer, redeveloped buildings and the neighbors above and below us don't live there full-time, so I don't bother anyone if I play the TV loud. And besides, we shouldn't have had to even think about moving because Mom and Dad had promised to take care of the rent no matter what. I should've known they'd lie about that, too.

I once told Gemma the first thing I did was ask Zadie, but Zadie was living with her boyfriend and wasn't looking for a place. Sarah asked around at work, but nobody there needed a room either. I even asked if that boy she'd started seeing wanted to move in, and she shut that down right away. So that left us with online ads. Complete strangers.

Hence, the interviews.

I always thought that was how Gemma found me. Found us. The ad. I mean, that's what she told us, but now, like everything else she said, I'm not really sure.

So anyway, the morning after the interview, Gemma called Sarah and said she'd show up around noon, so I spent the morning getting a key made and texting Zadie. I invited her over that night to meet Gemma, mainly 'cause I thought the more people that were there, the less awkward it might be and Zadie's really good at making people feel welcome. But she couldn't 'cause she had her shift at the hospital. So it was just going to be me and Sarah and the new girl.

Sarah and I were both feeling nervous. What was she going to be like? Would she play her music loud? Would she have boyfriends over all of the time? Would she show up with, like, three dogs and a gerbil or something? We didn't know. After we saw the money, we didn't ask any more questions. Even if we should have.

Well, noon came and went and Gemma hadn't shown up yet and she hadn't texted or anything, either. Now, if there's one thing Sarah is, it's punctual. She's never late for a shift at work, and if she's meeting her friends, she's always ten minutes early. I'm the friend that'll text you saying I'm five minutes away when I haven't even left home yet. So I was fine with Gemma being late, but Sarah was getting annoyed, and to be honest I was finding it easy to distract myself with all the articles and social media posts about the Phillies signing Trea Turner because the news had broken earlier that day, and I was all like, "Fuck yeah, we're winning the World Series this year, no doubt." (And now we're only eight wins away, so I was right.)

Anyway, then one o'clock came and went. No Gemma. Again, all I thought was she was running late 'cause moving days are always stressful, right? Nothing ever goes as planned. But Sarah was worried. I told her to relax. Then two o'clock passed. Then three. Sarah was pacing, kept asking me to check my phone to see if Gemma had texted or something.

And I was like, "Sarah, calm down. She'll get here when she gets here."

And she was like, "She said she'd be here at noon. It's been hours. Why isn't she here? I've been waiting all day."

And I said, "Sarah, she's a person. Not FedEx. She'll arrive eventually."

Sarah only seemed more put out by that. So I told her to start making dinner, which she did, and that shut her up for a little bit. It's not that I didn't care, but like, Gemma had already given us her money, so if she chose not to show, that was on her, right? We could use the money to cover the next few months and take our time finding someone else.

But Gemma did show.

It wasn't until, like, six o'clock, but she finally turned up, the Adidas bag over her shoulder, a bunch of reusable shopping bags in her hands. And before I could even say hello, Sarah was all over her, like, "Are you okay? Where have you been? You said you'd be here at noon."

And because I know Sarah, I knew that was just her maternal instinct going into overdrive, but I can see how it could come across as rude. Gemma stood there with this really neutral look on her face, and said, "Oh. Did I? I thought I said I'd be here sometime after noon."

That calmed Sarah down, so she said, "Sorry. I could have sworn you said . . . Anyway, I was just worried. I made dinner, though, so as soon as you get settled, we can eat!"

But Gemma said, "No thanks. I'm not hungry. Is there a key for the mailbox?"

We gave her Sarah's key because Sarah always forgets to check the mail anyway. The other year, Zadie and I took a week-long vacation to the Jersey Shore, and when I got back the box was so full the mailman couldn't fit anything else in because Sarah hadn't bothered to open it the entire time I was gone. Anyway, after I gave Gemma the mailbox key, she went to what was now her room and closed the door.

I figured she was acting that way 'cause she was an introvert like me and she must've been nervous, too. After all, she was moving in with two strangers. Two strangers who didn't only know each other well but who were sisters. That had to be awkward for her, right?

So me and Sarah sat down to eat—homemade lasagna and garlic bread—and it smelled really good 'cause, unlike me, Sarah can actually cook. And I was about to take a bite when I smelled something else. And I was like, "Sarah, did you leave the oven on?"

And she was like, "No."

But then she smelled it, too.

"It's not coming from the kitchen," she said, and she was right. It was coming from down the hall, from where the bedrooms are.

We both got up, and I was wondering if Sarah left her hair curler plugged in or something, when Gemma opened her door and walked out waving around a burning torch. Well, not burning. Smoking. Smoldering?

She was staying stuff like, "I am moving into this space. I want to acknowledge those that have come before. I want to state my intention of making my home here. I want to state my intention of making this a safe space."

Saying it over and over again, totally ignoring us as she walked around the living room. She waved this torch thing over the dinner table, and ash fell onto Sarah's lasagna. Once she got to the kitchen, Gemma dropped the stuff in the sink, ran some water over it, and left it there. Then she went back to her room without saying a word to us, and that was the last we saw of her that night. When we cleaned up the sink after dinner, I saved a bit of the burning stuff in a plastic bag so I could figure out what it was later.

Sage, I found out. It's used in cleansing rituals. I thought it was funny, but Sarah took it personally and after that first night never missed the opportunity to snipe about Gemma whenever the two of us were alone. Nothing bad, just little comments here and there. And, like, I get that people change, grow, and mature and all that, but I thought it was really rich of Sarah to say, "I bet she got all that money stripping."

That was maybe a week after Gemma moved in? Sarah and I were home alone. Gemma was out somewhere, and I had gone to the bank to deposit her security deposit and rent. The bank knew us 'cause of Mom and Dad, so they didn't think much about me walking in with all this cash. When I got back, I mentioned that to Sarah, and that's what started the conversation. And when she made the comment about stripping, I remember I actually said, "That's real rich coming from you."

Sarah shot me this look, the one she gets when she doesn't want to talk about something, and I said, "What?"

And she said, "I just think it's weird. She's weird. Carrying around all that money."

I said, "Pop-pop doesn't trust banks, either. He keeps everything in that box under his mattress."

And she said, "Yeah, but Pop-pop's old. That's an old person thing."

And I said, "Well, you didn't think she was too weird to move in. You'd rather we'd gone with Catwoman?"

"Christ no," she said. "It just makes me uncomfortable, that's all. Having all that money around. And you know Jeremy's over all the time, and I think he still owes the Davy boys something and if he knew—"

"He won't. 'Cause I won't tell him and neither will you, right?"

"'Course not," she said. But I could still tell how uncertain she was about the whole thing.

So I said, "Look, she seems normal enough, right? Apart from the sage stuff that first night?" I didn't mention I thought I heard chanting now and then coming from Gemma's room. "At least as normal as anyone else we interviewed. Let's just leave her alone, and if she gets weirder or you start to feel more uncomfortable, we'll tell her she has to go, all right?"

"Promise?" she asked.

And I said, "Promise."

We even pinky-sweared on it.

Maybe that's why Sarah's gone missing. Because I broke my promise.

I don't mean to ramble. It's just, you started asking about Gemma, so I thought you wanted to know. But I mean, I could've sworn I told you all of this before—about how Sarah and I first met her.

I didn't mention the part about the money? I swear I did. Not even when you first came to see us? I guess I don't remember exactly what I said back then. I do remember thinking, *Thank god you're here*, because it meant someone was finally taking Gemma's disappearance seriously. I didn't know that, like, five months would pass and there still wouldn't be any news.

But anyway, when you came by the apartment that afternoon, I could've sworn I told you everything. But no, I guess I am wrong. It must've been after you'd left that Sarah brought up the money.

Yeah, now I remember. She pressed her hand against her stomach. She wasn't even showing or anything yet, but she pressed her hand there and said, "Do you think they'll find her?"

And like I said, I was full of optimism back then, so I was like, "Yeah, of course they'll find her."

And she said, "What about the money?"

And I said, "What do you mean what about the money?"

And she said, "All that money she had when she moved in? It's gone. The bag, too."

And I was like, "I don't know why that matters. She probably just spent it or took it with her or something."

But Sarah still looked unsure, so I stuck your business card to the fridge and said, "You want to call them? There's the number."

And she said, "I just want to make sure we told them everything we could."

And I knew she wasn't really thinking about the money. I knew from her look that she was thinking about the times Gemma and I went out together, the times I came back with dirt on my clothes or my knuckles scraped or . . . But none of that's important. Sarah only mentioned those things to Jeremy in the first place because she got jealous that Gemma and I were hanging out so much, and Jeremy probably mentioned them to you back in May because he knew he was already in trouble for being the last person to see Gemma.

No, that's not true. I didn't say Gemma and I *never* went out together. We did. Just not the night she went missing. And, when she first moved in, it was true that we didn't hang out at all. Things changed. But later. I can actually remember the first time she and I spent more than two minutes in the same room together.

It was maybe two weeks after Gemma moved in? I remember it was around Christmas but before New Year's. Sarah and I had just had this fight, nothing major. Just one of those stupid things sisters fight about. We were already both annoyed because Mom and Dad told us they weren't flying up for Christmas that year and wouldn't pay for us to fly down to see them in Florida. And then I thought she'd used the last of my body wash and she swore she hadn't even though she uses my stuff all the time, and somehow that turned into an argument about her new boyfriend from Walmart and why I hadn't met him yet. Anyway, she left in a huff, and I plopped myself on the sofa to watch *People's Court*. Gemma came in and sat in the armchair, sitting up super straight while I was the opposite—slouched on the sofa, legs sprawled out, crumbs all over my chest.

And she said, "You and Sarah okay?"

And I was like, "Oh yeah. Just a sister thing, you know?"

She looked away and said something like, "Yeah, I know."

So I figured this was an opening, and I remembered the comment she'd made during our interview, so I asked. "Do you have any sisters? Or brothers?"

But just like when I tried to ask her before about her family, she sort of stared at the floor, and then she said, "I wanted to thank you for the clothes. Now I owe you a favor."

I sat up, brushed off the crumbs, and said something like "It's no trouble" or "it's fine." While in my head I was thinking, *Finally, she says thanks* and *why didn't she answer my question?* So I waited for her to say more. She didn't. But she didn't leave either. So I pointed at the TV.

"It's *People's Court*," I said. "You ever watch it?"

She said no. And I was thinking, it's been on, like, thirty years. How can you not have seen it? But I guess some people don't watch TV at certain times of day, so I explained what the current case was—something about landlords and rent—and once I ran out of things to say, I waited for her to get up and leave. To say something like, "Oh, that's fun, well bye," or roll her eyes at me like Sarah always does. But she didn't say anything. I peeked over to see what she was doing, and I saw she was wearing one of my old long-sleeve tees, one from college that I used to wear all the time 'cause it was super comfy, and even though I hadn't worn any of my college stuff since I dropped out, for a moment I wished I had it back and there was this little blip of anger in me.

Then she asked, "Can I watch it with you?"

And that blip went away.

Because no one had ever done that before—asked to watch something with me. Sarah's always telling me to at least put something good on and Zadie's always telling me to turn the TV off and go on a run with her.

So I said, "Yeah, sure."

And for the first time since she moved in, Gemma didn't look like she was going to run off.

After that, watching TV with Gemma became, like, a regular thing.

Instead of hiding in her room when she came back from wherever she went, after she checked the mailbox she'd change into more comfortable clothes, like my Albright sweatpants, and then she'd ask about what I was watching. She didn't seem to know anything about anything. So we'd watch whatever I wanted: *People's Court, Judge Judy, Judge Mathis, Wives with Knives, Homicide Hunter, Evil Lives Here.* Whatever courtroom show or true-crime show was on. Sometimes we'd watch quietly together, me with a Coke and Doritos, her with some water and Cheerios. Other times, she'd ask me questions about the show, and I'd answer. When she started to get more familiar with the shows, we'd sometimes make fun of the people on them. Once I joked about who I could see myself living with and who I'd end up murdering, which turned into a one-sided game of "fuck, marry, or kill." One-sided because Gemma wouldn't play. She just said, "You shouldn't do any of those things" and clammed up. But she still seemed to like watching TV with me. She even bought me a new Roku, too. When I told her she didn't have to, she said, "I'm just repaying you for the clothes. We're even now."

But we never really talked about anything. She never told me where she went during the day or why she went out in the first place. She never talked about any friends or anything from her past. And she never ate dinner with us. Not once. Most days, Sarah would come home tired and sweaty from work, carrying whatever groceries I'd asked her to get. She'd roll her eyes when she saw us sitting on the sofa, but she wouldn't say anything because I'd jump up and take the bags from her without asking and hand over the money for my half of the grocery bill. Then she'd shower and change and be in a better mood while I put something together for dinner. By the time I'd be setting the table, Gemma had already hidden away in her room.

I guess that's one of the reasons why Sarah thought she was weird. 'Cause Sarah only saw the quiet side of her. Sarah doesn't understand shy people. Like, you know what the very first thing she said to Zadie was? Okay, so since my family lived in town and Zadie's lived in New York, sometimes I'd invite Zadie over to have dinner with us on the weekend. That's how Zadie and Sarah first met. So picture this: Zadie's in the family room of our old house, and I go to the kitchen to get us drinks. Sarah wanders in tearing strips of prosciutto ham straight from the package, twirling them on her fingers before eating them, and she plops down next to Zadie and says, "Do you ever worry you'll end up dying alone?" No hello, no introductions. Just an existential question. But that's Sarah. It's off-putting to a lot of people, so with Gemma being so shy, I could see how it made her go quiet whenever Sarah was around. I guess it was sort of like Gemma didn't know how to act around us.

No, I know how I'm making it sound, but Sarah and Gemma didn't have any real issues. Nothing serious. They just didn't get along. And it's probably my fault. It's probably because there was so much about Gemma that I held back from Sarah that I created this distance between them. Not that Sarah didn't try to be nice at first. I mean, she's the one that noticed about the clothes in the first place, and she even tried to get Gemma a job at Walmart.

I remember Sarah and I were in the living room, just hanging out, talking about I don't even know what. Probably the latest email from Mom and Dad.

Gemma came out of her room, and Sarah stopped herself mid-sentence and said, "Oh, Gemma! Do you have your social security number?"

Gemma froze. Stared at Sarah, then looked at me, like she was accusing me of something, like we'd been talking about her behind her back when, honestly, we weren't.

And Gemma said, "Why do you need my social security number?"

And Sarah said, "My Walmart is hiring and I thought I could put in an application for you. Since you're still looking for a job. You don't need much for the form. Just name, address, and SSN. They, like, don't even care if you have any experience or anything. So all I need is your last name and SSN and I could put that in for you tomorrow."

Gemma just stared at her.

"I get a referral bonus," Sarah added. "I'd split it with you."

Gemma kept looking at Sarah like Sarah had insulted her mother. I had no idea what was going to come out of her mouth. And finally she said, "I'd rather you didn't." Then turned and went back to her room without doing whatever it was she had come into the kitchen for.

I said something like, "Don't you dare put my name in. You know I'm not working at Walmart."

And Sarah said, "We're not really even hiring, so forget it. But don't you think that's weird? That she won't tell us her last name?"

I didn't say anything.

But no, I never saw any hostility from Gemma's end. I don't want you to think that, either. Whenever there was an argument between them, it always seemed to start with Sarah. So Jeremy's wrong about that. Gemma never provoked Sarah. Gemma had enough shit to deal with. She didn't care enough about Sarah to hate her, to be honest. And she even gave Sarah a gift card once. I thought it was because of all the times Sarah had offered to cook her dinner and Gemma turned her down. See, the day after Sarah asked Gemma about her SSN, I was on the sofa, playing Minesweeper on my iPad, and Gemma came into the kitchen while Sarah was cooking and handed her this gift card.

Gemma said, "Here."

And Sarah said, "What's this?"

And Gemma said, "A little gift. I heard you really like Giorgio's. That you love to take your boyfriends there."

Giorgio's was this new Italian restaurant near Center Ave. Kind of a hole-in-the-wall, but I've heard the food is good.

Then Gemma said, "Thanks for trying to help me find a job, but I'm good."

And then she went back to her room.

Sarah didn't even say thank you. She looked too shocked, by Gemma's kindness I guess, to say anything.

I thought maybe Sarah would take the three of us out, and I kept waiting for her to bring it up until I found the gift card in the trash. I thought Sarah had used it without telling me. But if she had used it, I don't know why she wouldn't have just thrown it out at the restaurant. Anyway, after the gift card thing, Sarah and Gemma didn't talk too much.

Can I smoke in here? Jesus, never thought I'd be a smoker. I mean, both my parents smoked, and I'd sneak a cigarette here and there when I was a teenager, but I never even bought a pack myself until college. That's when I figured it out, I guess. That I was a smoker. There was this day when there wasn't anyone around that I could borrow a cigarette from, but I really wanted one, so I went down to the Sheetz. Needed to buy my own lighter, too. I was headed back to my dorm when I realized, "Huh, guess I'm a smoker now." But what can you do? Not like my lung capacity matters much. Sounds terrible, right? But I'm not playing field hockey anymore. Don't need to run, so why not? Honestly, if it weren't for the baby, I wouldn't bother trying to quit. Funny how life can turn like that, isn't it?

That was my life for years, you know, field hockey. I started playing when I was about eleven. Continued all the way through high school, then college. Years and years of conditioning and practices and games. I once told Gemma how I spent more of my life on the field than in my house, the sun burning my face, sweat dripping off of everywhere, hair and clothes stuck to my skin. Calluses and blisters on my hands. Bruises all over.

I loved it, though. I really did. Loved every minute of it, even the most miserable ones. There was something about being out there on the fresh-cut grass, the stick in my hands, chasing the ball down with my teammates on either side of me, taking a shot and sailing that ball past the goalkeeper. Whenever I was playing field hockey, my brain didn't have to think as much. And it kept me in shape, too, all that running. I could eat as many doughnuts as I wanted for breakfast, lots of Subway for lunch, as much pasta as I could handle for dinner, and it wouldn't matter. I'd run it all off during the day, work it off in the weight room. Sometimes I'd go to bed hungry even though I'd already consumed something like five thousand calories. The coaches, especially Barton—the assistant coach—would make us keep track.

I still count calories even though I don't play anymore. Force of habit, I guess. Hard to shake some things, you know? Sad thing is I can still eat five thousand calories a day if I want. Well, maybe not quite, but a lot. But I'm lucky if I do a thousand steps a day, let alone ten thousand. And I don't run at all anymore. I'm done with all of that. I told Gemma, once I dropped out of college, I put all that away. I suppose it's because I didn't want to think about any of it anymore. And the running was all tied up with it. I could've tried a different kind of exercise, like swimming or CrossFit or something. Cycling maybe? But, too late now, isn't it? Only twenty-six, and I can barely walk the five floors up to our apartment without running out of breath, which is why I almost always take the elevator.

I know I don't look so bad, especially sitting down and wearing a sweatshirt. I don't gain weight around my face, which is nice. Seem to store it all around my hips and ass. So you might think I look fine, but if you would've seen me in college? I mean, like, my first day? God, I was hot. I've gone up, like, three sizes so far. I lost a little over the last year but not much. Not really.

I kept my clothes from back then, though, as like, motivation. Some of my favorites. It's only been a few years. I mean, I could fit back into them if I really tried, but, you know. Who actually does that? Gets in shape enough to wear their old clothes? I guess it's nostalgia, why I held onto them. I told Gemma, my parents always say to us, "You know what's wrong with you girls? You're both stricken with nostalgia." Stricken. Like being nostalgic is some sort of cancer. Not even sure they know what the word means. Just heard it on TV and decided it sounded nice, probably. Yeah, Mom and Dad, we didn't want you moving to Florida and leaving us on our own because we're "nostalgic."

Anyway, to answer your question, those are the clothes I was just talking about—why Gemma was wearing my Albright stuff and my other clothes all the time. Most of my old clothes fit her so I gave them to her because she didn't have much to wear.

I honestly didn't think about it too much back then—why she had so few things with her when she moved in. I mean, not everyone's a pack rat like me and Sarah, so if all she had was that gym bag and a few reusable bags, how was that any of my business?

It was Sarah who noticed that Gemma was wearing the same clothes day in, day out. Yeah, I was the one who was home all the time, but Sarah's the one who's always been into clothes and jewelry and stuff. The typical girly girl. She'll do laundry almost every other day to make sure she has her complete wardrobe at the ready, whereas you can only get me to use the washing machine when I've run out of my favorite T-shirts. And even then, I might put it off for a few days, re-wear the same clothes. So I didn't really catch on to the fact that Gemma only had like, one pair of jeans and maybe—*maybe*—three T-shirts. But Sarah did.

When Sarah brought it up, I said, "Who cares? It's none of our business what she wears."

But Sarah was like, "Just ask her if she needs anything. You've got boxes and boxes of extra clothes"—she was exaggerating when she said boxes and boxes—"and she likes you better, so it'll be better if you ask."

I could've left it, but when Sarah gets an idea in her head, she won't let it go. She would've asked me day after day after day if I'd talked to Gemma about the clothes, and I didn't feel like putting up with all her mother hen-ing. So one day when Sarah was at work and it was just me and Gemma at the apartment, I asked her.

I said, "Do you need clothes?"

Flat out, just like that. Not very tactful, I know, but anyone will tell you I'm not really known for my tact.

Gemma was in the kitchen, pouring herself a big bowl of Cheerios, and she didn't say anything, and I was thinking I've gone and fucked this up—and I don't even know what *this* is—and it was all Sarah's fault. But then Gemma put down the Cheerios box and smiled. Sort of. She didn't smile much, and even this wasn't a full-on smile. More like a little twitch, but definitely in the category of a smile, I guess?

And she said, "Thought it would take you longer to notice."

She could've been mad, saying that, but she wasn't. I could tell she was joking, but I still felt myself going red.

I said, "Sarah noticed. I don't give a shit what you wear." But then I thought that sounded like I didn't care at all if she was struggling or something and we were all living together, so I didn't want to sound that mean. So I added, "I mean, some people are, like, minimalists. Like that Japanese woman, what's her name?"

Her name's Marie Kondo, and I knew that 'cause I'd just binged all the episodes of her show, but I didn't feel like admitting that.

And Gemma said, "Marie Kondo?"

And I was like, "Yeah, that's her."

And she said, "I'm not like Marie Kondo."

Then I felt bad because I may have been through some stuff, but at least I owned more than three T-shirts. And here was this girl who literally had, like, nothing but what she had on, who only ate Cheerios and whispered weird things to herself in her room at night, and what could've happened in your life to make you like that?

Yeah, I did wonder then why she didn't buy some new clothes if she had all that money. But I didn't ask. Like I said, it wasn't my business.

So I brushed the Doritos crumbs off my shirt and dragged my fat ass off the sofa and said, "Well, I've got some extra clothes, if you want. Stuff I don't wear anymore 'cause . . ." And then I told her about field hockey and how I used to be thinner. Then I almost told her why I dropped out of college. I don't know why. There was just something about her, standing there in the only shirt and jeans she owned with nothing to eat but Cheerios that made me think she'd understand.

But I didn't tell her. I just said, "They're nice clothes. Clean, too. I don't wear them anymore and Sarah's after me to do something with them so they stop taking up space, so if you want to have a look through . . ." And I shrugged, like it was no skin off my back.

And Gemma said, "That'd be really nice."

So, after she finished her cereal, I got one of the boxes from my room and brought it to her so she could sort through it. She was skinnier than even old-me was. I had a lot of muscle then, but Gemma just looked malnourished. So the shirts were a little baggy on her, but not too bad.

While she was changing, I went back to my room to grab another box, and I took this concert T-shirt off the floor of Sarah's room because I figured she should contribute something, too, since it was her idea, and she never really wore that shirt anymore, either. It was only on the floor because she'd yanked it out of her dresser while she was looking for something else. And as I walked this stuff back to Gemma's room, I saw Gemma peel off a shirt she was trying on. Her back was to me, and she wasn't wearing a bra. But I only want to point that out 'cause that's the reason it was so easy to see the scars that were all down her back.

I never asked her about them. Who would do that? Sarah, maybe, if the two of them had been closer. Sarah has that way about her, where she can ask really personal questions without coming across as overreaching. That's definitely not me. It's better if I just keep my mouth shut. I figured if Gemma ever wanted to talk to me about them, she would. She didn't. Of all the things she did end up telling me, that wasn't one of them.

So every time I think about Gemma and what happened, I think about those scars. I don't know if it excuses her, but I think it explains her a bit. Scars can do that, don't you think? Explain our past. Like, this scar on my knee, or this one here on my chin, or this burn on my wrist—each one of these has a story, you know? If people could read our scars like you can read a book, I think there'd be a lot more understanding in the world.

Or maybe I'm just talking shit because I've been up for, god, what time is it? Five in the morning? Six? Shit. That means I've been awake for almost a whole day.

No, Gemma and I never got close. That's not what I said. I said we got closer. Went out a few times. Mainly because I was helping her with some things.

No, some things related to something that happened before she moved to Reading.

And I only helped her because I was trying to protect myself. And Sarah.

Okay, look. That story Sarah told me about seeing Gemma scratch the bricks until her hands went bloody? That's not why Sarah was scared when she thought she saw Gemma last night. To explain that, I have to start at the beginning of when things started getting really, well, fucking weird.

It was a month after Gemma had moved in. Almost a month. I remember because it was right after New Year's and Zadie had invited me to spend it with her and her boyfriend, but I didn't want to be a third wheel so I stayed home and ate crescent roll-wrapped brie. It's a Pillsbury recipe. I ate the whole thing even though it's supposed to be for a group.

Anyway, it wasn't New Year's Day because it was a day we got mail, so it wasn't the holiday. But it was soon after New Year's Day. We'd already forgotten about the sage burning thing and had sort of settled into a new routine with Gemma, though neither me or Sarah was really comfortable with her living there yet.

I remember Gemma had been a bit edgy that day after she'd checked the mailbox. She'd come back home in this huff I'd started to recognize, and I said something like, "Do you want me to help you track it down?"

And she was like, "Track down what?"

And I said, "Whatever it is you're looking for."

And she said, "I told you to stay out of my business."

She went to her room and shut the door, and I thought maybe this was one of those nights where she wouldn't come back out. But, a few hours later, after *Hot Bench* ended, she did. We started watching *Paternity Court*, but not for long because it was so boring and I put on a murder show instead. You know, those true-crime documentaries about a murder? Usually a woman's. Usually in a small town. People talking about how they never thought it would happen here and saying how the person who died, oh they were the most wonderful person in the world, weren't they? Just one time I'd like to hear someone say about the victim, "Oh, they were a complete asshole." Anyway, I watch these true-crime documentaries on *Investigation Discovery* all the time during the baseball offseason, so I didn't think anything of it when I changed the channel. I didn't realize I'd never watched one with Gemma before.

Anyway, I had this murder show on and I'd finished my soda, so I went to the fridge for another. And I heard this crash.

I spun around, expecting to see that the TV had fallen off the wall—I never thought I mounted it properly—but it wasn't the TV. It was the pot that was on the stand next to the TV. Except it wasn't on the stand anymore. It was in pieces on the floor—the Japanese peace lily Zadie bought me as a housewarming gift way back when—lying in its own dirt. I couldn't figure out what happened until I saw the remote on the floor next to the shattered pot. Gemma was breathing heavy and her face was red, and I was about to offer her a glass of water when someone said, "What the hell?"

Sarah was standing in the doorway in her work uniform holding our groceries. I didn't even hear her unlock the door. She was staring at Gemma like Gemma was nuts. And, to be honest, it was a crazy reaction to I don't even know what. Before I could calm everyone down, Gemma ran to her room and slammed the door. I wondered if I should check on her, but you don't slam a door like that when you want someone to come after you. So instead, I picked up the remote and started cleaning up the pot shards and dirt.

Meanwhile, Sarah set the shopping on the counter and said, "What on earth was that about?"

And I was like, "I don't know. We were watching TV and she just . . . freaked out."

We were both being quiet even though Gemma couldn't hear us from her room. Sarah eyed Gemma's door but didn't say anything else, even though I could tell she wanted to. When she's holding something back, she chews her lip, like this. And that's what she was doing. And instead of putting the groceries away like she normally did, she left them sitting all over the counter and said, "I'm getting a shower. Figure something out for dinner."

She seemed more upset about the plant than I was, and it was *my* plant. Or maybe something else was bothering her. I don't know.

Anyway, as soon as I finished cleaning up, I turned the TV back on but the show was over by then. All I could remember was that a woman or her son—and her son?—disappeared or were murdered or something. The same thing all of those shows are about.

That night, though, Gemma's voice in her room was louder than before, and I didn't know who she was talking to but I finally caught a few words:

Give it back.

The next day is when I checked the mailbox and found . . .

But that's not really important. What you want to know is about last night, right?

Okay, so last night—Sarah's just told me this story about seeing Gemma near the Quick Stop, right? And before I even have time to process that, Jeremy comes bursting through our front door, sweating like a pig.

So when you find him, if he tells you I asked him to come over, he's lying. I never even had the chance to call him because I was too busy listening to Sarah's story when *BAM!* The door bangs open and he's standing in the doorway of our apartment with this look in his eye that makes me think he's been huffing computer duster. Before I can ask him to close the door, he says, "Where have you two been all night?"

I see Sarah looking at me from the corner of my eye, wanting to know what I'm thinking. She wants to know if she should tell Jeremy what she saw or not. But I keep my eyes locked on him.

He asks again, "Where have you been all night?"

And I say, "Right here. Does it look like we've been anywhere?"

And he looks at Sarah and says, "Then why does she have her coat on?"

So I say, "Because it's cold. And we're trying to save on electric."

Our parents used to say that to us all the time, so it was the first thing that popped into my head, even though it's stupid. So I ask him, "Could you please close the door?"

He hesitates. Not long. Just, like, a split second, and it's enough to tell me he doesn't want to, but I don't know why. I don't know why he'd want to leave the door open, and I don't know what he's afraid will happen if he closes it. But like I said, it's only for a split second. And maybe it's nothing at all. Maybe I'm imagining things. Anyway, he closes the door and the room is pretty warm, so Jeremy knows what I said about the electric is shit, but he doesn't press us on it. In fact, he doesn't say anything. After his grand entrance, he stands there like he forgot why he came over.

So I say, "Why are you here?"

And he says, "Why are you up so late?"

And I say, "I asked first."

Which, yeah, I know is childish, but Jeremy's basically got the IQ of a six-year-old so it works, and he says, "I needed to ask you guys something."

And I say, "Ask us why we're up?"

And there is a lot of sarcasm there, but it's like he doesn't hear it. He just says, "Have you seen her?"

My blood goes cold. 'Cause that's twice in one night she's come up in conversation. Twice after weeks of not mentioning her at all.

I don't give him a direct answer. I mean, I haven't seen her, but I don't want Sarah telling him what she saw. Not yet.

So I say, "Why? Have you?"

And he doesn't answer right away. Just looks down the hall to her room. The room that was hers. And then he sort of nods, sort of shrugs. I'm not sure which.

"Where?" I say. "When?"

I don't want him to say anything. I want him to change the topic. Make up another reason for being here.

But he says, "Tonight. On the corner."

"What corner?"

"The one in front of Redner's," he says.

He means a different Redner's. Not the little Redner's Quick Stop near our building, where Sarah's crush works. This is the regular Redner's in the shopping center with the Applebee's.

I say, "Jeremy, that's good. That means she's back. You can tell the police."

Those are my exact words. I swear to god. I tell them both that we should come here—to the police station—and they should tell you they saw Gemma.

But Jeremy keeps talking like he never heard me. Instead he says, "I tried to follow her. But she kept moving away. I tried to get her to turn around, but she wouldn't. I couldn't see her face. No matter what I did. I couldn't see her face. She didn't have a face."

Sarah starts shaking then. Like you would've thought she was having a seizure, the tremors are that bad. And she's super pale. So any thought I had about this being some sort of practical joke goes right out of my head. Because this fear on Sarah's face, it's one hundred percent real. A Level Six fear. I've never seen Sarah hit a Level Six. I only ever had five levels.

So that's when I know I can't let this go on. Whatever is happening, I have to stop it because it's hurting Sarah. Sarah is . . . She's too kind. Open-hearted. Fragile, Mom used to say. And I can't say I'm the most maternal person, but I protect my family. I protect my sister.

So finally I stand up and I'm like, "That's it."

And Jeremy says, "That's what?"

Because, like I said, he's an idiot. So I say, "We're gonna find that stupid bitch."

Actually, I don't say bitch. But I say something like, "I'm so sick of her playing games with us. We're going to find her."

'Cause first she goes missing for five months, right? And after everything we did together, after everything she made me do for her, and now she's trying to scare my little sister half to death? Nuh-uh. No way. If she's out there, we're going to find her. That's all I want to do. Find Gemma and tell her to stop.

So I get my coat and Sarah puts on a scarf and a hat.

And all I'm thinking is, *God, Gemma, what are you up to now? Can't this be over?*

If I'd known everything that was going to happen after that? No. Of course I wouldn't have said we should go. I would've kept my fat ass on that sofa until I fell asleep watching *Simpsons* reruns. But I didn't know. Maybe Jeremy knew, maybe Sarah. But not me.

All right, so I guess I was wrong. It was my idea to go out. But I never planned on going to the river.

No, I don't have a picture of Gemma. I didn't have one to give you for the missing person report, and I don't magically have one now. So I can't prove what she looked like. But I'm telling you, this girl here isn't her.

No, I don't think there's anything else about Gemma that I forgot to tell you.

I mean, there wasn't much else to know about her, period. I googled her once, but it was hard to find anything because she hadn't told us her last name. I tried "Gemma New York" and "Gemma New Jersey" and "Gemma Philadelphia," even "Gemma lottery winner." Nothing. I scoured Facebook, too, but do you know how many Gemmas from New Jersey there are on Facebook? Everything I tried came up with thousands of results. I had all these tabs open. Page 502 of this search. Page 712 of that one. Honestly, if you looked at my laptop, you'd think I was some kind of stalker. I didn't know the surname Horne. Why would I? So I couldn't search for a Gemma Horne. Check my laptop. You took it, didn't you? Well, if you're able to piece the fucking thing back together, you won't find any searches for a Gemma Horne.

No, I wasn't actually stalking her. Don't say it like that. It wasn't like that.

I was just curious.

See, all Gemma did each day was—number one—check the mailbox and—number two—leave the apartment at random times. Like, I'd be on my laptop or watching TV or whatever and suddenly the front door would open and shut and Gemma would be gone. Sometimes she'd be away for only, like, half an hour. Sometimes she wouldn't be back until dinner. She never said hello or goodbye, but sometimes she'd rush back in like she was being chased or something. I never saw her with a phone, but at night, through the wall, I could hear her talking to someone, so I figured she must have one. At least, that's what I thought at the time.

I mean, we hung out when we watched TV, but that was it. Most of the time, it was like she didn't even want us to see her because she'd do things like only come out to the kitchen if Sarah and I weren't there. Like, as soon as we'd go to bed, or if say Sarah was out and I was getting a shower, as soon as I'd turn on the water, I'd hear her door open and listen to her go to the kitchen. She'd be back in her room by the time I opened the door. And I only ever saw her eat Cheerios, so it's not like she spent a lot of time prepping meals. Once in a while, I'd catch her staring out the living room window like she was watching for someone. Then she'd notice I was there and hurry back to her room, muttering things like "Not enough time."

Honestly, it was like living with a fucking ghost. Hearing noises but not seeing the person making them. Stuff moved around from the last place you left it. It was, like, this dark presence had formed inside our own home. No wonder Sarah didn't like her.

No, I don't know why Sarah didn't mention any of this to you when you interviewed us in May. Maybe she didn't notice. She was always at work or with her boyfriend a lot. I was the one who was at home the most. I really was looking for work, but none of the jobs I came across seemed like the right fit. And then my ex-manager from the Santander started emailing, saying we needed to meet . . . but I don't want to get into all of that.

I said don't I want to talk about it.

But anyway, when Sarah and I would talk about how weird Gemma was, Sarah became convinced Gemma wasn't a stripper but a prostitute. I mean, it did make sense—the weird hours, all the cash. But it turns out Gemma really didn't have a phone. Remember, you asked us that back in May. You said you were trying to find ways to track her down and you asked me about her cell phone, and I told you she didn't have one. No phone. No tablet. No laptop. And you never found one, did you? Well, if there's anything I've learned from watching documentaries on *Investigation Discovery*, it's that prostitutes always have a phone.

So, like, there I was at home, nothing to do, and Gemma was interesting and I was thinking, *There's a story here, and I'm going to find out what it is.* I mean, no one just walks around with a bag of cash, right? Who would do that? Where did it come from? What's her story?

It didn't have anything to do with the money. We didn't need the money. I told you, I was just curious. And I didn't stalk her. I was investigating. But I'm not really that good at investigating. I'd never make a good detective. Like, I didn't want to keep any notes about anything I found out because that would've been really creepy, especially if Gemma found them or something. I mean, who keeps notes on their roommate? So I was keeping everything I knew about her in my head, and even though it wasn't much, I couldn't piece any of it together because everything I found out led nowhere.

No, it was only *after* I tried looking around on the internet that I went in her room. And I didn't make a habit of it. Jeremy lied about that. When did he tell you that?

No, look, I know it was wrong, okay, but after about a week or so, I decided why not have a quick peek while she was out? Like, what the fuck does she do in there all day? Plus, I was like, this is my apartment, that used to be my spare room. Why shouldn't I be allowed to go in? I'd never been a landlord or a subletter before or whatever. I didn't think about it being illegal. And it's not like I was going to take anything. So this one afternoon, as soon as Gemma left the apartment, I knew I'd have at least half an hour before she got back, and I figured it wouldn't take me more than fifteen minutes.

No, I wasn't looking for the money. All I wanted was to find something I could research later, like a last name, a bus ticket, anything. So, after she left, I waited five minutes, then I went down the hall to her room.

It's funny, but when I got to her door, I had the strange feeling it was gonna be locked. Which was stupid because none of our bedroom doors have locks. I turned the knob and of course the door opened.

It was a pretty bright afternoon, so I didn't have to turn on a light, and the first thing I noticed was how orderly the room was. I mean, for years it had been a junk room—suitcases, boxes, a bicycle of Jeremy's that I made him take back, spare furniture. I'm used to it looking like a storage unit. So the order—even though it was me and Sarah who cleaned it up in the first place—was still kind of a shock.

The bed was very neatly made, and the doors to the closet were shut. Same with the dresser. No ends of shirtsleeves or anything sticking out. The top of the dresser was also clear except for three red candles and the spare mirror Sarah had put there. But the mirror was covered with a black cloth. Otherwise, the place looked more like a hotel room that had just been cleaned instead of a room someone had been living in.

There weren't any decorations or anything, either. No pictures or posters. None of the little knickknacks people take with them from place to place. Everything was just so plain and neat, and I knew if I touched a single thing she would know. So I was like, *well shit, how is this supposed to help?*

But yeah, I went in anyway.

Back in the living room, the TV was yammering away while I searched. I didn't want to open the dresser drawers or go into the closet—that seemed too personal—so I looked on the bedside table and found a book there—*Llewellyn's Complete Book of Names*. And it had this really long subtitle I can't remember, but it was something like *For Pagans and Witches and Mages Who Are Curious About Names*. Then I got on my hands and knees and looked under the bed. First thing I saw was the Adidas bag. It was a bit dirtier than I remembered. I pulled it out to look for some sort of name tag or something, but there wasn't anything. So I put it back. I never unzipped it. I told you, I didn't care about the money. Next to it were a couple of the shopping bags she brought with her. They were empty now, folded up.

I slid them out from under the bed anyway, not expecting to find anything, but on the inside edge of both of them, someone had written a name—a last name—in faded permanent marker.

Baker.

That's it.

No, not Horne. Baker. How would I get those two confused?

No first name or even first initial. I checked the other bags and found the same name in the same handwriting. Blocky capital letters with this little swirl on the *K*. Later, while I was eating my ramen noodles, I did google "Gemma Baker," but nothing came up.

Anyway, since I'd found what I came for, I decided it was time to go, and I was folding up the bags so I could put them back, when this shadow came over me. At first I thought it was a cloud passing by. Then a voice said, "What're you doing?"

I turned around and there was Jeremy, standing there with this smirk on his face, like he'd caught me robbing a bank or something.

"Let yourself in, why don't you?" I said, then I finished folding up the bags and put them back where I found them.

He said, "It's why I have a key."

And I said, "You have a key in case of an emergency."

I had to shove past him to get out of the room.

He asked again, "So what were you doing?"

And I was like, "Looking for something I thought I left in there."

"I thought you and Sarah cleaned that room out," he said.

I reached around him to close the door, and he flinched when I slammed it shut.

"I thought I did," I said.

He said, "You know, you really can't go into someone's room without permission when they're paying you rent."

And I said, "Well, how about going into someone's apartment without permission?"

Then the front door opened. Gemma came in, and she saw us standing there in the hall in front of her bedroom door. The door was closed, but still. It seemed pretty obvious that we'd been talking about her. But she didn't say anything.

So I said, "Jeremy was looking for his tire pump. For his bike. He thought he left it in there. I told him we got rid of all his junk."

Jeremy didn't even try to call me out. He just stood there with that stupid grin on his face and said, "Hi, Gemma."

I could tell Gemma was trying to figure out if I was telling the truth or not. Then she shrugged and said, "I haven't noticed a tire pump, but I can check."

And Jeremy said "Thanks," like Gemma was doing him this huge favor. I just rolled my eyes.

We moved out of the hallway to give her more space, and I went to the kitchen 'cause it was lunch and I was hungry. Jeremy followed me, and I said—well, more like whispered—"I don't care why you're really here. As soon as she says there's no tire pump, you're leaving."

"But I just—" he started.

And I jabbed my finger into his chest, like this, and I said, "You're leaving. And don't come here again until you're invited."

I had just finished saying that when Gemma came out of her room and said, "I didn't see it. Sorry."

And I looked at Jeremy and said, "See? Told you. I don't know what you did with it. Just go buy yourself a new one."

And Jeremy, he was staring at Gemma, he said, "Yeah. Guess I better." Then he said his goodbyes and left.

Then it was me in the kitchen and Gemma standing there in the living room, and the quiet was really awkward, and I could tell she didn't believe my story but she went along with it anyway instead of calling me out, so as I was getting my ramen ready, I said, "I'm sorry about him. I honestly don't know what goes on in his head. I'm going to talk to Sarah about taking away his spare key. He can't just turn up any time he wants. I'm glad I was home. I mean, I know I'm pretty much always home, but —"

And Gemma said, "You don't have to do that for me."

And I said, "No, of course I do. You have a right to your privacy. You shouldn't have to worry about that idiot turning up whenever he feels like it."

She knew I'd gone in there. Of course she knew. But she didn't say anything, not at first.

And then she said, "It's best if you leave me alone and pretend I'm not here. Can you do that?"

I didn't really know how to answer that, so I just nodded.

And then she said, "Good. So here's what's going to happen. You don't ask me any questions. You don't google me. You don't go through my mail. I keep paying my rent. Soon I'll leave and, when I do, you can forget all about me."

She didn't wait for any response. Just turned on her heel and marched back to her room and shut the door.

I went back to my ramen and let out this big breath. I mean, I felt like I got away with something even though I hadn't done anything wrong. I looked up to see if her door was closed, and that was when I noticed the smudged white line that ran across the floor. Salt—a line of it in front of her door, now scuffed up by my and Jeremy's shoes.

I didn't tell Sarah what happened. I figured it was better not to because she'd flip out at me for going into Gemma's room and making things worse between all of us. So I decided I'd keep my mouth shut and bear the brunt of whatever increased weirdness we were going to get from Gemma. I mentally prepared myself for how shit things were going to be, and for a few days they were. Gemma would do her leave-and-come-back-at-random routine. I wouldn't say more than "Hi," and at night Sarah and I would pretend she wasn't there.

My theory—back then anyway—was that Gemma was looking for someone. I caught her coming out of the library on Fifth Street once and she didn't have any books, and the only other reason people go in the library is to use the free internet. As far as I knew, she didn't have her own computer. Plus, she always seemed to be looking over shoulder. And when she came home once with some shopping, I saw a map of Reading in her bag.

No, I said I wasn't stalking her. It was just coincidence I saw her that day.

I told you Jeremy's a liar. When did he tell you this? Back in May? I bet it was another of his "Gemma saids." *Gemma said you were stalking her. Gemma said you and Sarah could never leave her alone. Gemma said . . .*

Yeah, he came out with a whole load of that bullshit after Gemma disappeared. Like Gemma was his long-lost love or something, even though they barely spent five minutes alone together at a time. *He's* the one that was always asking me and Sarah about her. Always trying to come over and hang out when she was around. And it sure as fuck wasn't because of "true love." It's because Sarah must've told him about the money even though she said she wouldn't. I certainly didn't tell him. But there was a time when we had actually been seeing less of him finally and then, after he met Gemma, suddenly he was back at our apartment all the time. That's not a coincidence.

Yeah, he was just as interested in that money as anyone else. No, I never saw him go into her room when I was home, but I wasn't home all the time, and he had his own key.

So no. Despite what Jeremy might've told you, I wasn't Gemma's stalker. I only followed her the *one* time. And no, my reasons for following her had nothing to do with the money. I told you the money didn't matter to me.

I was curious because there was never any rhyme or reason to when Gemma went out, but I figured there had to be a pattern. Plus I was bored and needed something to do. So I started keeping track of the time she'd leave and the time she got back. Just, like, in the Notes app on my phone. But I never figured anything out. The times seemed so random—when she left, how long she was gone, when she returned. Though, to be honest, I've never been good with puzzles, so maybe there was a pattern but I couldn't see it.

No, I don't have those notes anymore. I never said I didn't take some notes. I said I didn't *keep* any notes. I deleted them because they were pointless.

Anyway, this one day I was on the sofa watching *Paternity Court* and trying to figure out how to respond to that email from my ex-manager at the Santander—yes, *that* email—when Gemma came out of her room and walked out the front door without a word, and suddenly I was up and putting on my sneakers, and I realized I was going to follow her. I didn't plan it. It just happened.

Now our elevator is slow despite it being a new building, so I jogged down the stairs and when I got to the bottom, I saw her outside, on the street, turning right. I waited a second, and then I followed.

'Cause it was a weekday afternoon and the weather was decent, it was fairly busy, and I could blend in easily, or I thought I could. Gemma was wearing this old green T-shirt of mine, and that's what I kept my eye on. She never once turned around, but she kept taking quick turns, picking up her pace, like she thought someone was following her. But I managed to stay with her for, like, ten minutes. And I thought, we have to be getting close. Wherever she's headed, it's not to a bus stop, so it has to be in walking distance.

Then I lost her.

Just like that.

She made a quick left turn and so did I, and the street she turned onto hardly had any people on it, but she was gone. I didn't see her anywhere. I took my time, sort of strolling along, pretending to be window-shopping, but I never caught sight of her again. And then I came to a stop 'cause I realized that where I was standing was where Uncle Mitchell's store used to be. How's that for coincidence, right? Gemma didn't know Reading at all, she said, and yet somehow, by following her, I ended up at that exact spot.

I asked her about it later. I mean, I didn't tell her I'd been following her. Even after she started watching TV with me, I knew she still didn't want me involved in her business and I certainly wasn't going to tell her I'd followed her. I just brought it up in regular conversation that night.

Before that, after I lost sight of her, I went straight back to the apartment so that I was already home by the time she got back. She rushed in and closed the door quickly, and I pretended not to notice when she looked through the spyhole. Then she went in her room, came out a few minutes later, and settled into the armchair, and we started watching reruns of *People's Court*. I'd made sure to put on something really boring. Then, casually, I asked, "So you finding your way around Reading okay?"

And she said, "Yeah, it's fine."

"'Cause I could show you a few places if you wanted," I said. "My family's lived here since, like, the city was founded."

And she said, "Is that so?"

But not in an interested way. Like, you could tell she didn't actually want to know anything about my family and she'd just said that for something to say. But I pretended to be stupid and kept talking anyway. I'm good at that.

"Oh yeah," I said. "All my ancestors came over here before the US was even a country. German farmers. Pennsylvania Dutch or something. And they all married other German farmers and never really went anywhere. My great-grandma apparently still spoke German until World War II because she didn't want to be seen as a Nazi sympathizer. Or spoke PA Dutch. I'm not sure what the difference is, honestly."

And she nodded, so I knew she heard me, but she wasn't contributing anything to the conversation. So I just kept going.

"But yeah," I said. "We've been here a long time. I've got family all over the city. And some businesses, too. My Uncle Mitchell used to own a store on North Fourth Street, not too far from the big bus station. And a few blocks from GoggleWorks—that arts center place? Have you been there yet? Some of the stuff is weird, but I bought some really cool ceramic mugs there. And they have a life drawing class I was thinking of taking."

She kept watching TV, but she asked, "Your Uncle Mitchell, that's your cousin Jeremy's dad, right?"

The first time I had warned Gemma about Jeremy was shortly after Gemma had moved in. She'd come home and tossed all of the mail on the counter with this moody sigh.

And I'd said, "Our cousin Jeremy came over again. I know he was looking to meet you. If you see him . . . I don't recommend encouraging him. Not that you are. I just mean . . . yeah, he's family, but he's not a part of the family you want to get close to."

I was afraid she'd get angry with me or something, but she'd just looked at the pile of mail and said, "Families can be a fucking mess."

And so, this time, while we were sitting there, I thought, well, maybe I could get her to talk about her family if I told her about mine. That's usually how it works, right?

So I told her that yeah, Uncle Mitchell was my dad's brother. And I told her how people who met them both thought mine and Jeremy's dads were only half-brothers 'cause they were so different, but nope. Full-blooded. Nana and Pop-pop, you can tell when they talk about Uncle Mitchell—how they shake their heads—that they wish he was from someone else, but he's not. Once, when they didn't realize I was listening, they said Uncle Mitchell, God rest his soul, was the worst parts of both of them put together. Not that my dad is the best parts, but I never had to visit him in jail, you know? And my house never got visits at one or two or three a.m. asking to speak to my dad. Except the night of Uncle Mitchell's accident, that is.

I didn't need to tell Gemma all that, but I wanted her to understand where Jeremy comes from. What he's like. That I don't really blame him for the way he is. But that lying runs in his branch of the family tree. I did tell her that it must've been hard growing up with a dad like Uncle Mitchell and how that was why, when we were kids, Pop-pop insisted that Jeremy spend as much time with us as possible. We only lived a few miles apart, so I suppose it's not strange that Jeremy would be over a lot. Being an only child, he didn't have anyone to play with, not regularly. And even when he was little, his mom knew better than to let him play with the kids in their neighborhood. Although if she had that much sense, you'd think she'd never have ended up with Uncle Mitchell in the first place.

I told Gemma that it didn't bother me that Jeremy would come over. It was just we never got any warning. Pop-pop would show up unannounced on our doorstep, Jeremy's shoulder in that gnarled grip of his, and practically shove the poor kid through the front door. Then we'd have to change our plans 'cause now we had to look after him. Mom took it all in stride. I mean, she barely paid attention to me and Sarah, so what was one more? Besides, I think she felt bad for Aunt Mel, Jeremy's mom. Mom and Aunt Mel were never friends, but they got along okay. Mom's never said a bad word about her, at least not that I've heard. And Aunt Mel always seemed to have a harder time than Mom, even though she only had one kid and Mom had two.

Gemma asked me then why Jeremy and I weren't closer since we're the same age and both like sports, but I told her it was Sarah he took to. I guess I could be too bossy, and Sarah, well, Sarah's always been a people pleaser, and the mothering type. Like, when we were little, Jeremy would hang out with her and do whatever she asked. Unlike me, Sarah always asked, never ordered. Can I have that doll, Jeremy? Do you want to go on the swings, Jeremy? Should we sneak some Oreos from the kitchen, Jeremy? And he'd listen and let her talk while I was off doing whatever the hell I did at that age.

And I told her that it wasn't until we got older that he really started to—I don't know how to put this—be weird? Like more of his dad was coming out in him as he aged. I really started noticing it when Dad's business took off. Uncle Mitchell had died by then so at least he wasn't coming over and asking for money all the time. But we went from Jeremy visiting a few times a week to him spending whole weeks with us. Whole summers. Mom and Dad even made sure he had his own room when they bought the new house in Reinholds, even though his official address was always Aunt Mel's. That's when I really started to dread seeing him—when we moved into the new house, the big house—because I knew something of mine was going to get "lost."

I want to make this clear, and I told Gemma this, too—I never actually saw him take anything. But around the time he was thirteen, maybe fourteen, things started going missing. Small things at first, like a pair of Mom's cheaper earrings, books here and there, spare change from the jar. Things you might think you'd misplaced. And he still does it. My wallet went missing one day, with my driver's license and everything. Another time it was the backup hard drive I bought for my computer, and then a necklace of Sarah's she got from her last boyfriend.

No, I've never mentioned any of it to Jeremy because I've learned not to. Back when it first started, if you brought stuff like that up around him—not even ask him if he did it, just mention it casually in conversation, like, "Oh I can't find where I put that book. I only had a chapter left"— he'd get this look in his eye and he wouldn't say anything back. Just sort of shrugged, like this.

Some people are all like, "Oh, I'm so close with my cousins. They're like my siblings." And I'm instantly like, "No." No matter how much the rest of the family tries to pretend he is, he's not my brother. He's a cousin. Jeremy and I might see each other almost every day, but he is not my brother and we're not close. He is Uncle Mitchell's boy through and through, and I want nothing to do with him.

Yeah, I told Gemma all of that.

But what I didn't tell her is that I would've put more distance between us if it weren't for Sarah. I don't know. Maybe she ended up with a few of those bad genes Nana and Pop-pop passed on to Uncle Mitchell, but she started looking up to Jeremy like he really was her big brother. That's why she always believed him when he'd say her stuff was only missing, not stolen. Then she started skipping school around fourteen, like him. Going to more and more parties like him. Mom and Dad should've done something. She was their responsibility, not mine. But they were wrapped up in the business, planning for early retirement. Besides, I had field hockey after school. I couldn't babysit her, and it wasn't my job anyway. So I guess she latched onto Jeremy, at least for a few years, until what happened at Garters and Lace. Then she mostly sorted herself out. Started looking at Jeremy a bit more warily, the way she should've all along.

But anyway, when I finished talking, I waited and I thought, *Here we go, Gemma's got to give me something now. It's the normal thing to do.*

And she shifted toward me a bit, like she was building up the courage. I waited and kept my mouth shut, because talking too much can ruin a moment like that, and finally she turned all the way toward me, and she said, "I have no reason to go to the bus station."

Then she turned back to the TV.

And that was it.

Now that I'm thinking about it, that makes what Jeremy said about the night Gemma went missing even weirder. Because he told you he took her to the bus station, right? Because that's what he told me and Sarah.

I remember it was the morning after that night and he came over to our place unannounced—just like last night. And just like last night, I could tell something was off. He looked really pale, and he was shivering except it wasn't cold. That was the weekend we had that heat wave, and it got up to like ninety degrees later that day.

Sarah was still asleep, so I was the only one up, eating Pringles and watching *Dr. Pimple Popper* because the Phillies had lost embarrassingly to the Cubbies ten to one the night before so there weren't any highlights to rewatch. Then the peace and quiet of a lazy Saturday morning was broken when he burst in, pale and shivering, like I said.

I rolled my eyes and said something like, "Morning, Jeremy."

He grunted, which was a usual response from him. But instead of going into the kitchen to look in our fridge for something to drink, like he usually does, he just stood in the entranceway, hands in his pockets. Sort of shifting from side to side, like this. Like he was waiting for me to say something. And then he said, "Sarah up?"

And I said no. And he asked me where I was last night, and I said here, in the apartment.

"Didn't feel like going out?" he asked.

And I said, "When do I ever feel like going out?" And tried to go back to watching the show. But he kept talking.

"Were you up when she came home? Have you talked to her?"

And I was like, "No, I wasn't going to wait up."

And he said, "So you haven't seen her?"

And I said, "No, I haven't seen Sarah."

And then he said, "What about Gemma?"

And before I could answer, Sarah opened her door. It was clear she had just woken up 'cause she was still in her pj's and was rubbing the sleep from her eyes. And the two of them just looked at each other for a second.

And then Jeremy said "Hey," and Sarah said "Hey" back, and then neither of them said anything else for so long that I thought, *What is it? Did you two have an argument or something?* Then Jeremy said, "I'm going to see if Gemma's up," and he marched down to her room and knocked on the door.

That was when we realized she wasn't in, and I asked Sarah, "She didn't come home with you?"

But Jeremy was the one who answered. He said that he'd stayed out with Gemma after Sarah had wanted to head home for the night. And that was the first time I learned that Jeremy had met up with the two of them that night. Then he said Gemma had wanted him to drive her to the bus station—yeah, the big Barta Transportation Center one—but she hadn't said why, and once they got there, he was going to wait, but she told him not to worry about it and she'd walk home herself. Which, yeah, sounded a little weird at the time, but I didn't press him because we weren't too worried then. We figured she'd turn up later.

When she didn't, we called the next day to report her missing, like you know.

But it wasn't until a week or so after she disappeared that I made Jeremy give me more details. He didn't want to at first. Said he didn't know any more than what he'd already told us, but I literally slammed my fist on the table—we were at the Tavern and it was loud anyway, so it didn't really have the effect I wanted—and I said, "Jeremy, there has to be something else."

And he was like, "Look, I told you. After Sarah decided to go home, Gemma and I stayed out for a while. When she was ready to head home, I offered to drive her and she said she wanted to go to the bus station first."

I asked him what her exact words were and he was like, "I don't remember her exact fucking words."

So then I asked him, "Well, why did she want to go to bus station?"

And he said, "I don't know. She didn't tell me."

I looked at Sarah and asked if Gemma had mentioned anything to her about going to the bus station, and Sarah shook her head no and said, "Whatever Jeremy said."

And I was thinking she'd probably been too drunk to remember—that night they went out, I don't think Sarah knew she was pregnant yet—and

I was like, "There wouldn't have been any buses for hours. So why did she want to go there?"

And Jeremy was like, "How should I fucking know?"

Then Aunt Joanie shot him a look from the bar, I figured because Jeremy's voice had got too loud and she doesn't like that kind of language.

So he lowered his voice and said, "She asked me to take her there, and I did. And when we got there, I asked her how long she'd be and she said not to worry about it. I could leave and she'd make her own way home."

And he'd watched her walk into the station and he'd waited five minutes anyway, and when she didn't come back, he took her at her word and he left. He said he was sort of drunk himself and shouldn't have been driving anyway, so he was more focused on getting home without getting arrested and it wasn't until he woke up hungover the next morning that he felt worried about what he'd done, which is why he'd come over to check on her.

And I was like, "Jeremy, do you know how stupid that all sounds?"

And he was like, "Of course I know it sounds stupid. That's why I don't want to tell it to the police. But you know what Gemma was like." And then he asked, "Have either of you gone in her room yet? Have the police searched it?"

I looked him dead in the eye and I said, "The money isn't there, Jeremy. That money wasn't meant for you."

That finally shut him up, at least for a little while.

When he gets here, make sure to ask him about Gemma's money.

The mailbox? Oh, I'd forgotten about the mailbox thing. But it wasn't . . . yes, it was weird, but it really doesn't have anything to do with Sarah. But if you want to know . . .

Okay, so I didn't realize until then that I hadn't actually checked the mailbox myself since Gemma moved in. I mean, I wasn't going out much and Gemma was. So it seemed normal that when she came home, she'd check the box and bring the mail up with her. It didn't occur to me that she was deliberately getting to the box before me.

But that day, Zadie had wanted to meet me for breakfast because she had the week after New Year's off since she'd had to work the week of Christmas. I tried to get her to push it to brunch or lunch, maybe even dinner, but she insisted that it had to be breakfast. She point-blank told me she wanted me out of the apartment before eleven. For as long as she'd known me, I'd always been a morning person, and she didn't like it that nowadays I wasn't normally up and dressed before noon.

"You have to move on," she'd say. "We have to move on."

So I agreed to breakfast but only because it was Zadie. We met around nine in the morning, and I was back at the apartment around twelve thirty and by then I was exhausted. From a lot of things. From Zadie haranguing me about either getting a new job or going back to college. From my ex-Santander manager emailing me that the deadline was next week and how she was going to call the police, and now I was getting emails from my ex-supervisor from Staples, too, where I'd worked before going to the Santander. All I really wanted to do was to curl up on the sofa and watch some *Judge Judy* reruns or something.

I shuffled into our building trying to get Zadie's voice out of my head, and I figured I'd check the mail since I was right there, and I pulled out a stack of letters and this small package. I got excited because Mom and Dad sent me and Sarah stuff from Disney World every now and then, you know, out of guilt, and they hadn't sent us anything—not even a post-card—in a while. Not even anything for Christmas. But the package was for Gemma. No return address. And it only had her first name on it, which was weird, like she was Zendaya or something.

As I waited in the elevator, counting the floors till ours, I noticed my fingers were damp. I thought it was sweat 'cause at Zadie's insistence, I had walked home to get some fresh air and exercise since it was sunny and, like, almost sixty degrees. But when the elevator stopped at our floor and the doors opened, I looked down at my fingers, and they were red. Like, you know, blood. Gemma's package was leaking.

The elevators doors started to close, and I put out my hand to stop them. As I walked to our apartment, I kept staring at my fingers. I had a spare tissue in my pocket, so I wiped my fingers on that before I got my keys out and let myself in.

But it couldn't be blood, I was telling myself. That would be ridiculous. So I placed all of the mail, including the package, on the counter, and I sniffed my fingers. It was kind of a metallic smell. I figured it was probably pens that broke during shipping or something, even though it didn't smell like pen ink.

I washed my hands, and I was getting a paper towel so I could wipe the package off when Gemma came in through the front door, out of breath.

And she said, "Did you get the mail?"

Her voice was sharper than I'd ever heard it and, before I could answer, she spotted the package and went straight for it.

"Why did you check the mailbox?" She said it like I'd committed some sort of offense. And her reaction was so ridiculous, I almost laughed, but she looked really serious.

So I said, "Because it's my apartment."

And I was already annoyed after breakfast with Zadie, so to rub it in I added, "Your package finally came. Whatever you ordered broke."

And she looked at me confused, so I said, "It's leaking."

That was when she noticed the damp corner and dropped the package on the counter. At that point, I wasn't annoyed with her anymore. I was worried 'cause I'd never seen her like this before. I mean, not since she threw the remote at the TV. I asked her if everything was all right, but she didn't say anything. She didn't even move.

And I was like, "Gemma? Are you okay?"

But she ran to her room and slammed the door shut.

I probably should've gone on with the rest of my day like normal. I shouldn't have pried. But I'd spent weeks trying to find out something—anything—about her and got nothing. And here was my chance. So I opened the package.

I don't have it anymore. Not any of the packaging, either. We got rid of it in a dumpster behind a McDonald's so it's long gone now. Gemma never threw anything out at the apartment in case it could be traced back to her. She would always take her trash someplace else.

But I remember the package was wrapped in brown paper, and all that was written on it was Gemma's first name—no last name, like I said—and our address. Normal handwriting. Different from the handwriting on the bags under her bed. Looked like black Sharpie. And the box was a plain brown cardboard box. It didn't have any writing on it or anything, and the one edge was sealed with plain packing tape. You work at Staples, even for a little, you get to know your office and packing supplies. I slit the tape open with some scissors and lifted the lid.

The first thing I saw was a disposable ice pack. The kind companies use when they ship food, but it wasn't very cold anymore. I lifted it out, and underneath was a lump covered in brown packing paper. The corner of the paper was red and damp. I don't remember if I hesitated before I lifted it out or if I just took it right out of the box. But I do remember that when I removed it and saw what was inside, I carried the box down to Gemma's room and knocked on her door.

I thought she'd be angry at me for opening her package. I mean, that's totally illegal. She opened the door and saw me standing there with the open box, but she didn't shout at me or anything, so I came right out and asked her.

I said, "Gemma, why did someone mail you a dead rat?"

I'm not sure why I didn't freak out. Why I was able to be so calm when I first saw that rat even with how bloody it was. I guess I was sort of on autopilot. A friend was having a crisis, so I did what I had to do. Not that Gemma was a friend then. Not quite. She wasn't a friend until later, until she wasn't.

Right then, though, what I thought was (a) *Hey, at least someone's life is more fucked up than mine*, and (b) *She'll move out*. I mean, she had to. Who gets something like that mailed to them and stays put? I sure as hell wouldn't. And it wasn't like she enjoyed living with us anyway. She always seemed to be on edge, even when we were just watching TV. And ever since I'd snuck into her room that first time, she kept watching me. I mean, I don't think she actually was spying on me, but it felt that way. I often got this feeling when I was out running errands or even just hanging around the apartment that someone was watching me.

It was a few days after the package arrived that she finally decided to talk about it. Like I said, I assumed she was going to say she was leaving.

Sarah was at work. I was on the sofa, and Gemma sat down in the armchair, wearing one of my old Albright hoodies. While I waited for her to say something, in my head I started preparing my response: *I understand. Best of luck. See you around*, etc.

But what she did was ask, "Have you ever done anything you regret?"

I looked at the Albright logo on the hoodie. I thought of the burn mark on my wrist. And then I looked Gemma in the eye.

"No," I said.

She smiled and said, "Me, neither."

And that's when she told me where the money came from.

You're the one that wanted to know. I told you it has nothing to do with this other girl you keep showing me. This Gemma Horne. I don't know who that girl is, I've already told you. How many times do I have to say it? If her name is Gemma, then it must be a coincidence because this person you're calling Gemma Horne is not our Gemma.

Look, if you think there's some connection between this girl's disappearance and our Gemma's, or this girl and Sarah, why don't you just come out and tell me?

Have you found anything on Sarah yet? Have you even checked?

You checked the river?

Was Jeremy there?

What do you mean he's *here*?

VERSION 2

I have dreams about dead rats. I dream that Pop-pop has all of these fuzzy brown bodies piled on the table and he's skinning them and talking about the new subs he's putting on the menu, and little Jeremy is handing him the rats one by one except it isn't little Jeremy. It's Gemma, and when I realize it's Gemma, I realize it isn't Pop-pop doing the skinning, it's me. And my hands are covered in blood, and Zadie comes into the kitchen and starts yelling at me, asking me what am I doing? What am I doing with Gemma? And I look back into the sink and it's not a rat I'm skinning, it's . . . and then I wake up and I check my hands but there isn't any blood. It's been almost a year, and I'm still having these dreams.

That's why I didn't tell Sarah about any of this—the rat or what Gemma told me after. Because if Sarah didn't know anything, she wouldn't have to be scared. I could be scared for the both us. I'm the one who can handle being scared.

No, I'm not nervous Jeremy's here. What makes you say that? I don't care. He should be here. It's just that I really want to find Sarah, and I don't see how sitting here talking to you is helping. I know, I mean I think, someone was following me last night. And if someone was following me, they were probably following Sarah, too. How long ago did he get here?

No, I didn't see anyone, but ever since I left the river, ever since I drove away, it feels like someone's been following me. Like they're just outside these walls, waiting for me, and . . .

Forget it.

I don't know what I'm saying. I'm just being paranoid.

It's nothing. I'm just saying, if anything's happened to Sarah, I wouldn't be able to live with myself. And if you're telling me the truth—that Jeremy is across the hall saying Sarah's not missing—that means he knows where she is. What other option is there? Like, she wouldn't have run away or anything. There's no reason for her to do that.

So I'm telling you, whatever you think happened, Jeremy's behind it. I know he is. Everything you say he's telling you about how I've been treating Sarah and the tracking app and the stalking and all that is just him trying to distract you.

No, I don't have anything else to say about the river because I don't know what happened at the river once I left. If Jeremy told you any different, he's lying. The two of them ran off and left me alone, so I went back to the car and I drove off. That's it.

If Jeremy's saying he heard me drive off really fast, I don't know, maybe I did. But the only reason I went fast is because I thought I saw . . .

Look, I didn't bring it up before because it sounds stupid. It really is stupid, sitting here, dry and warm, under a bright fluorescent light that's giving me a headache, in a building filled with police officers, to think what I saw was real. It makes me want to laugh. Like how a dream terrifies you in the middle of the night and there—in the darkness, right after you wake up—you think you'll never sleep again. But somehow you do. And when you wake up the next morning, and you see your bedroom in the daylight, you feel ashamed of how scared you were.

See, before I tell you, you've got to remember what it was like last night.

By the time we leave the Tavern, we've already been out looking for Gemma for, like, hours and we haven't seen anything. I'm tired and cold and annoyed, and I just want to go home at this point. I mean, it would've been nice if we'd actually found Gemma. Found out this had all been one big stupid joke. But even as we're driving, I know we aren't going to find her. Not if she doesn't want to be found.

But Sarah and Jeremy insist we check the river before we call it a night. I don't have much of a choice but to go with them. When we get there, they start having this argument in the car. I don't remember what it's about. Something like how to go about searching the river or if they even should. They're completely ignoring me. It's like I don't exist. I'm sitting in the back, resting my head against the window and looking out in the dark while they bicker, and I start thinking about all the trips Gemma and I took in Jeremy's car, the conversations we had, the way she looked at me toward the end, and it's like I start hearing Gemma's voice in my head and it feels like I'm being pressed in by all this heat and noise, so I get out. I don't say a word. I just open the door and leave them to argue.

I'm standing outside the car, hands in my pockets, shuffling back and forth in the cold, when Jeremy and Sarah finally get out of the car. That's when I notice Sarah's lip is bleeding. I thought it was because her lips were chapped from the cold. Honestly, I don't know how it happened. But no. Despite what Jeremy's telling you, I never hit my sister.

Anyway, both of them are just standing around like they're waiting for me to say something, so I tell them, "Let's just walk down to the riverbank, see if there's any sign of her, and if there's not, we go home."

Jeremy and Sarah don't say anything. They just share this look. It's, like, the billionth time they've shared that look tonight. But they don't argue with me.

No, there is no argument.

There is no fight. Not between the three of us. The two of them were arguing. I wasn't a part of it.

We agree to walk down to the embankment together, explore a stretch of the river, then head back to the car.

I start walking before I get the flashlight on my phone turned on because I'm stupid, so I trip on my way down. That's how I got this cut on my chin. That's also how I lose sight of them. Because by the time I get to my feet and dust off my knees, Sarah and Jeremy are gone.

There's nothing around me but darkness. The only warmth is the blood on my chin, and there's this smell of rot drifting off the water. Like a deer or something has died nearby. But I don't hear a thing other than the sound of the river and some cars on the highway in the distance. No voices, no footsteps.

I call out their names a few times, but there's no answer. And I'm like, how could they vanish like that?

That's how I know they must have run away. 'Cause that's the only way they could've moved so fast. Even with her belly, Sarah can still move pretty well. So no, I didn't actually see them run away, but it's the only explanation, right?

And while I'm standing there in the dark, trying to listen for them, I think back to some of the other things they've said tonight, and I start thinking maybe they're hiding from me on purpose. That maybe they were planning on leaving me here. Or something. Maybe that was what they were arguing about in the car. And then I really don't like that I can't see them or hear them . . .

But the cold and the dark and the quiet—they do funny things to your mind. And it's not like I've been sleeping great lately, either. All I know for certain is that I'm alone. But I've lost my phone. I don't remember exactly when it happened, but I don't have it at that moment, so I can't text them. And I can't use it as a flashlight. The only light is what's coming from Jeremy's headlights. He left the car running, which is weird. He's usually big on saving gas. So that makes me think maybe they are back up at the car. Maybe they're about to drive off. And I look back up at the car and in the lights . . . in the lights I see . . .

I told you it sounds stupid, but okay.

I think I see Gemma standing in the beam of the headlights.

About as far from the car as I am from that wall. Her back to me. Just like Sarah said.

I know it's not real. It's not. Because by the time I run up to the car, there's no one there.

But that's why I don't hang around longer to look for Sarah and Jeremy. Like, Sarah's story had been bad enough, but *seeing* Gemma myself?

All the things Gemma had told me about the money—her ex, the threats, the curses—it all comes flooding back.

So yeah, I guess I freak out a bit. I jump behind the wheel, drive off, and leave the two—or maybe three—of them behind. And I go to Zadie's instead of coming here.

But what does that matter? I came here in the end, didn't I?

I'm telling you right now, Jeremy doesn't know shit about Gemma's ex, so you can ignore whatever he's saying about him in that other room. And I know he doesn't know shit because he mentioned a few things to me before Gemma went missing that told me he didn't know shit. Like, I know he thinks Gemma's ex started out like this knight in shining armor that saved her from a bad situation. That his family took her in, pretended they cared about her. And then he started cutting her off from the few friends she had. That little by little, he made her completely dependent on him. That the rest of the family treated her like a pet—a pet they began to ignore and abuse. He thinks that when she finally escaped, her ex came looking for her. That she needed protection. That he was the only one who could save her.

Jeremy called me a stalker? Please. He was the one that was fucking obsessed.

He's told you I tried to set him up with Gemma, hasn't he? That was his story to me, too. That Gemma was texting him, saying how I said the two of them had a lot in common and she should get to know him.

Uhm, seriously? She didn't even have a *phone*, Jeremy. How was she texting you?

He always thinks I've tried to set him up with my friends when really it's the complete opposite. Look, he's not good at dating. He just isn't. I mean, it would be hard anyway with his acne and everything, but it's not like he has the world's most sparkling personality, either. Like, he might brag about girls like any other guy, but he isn't any Don Juan. Believe me. You could probably count on one hand the number of girls he's actually kissed, let alone slept with. God, you want to laugh? Check out his Tinder profile, if he hasn't already deleted it. I showed it to Gemma once. It's, like, every cliché mentioned in those "creepy men on Tinder" Buzzfeed articles. Honestly, if I didn't know him and just saw his online profile, I'd deactivate my account. I mean, I don't have an account, but hypothetically speaking. So yeah, he might brag about his "hookups," but I don't think he's ever met up with anyone from that app.

Yes, I did talk to Gemma about him before they met, but not to try and set them up. I did it to warn her off him. I told you that.

Did Jeremy even tell you what happened when he and Gemma first met? He probably said he was real slick or something. The truth is he showed up unannounced, bursting through our door at something like ten o'clock at night with a bloody lip. Bloodstains on his shirt and everything.

Sarah closed the door behind him pretty quickly, before anyone could yell at us for the noise, and he didn't even notice Gemma at first, who was standing in the hallway. She must've been on her way to the bathroom or something. But he was so wrapped up in himself he didn't notice, pushing his way into the kitchen like he owned it.

"What on earth happened to you?" I asked, because Sarah would've been too nice about it.

"Nothing," he snapped, and used one of our Christmas tea towels to dab his lip.

"Right, definitely nothing," I said, and Sarah shot me that look that means *be nice* and I shot her one back that means *shut up.*

And he said, "Just the Davy boys, all right? It's nothing."

I asked, "What did you do to them this time?"

Although I didn't really care. Whatever it was, he probably deserved it. That's what he got for messing with the Davy boys. They're these low-level shits from his old neighborhood. Stolen goods and fake IDs and god knows what else. Boys like them were the reason Pop-pop would bring Jeremy over to our place all the time.

As Jeremy was dabbing his lip, he finally spotted Gemma.

He's never been one to take a hint. He looked right at her, puffed his chest out a bit, and said, "Oh, hey. I'm Jeremy. You must be the new room-mate. Gemma, right?"

Gemma didn't say anything. She just turned around, walked back down the hall to her bedroom, and closed the door.

Jeremy went back to poking at his bloody lip and said, "What's with her?"

Sarah started to say something, but I cut her off.

"Have you seen yourself?" I said. "No wonder you scared her away."

Jeremy grunted and then Sarah started babying him, telling him to take off his bloody shirt. She'd get a clean one and some hydrogen peroxide and blah blah blah, and he didn't bring up Gemma again that night and I thought that would be the end of it.

Yes, I am well aware that even though I was the one that spent the most time with Gemma, I wasn't with her twenty-four seven. I never said I was. So no, I wasn't there every single time she and Jeremy were together. I understand that. And no, I don't know what she was like when it was just the two of them. I don't. But I do know what I saw when the three of us were together. And that wasn't flirting. That was fear.

So all that "she said she loved me" crap you say Jeremy's spouting in the other room? I'm telling you it's bullshit. Gemma didn't love him. I'm not sure she's ever loved anyone. Especially not her ex.

No, that's not it. The reason I didn't tell you about the rat back in May is because I didn't want you to think I was crazy. But if you, like, really want to know, just keep in mind these are Gemma's words, not mine, okay?

So a few days after I found the dead rat, Gemma and I were sitting in the living room, remember? And Gemma had asked me if I'd ever done anything I regretted. I said no, and then she told me this story.

She said that about a year before, she'd started dating this guy and was hoping to move in with him because the people she was living with at the time were sort of bad news, although she didn't tell me exactly why. Anyway, she wanted to move out, but she couldn't 'cause she was on the lease and couldn't break it. I don't know if she was working or not, she didn't say, but if she was, she wasn't earning much. So anyway, she's trying to figure out what to do, trying to figure out if there's any way she can get out because it's getting really bad there, but she's coming up blank and she doesn't want to tell her boyfriend how bad it is. They hadn't been dating for too long and she didn't want to dump this on him.

And then, she said, she's at a bar one night. I don't know if she was working there or just having a drink. She never said. She never told me what bar, either, or what city.

But she's at a bar and this woman comes up to her—long blond hair and a black beret—and this woman says she noticed how sad Gemma looked and was there anything she could do? And Gemma tells her no, it's nothing, she's fine. Because she doesn't know this woman, right? And Gemma's a fairly private person, so she's not going to start blathering on about her personal life, you know? The woman leaves her alone, and that seems to be the end of it. Gemma doesn't think any more of it.

But when Gemma leaves the bar that night, the woman with the beret is waiting for her, standing on the corner underneath a streetlight, and there's this bag at her feet. It looked like a scene from a movie, Gemma said. And there's no doubt she's been waiting for Gemma. She's staring right at her. The woman doesn't say anything. Just waits. And Gemma knows she can walk away, she says. She has this feeling that she can just turn her back and walk away and that'll be the end of it.

But she doesn't. She pauses, and then she walks across the street to where the woman is standing. And maybe it's the light from the street lamp, but now Gemma can see how tired the woman looks and how worn her clothes are and how her long hair looks greasy, and she doesn't remember the woman looking like that in the bar. So that, plus this big bag at her feet, and Gemma's wondering if maybe this lady's homeless and maybe she should go, except now it doesn't feel like she can. Like she made her choice to walk over here and now she's stuck with it.

So Gemma's standing there in front of this woman and she doesn't know what to say 'cause she doesn't even know why she walked over in the first place. Her brain's sort of all foggy about that. But she doesn't have to wait long 'cause the woman says, "You need money."

Gemma says, "Don't we all?"

And the woman says, "No. You really need money. You need to get away from them."

And then, Gemma says, she tells Gemma all about her situation—*Gemma's* situation. She knows all about being trapped in that shitty apartment with those shitty roommates, but she knows more than that. She knows details, names, dates. She knows Gemma's whole life story. She knows details about Gemma's past that Gemma had never told anyone.

And Gemma doesn't know what to say to that. But she doesn't have to say anything because then the woman says, "So I know you need the money."

And Gemma says, "What money?"

And the woman bends down and unzips this bag.

It's filled with cash. Gemma thinks it's a scam, of course, like it must be mostly newspaper or something. So she bends down and riffles through it, but it's real. It's all real.

And then Gemma's like, "I don't understand. Who are you? Why are you giving this to me?" She also wants to say, *you don't even know me.* But she doesn't because the woman clearly does know her. Somehow.

When Gemma looks up, she expects the woman to be gone because that's what you would expect, right? Poof. Vanished into thin air. But she's still there, looking down at Gemma. Her beret has shifted a bit.

And the woman says, "This money wasn't meant for me."

Then she turns around and walks away. Gemma keeps watching her until she disappears around a corner.

As soon as she's gone, Gemma realizes she's crouching on the pavement next to a massive bag of cash, so she zips it up. Takes it home with her. Roommates are out, so she's able to stash it under her bed without anyone seeing. Figures she'll decide what to do with it later.

Less than twenty-four hours later, her building burns down. She was able to grab the bag and get out safely. At least one of her roommates didn't.

She calls her boyfriend—his name is Ian, she says—because she has no one else, nowhere to go, and he's such a nice guy, she says, he agrees to take her in. It's so peaceful at his house, so calm and quiet, and she feels so welcome that she falls into a deep sleep thinking everything is going to get better now.

But the next day, she says, that's when everything started to go wrong. It was her sleep at first. After that one good night, she started having these terrible dreams, and she chalked it up to guilt over being happy that her building burned down. But the dreams only got worse. She didn't say exactly what happened in them, but she'd wake up sweating, with this feeling that someone was coming for her. But they were just dreams, so she tried to ignore them.

And then, after a few nights of these nightmares, she caught Ian taking money from the bag. He said it was the first time. She forgave him. She hadn't told him about the money, but she used some of it to replace the clothes and things she lost in the fire, so he must have seen what was in the bag at some point.

Two days later, she recounted the money. More of it was missing.

When she confronted him about it, he grabbed her neck and threw her against the wall. Nearly choked her.

A few days after that, Ian introduces Gemma to his family. To his mother.

It was the woman in the beret.

The woman looked just as shocked as Gemma. They pretended not to know each other, but as soon as they were alone, the woman started yelling at Gemma, asking her how does she know Ian and what was she doing, et cetera, et cetera. Gemma told her what'd been happening with the money and what it'd been doing to Ian, and the woman crumpled to the ground, started muttering about how Gemma shouldn't have brought the money back to her, how she shouldn't be spending it, how it needed to keep getting passed on.

She told Gemma then that money was cursed. That she couldn't use it because every time she would use some, things would get worse—the nightmares, the violence. Until Gemma got rid of it, she said, it would turn the hearts of everyone around her black, no matter how good they started, no matter how kind.

Then Ian came back in the room, and his mother pretended she'd lost a contact lens—that this was why she was on the floor—and never said another word to Gemma about the money. Not until Gemma and Ian were leaving. The woman pulled Gemma in close, pretending to hug her, and said, "If you don't get it away from my family, I will."

That night, after Ian had fallen asleep, that's when Gemma ran. And she'd been running ever since.

I looked at her and I was like, "So your ex, Ian, he's after you for this money? And he sent you the rat as what, a warning?"

Because I thought I'd figured it out then. She'd run off with the money, went into hiding. He came after her. That was why she was so adamant about checking the mail. She was looking for a warning, and it finally came.

Gemma didn't answer right away. She tilted her head to the side, was looking at the coffee table but not really seeing anything, or at least that's what it seemed like. Then after a few seconds, she nodded and said, "Yes. That's it. It's Ian. Yes. But the warning isn't what you think."

Then she said that she'd been trying to break the curse—searching for its origins, going on all sorts of websites, reading all sorts of books. Finding any ritual she could think of from any religion or belief. Anything to break the curse, cleanse her spirit. That's why she'd thought burning that sage would help, but it didn't do anything.

"And then what?" I asked. "If you do break the curse? Ian will turn back into a good person or something?"

"It's too late for that," she said. "But . . . but he's not looking for me. I'm looking for him. He sent me the rat as a warning but not a warning that he's close. He's warning me to stop looking. To stay away and leave his family alone. But I can't break the curse until . . . see, he took something from me. Something I need back. That's why I go out. I go out looking for him because I only have a few months left to pass on the money or break the curse."

"Or else what?"

But she wouldn't say.

So I said, "So what does he have? Some of the money? Is he holding on to some of it still?"

She hesitated, then nodded.

And I said, "And he's somewhere in Reading?"

She nodded again.

I said, "Why don't you go to the police? Tell them what's been going on? I mean, maybe not all of it, but—"

"I can't. They won't believe me. They'll think I stole the money and they'll . . ." She got up from the chair. "I've already told you too much. I never wanted to get you involved. You or Sarah. Just please, when you go out, be careful. I don't think he'll do anything to you. But if he thinks you're involved . . . I don't want to see anyone else get hurt."

And I said, "If you didn't want to get me involved, then why did you tell me all this?"

And she said, "You found the rat. I thought you deserved to know why."

I asked, "The money you gave us for rent, is that some of *this* money?"

But she left the room without answering.

Gemma was right. About not going to the police. I can tell from your face you think it's crazy. I thought it was crazy, too—cursed money. I mean, honestly, just 'cause I believe in ghosts and think witches and supernatural stuff are cool doesn't mean I believed her. Like, it was obvious there was more to this story than Gemma was saying. I'm not stupid. My favorite theory at the time was that this Ian hadn't been her boyfriend at all. He'd been her kidnapper. Like, you hear these stories about men who keep girls locked up in their basements or sheds for months. Years, even. It seemed to fit with Gemma and how weird she was, and it made perfect sense that she could've been held captive for years and then escaped. I mean, the lack of pop culture knowledge? The scars? But even if I was wrong, what I *did* believe was that there could be some angry-as-fuck ex-boyfriend after her, and if he was after her and she was living with us, then he'd be after us.

But it wasn't until about a week later that I really believed even that.

Sarah had started picking up extra shifts at work and spending more time with that guy she was dating, the one who'd get her pregnant. That night, Sarah called me from work. I started telling her what to pick up for dinner but she cut me off and said she wouldn't be home. She was helping out a friend by picking up an extra shift. And I was like, "You have friends at work now? I thought you hated that place."

And she was like, "Not everyone hates people like you do."

And I was like, "I don't hate everybody."

She was being real snippy, and I could tell it was because something was bothering her and she was taking it out on me, you know, like most sisters do. But before I could figure out what it was, she said, "I have to get back to work. Get your own dinner." And she hung up.

I was really mad at Sarah after that. Like, she couldn't have told me earlier that she was taking an extra shift and wouldn't be getting dinner? So that I could've gone to the store earlier when it wasn't so busy? I swear she does this on purpose sometimes. Little inconveniences to annoy me when she's annoyed at something herself. Like I'm her punching bag or something. And I get it. We're sisters. I take things out on her. She takes things out on me. Then we make up and move on. But as the older sister, I feel like I'm the one that has to put up with more, 'cause she's the baby. And I don't think she knows that's how I feel 'cause that's just how life's always been for her. I never asked, but I'm not even sure if she actually picked up an extra shift that night or if she was just going out with that guy.

Anyway, I didn't really feel like going to the store, but we didn't have anything I felt like eating. I thought about ordering takeout, but I needed to save money, so while some Mexican takeout sounded perfect, I figured I shouldn't order food for $20 or $30 when I could walk to the grocery store and pick up a decent frozen dinner version for around ten bucks. The

Redner's Quick Stop doesn't have good frozen Mexican, so I decided to go to the Weis, which is about fifteen minutes away.

Gemma was in her room with the door closed, so after I changed out of my stay-at-home sweatpants and into my running-errands ones, I knocked on her door to let her know where I was going and asked if she wanted anything or wanted to come along. I didn't think she would. She never did. But I didn't like the thought of leaving her alone. I mean, I know she went out by herself during the day, but leaving her home alone, I don't know. It just felt like I was leaving something fragile behind.

But I was also fucking starving for some enchiladas.

After she told me she was fine, I slipped on my sneakers and grabbed my keys and out I went. It was a Friday or Saturday night. I can't remember which, but the streets were pretty busy—people going out and stuff. It was a mild night for January. No chance of snow or rain. You could even glimpse a few stars through the city lights.

And it was really fucking loud.

No, you're right. It's only about a ten-minute walk—not fifteen—from our apartment to the Weis, but that's if you go the short way. I took the long way around so that I didn't have to walk past Staples just in case my ex-supervisor was working late. So it took me more like fifteen minutes, and by the time I got there my head was splitting. Sirens going off. So many people, all drunk and shouty. You know that type of shrieky laughter drunk girls make? The kind that you're not sure is a laugh or a scream and you whip your head around to check? I heard one of those right before I walked into the store and I fucking jumped in the air. Gemma's story about Ian had been swirling around in my head all week. Plus I hadn't slept well the night before. It was the first time I dreamed about the rats. I had thought going out with all those people around would make me feel safer, but all I kept thinking was that it'd be easier for someone to hide in the crowd. I mean, I didn't even know what this Ian looked like, so with all those people, how could it be obvious if some guy was following me or not?

I used to walk to that Weis all the time, especially when I first moved in, but ever since Sarah started working at Walmart, I haven't needed to get groceries as often. I sort of forgot what it was like going into a crowded store on a Saturday night. Honestly, one of my favorite things about COVID was that it was socially acceptable for people to stay away from you. Like, they had to. It was a safety measure. And you could tell people to back off and feel pretty righteous about it. Now, though, it's like people miss being close to other human beings, I guess? And people, strangers even, just gravitate toward you physically, like they want to make contact. So no matter how much I tried to step away from someone, there'd be another person there. Like there I was just trying to grab some frozen enchiladas, and it was like I was in a pinball machine, getting bounced around by people reaching for sodas and chips and Tastykakes. I could feel my heart racing. What if Ian was hiding in one of these aisles, watching me? What if he had a knife? Or even a gun?

So while I waited in the line for self-checkout, I kept myself all hunched in, hoping no one would touch me. Hoping I wouldn't see anyone staring at me. No one really stood out to me, but it felt like I was being watched. I could feel my back burning, like someone's eyes were drilling into me, and I became convinced Ian was in the line behind me, hiding behind another customer. I tried to pay for my groceries as fast I could, but the stupid-ass self-checkout machine kept yelling at me about an unexpected item in the bagging area, and I had to wait for the cashier person to come over and type in a code, and as they're doing that, I swear I heard someone say my name. I snapped my head around, but I didn't see anyone I knew. The cashier left, and I tried to pay but I couldn't get the tap-to-pay on my card to work, so I had to put in the chip and wait, and I looked around again as I was waiting for the transaction to go through. As soon as it did, I grabbed my bag and nearly forgot to take my card. I didn't even wait for the receipt to print. I just booked it out of there.

But it wasn't any better when I get out of the store. As I was walking home, the earlier crowds had vanished. I was completely alone. It was like one of those apocalypse movies where all the people disappear or have hidden inside buildings because they know the monster's coming. I picked up the pace, trying not to look behind me because I knew there was no one there, I couldn't hear anyone there. Even though it felt like someone was there. I was about a block from our apartment building when I swore I heard my name again, but before I could turn around, I was falling.

Someone had shoved me into the street just as a car turned the corner. The car's horn blared, but I managed to keep my balance and staggered back. I turned and swung the grocery bag to try and hit whoever had shoved me. But there no one was there. I could still feel someone's hands on my back where they had pushed me, but there wasn't anyone there that I could see.

I ran like I haven't run since I played field hockey.

By the time I got back to the apartment, I was completely out of breath. My lungs and my legs were burning. I jabbed and jabbed at the elevator button, checking over my shoulder to make sure no one had followed me inside, but the elevator wouldn't come. It said it was on the fourth floor and it wasn't moving, which meant that idiot that lives on the floor below us was keeping the door propped open so he could load up his two weeks' worth of trash and bring it down. And he's like, ninety, so it takes him ages to move a single bag. But I couldn't stand there and wait, not when it felt like someone was catching up to me, so I started running up the stairs.

By the time I reached our floor, the grocery bag was heavy in my hands and my stomach was all cramped up and I wasn't even sure if I was hungry anymore. I just wanted to get inside the apartment.

I unlocked the door, ran inside, and there was Ian, perched on the edge of our sofa.

I blinked. It wasn't Ian. It was Jeremy. Jeremy and Gemma on my sofa.

She was pressed up against the arm of the sofa, like she was trying to crawl away, and he was leaning over her. Not touching her, I never saw that, I never said that. Just leaning over like he *wanted* to touch her and he was close to doing it, too. Like, he would've touched her if I hadn't opened the door right at that moment. When I think back, it felt like I was standing there staring for five minutes, but it couldn't have been more than a second because they noticed me right away.

Jeremy leaped back, like he'd been shocked. Gemma stayed where she was.

I was too stunned to say anything. I just came in, and by the time I closed the door behind me, Jeremy was standing up like he was getting ready to leave.

I went to the kitchen to set my bag down, and I said—not shouted—"What are you doing here?"

And he said, "I was just leaving."

Which didn't answer the question. I looked at my phone and saw what time Sarah called and what time it was now, and it hadn't been much more than forty minutes, so he couldn't have been here long. And then he said to Gemma, "I'll see you around." But he didn't say anything else to me. He just walked out.

As soon as he was gone, I looked at Gemma, but she didn't want to meet my eye. She pulled her arms tight to her chest, like she was trying to shrink into herself. So I started apologizing for Jeremy and she said, "It's fine. I'm okay. I'm okay now."

And then she said she was going to bed and she left me alone in the kitchen with my frozen dinner, which I didn't bother to eat that night because it felt like I was going to throw up, so I just hid in my bedroom and watched a bunch of Bryce Harper postseason home run videos to try and calm down.

No, as far as I know, Gemma never initiated any texts or calls with Jeremy. I'm sure he says she did, but he didn't show you any of those texts or anything, did he? That's because they don't exist.

No, Gemma never asked him to come over. Not that night. Not ever. Not that I know of.

Thanks for the cigarette. I know you don't need to be this nice, but I really appreciate it. And I swear I'm doing the best I can.

I am trying to tell you everything.

No, Jeremy's not lying about the tracking app.

It's called Eyezy. It lets you track someone's phone in stealth mode. I picked it because it had a fairly cheap monthly fee. And yes, I was the one who installed it on Sarah's phone.

But it's not why you think.

I did it to protect her.

Before I installed the app, I had tried asking Sarah to text me about where she was whenever she went out, or to at least turn on the share location thing in her iPhone. It was important that I knew where she was and who she was with because someone had already tried to shove me in front of a car, and they were still watching me. So I needed to watch Sarah.

But she got fed up with me and stopped responding or would only respond with rude emojis. So one day when she was in the shower, I borrowed her phone, installed the app, and set up an account that linked it to my phone. I know all her passcodes and stuff. She always uses her birthday even though they say you shouldn't do that.

Jeremy's wrong, though. I did *not* lose my phone on purpose so I could hide evidence of the Eyezy app or so you couldn't use the app to trace Sarah. That's right, now I remember. I lost my phone when I tripped at the river. It fell out of my pocket. Plus, it didn't occur to me to use the app to find Sarah anyway because I haven't used it in months. I'd forgotten it was on there until you brought it up. Besides, if Jeremy already knew I'd installed the app, that means Sarah must've known. Because either he somehow found out and told her or she found out and told him. And if Sarah knew about the app then she probably already figured out how to uninstall it anyway. But Sarah would've been completely fine with the app if she'd known why I'd installed it in the first place.

No, the app was Gemma's idea, actually.

Because she wanted to make sure that Sarah would be safe. Just in case Ian came after Sarah.

Well, because I told Gemma what happened on my way home from Weis. That's how she knew. I didn't tell her right away, but I guess I was sort of different after it happened. Like, after that night, every time I left the apartment, I was looking for some guy waiting to jump me, throw me in his van, and lock me up in his garden shed. And I couldn't relax whenever Sarah was out of the apartment, even when I knew she was at work. Because who knew if he'd come through her checkout line at Walmart? Wait for her in the shadows as she left after her shift? I mean, I thought I was protecting her by not telling her, but what if he went after her anyway?

Gemma noticed I was acting a bit anxious, so I told her.

And it wasn't just my imagination. I knew he was still watching me. Because of the lighters.

One day, after the Weis thing, I was walking home from the Quick Stop, and right in the middle of the sidewalk was a lighter, a green one like I used to have back in college. I picked it up and tossed it in a trash can. The next day, there it was again, on that same spot of sidewalk. After that, I lost track of how many times I found it.

Well yeah, I've always looked out for Sarah. Obviously. It's what a big sister is supposed to do, isn't it? Our parents pretty much gave us free rein while they ran the business, so it was up to me to look out for her because no one else would. Like, I remember this one time when Sarah and I went to a carnival when we were little. Not *little* little. I guess I was about twelve and she was about ten. Dad took us because Mom was in the hospital again, and I don't think he knew what else to do with us. After he won us this teddy bear at the milk bottle toss, he said we were big enough to walk around on our own and gave us some money and off we went. We ended up joining up with some other kids around our age, as kids do, and Sarah took to this one boy. I don't remember much about him other than he was really, really blond. I think his name was Chase or Cole? Anyway, Sarah latched onto him, and the two were, like, inseparable the rest of the day.

I was the oldest of the group, so I took charge of leading everyone around and going on the different rides and stuff. But when we got to the Gravitron, I loved it so much, I wanted to ride it again. So I did. And then again. And then again. I know it makes some people nauseated, but I just felt like I was flying. I could close my eyes and feel it spin and spin and spin, and I didn't have to do anything at all, not even buckle a seatbelt because the force of the ride kept you pressed against that padded wall. I could just let go and let the ride do all the work.

By the seventh or eighth time, I realized I was the last of the kids still at the ride, so instead of going one more time, I went off to look for them. It was getting late, and most were probably headed home. I didn't care if I never saw them again, but I couldn't find Sarah anywhere and I knew Dad was going to kill me if I didn't find her. But just as I was starting to get worried, I spotted her by a cotton candy cart, sitting in the dirt and crying.

She didn't seem hurt or anything, and when I asked her what was wrong, she screamed, "Cole left me!"

The cotton candy man gave us this weird look, so I grabbed Sarah's arm and pulled her away.

I said, "He had to go home, Sarah."

And she kept screaming and said, "No! He left me! He said he didn't want me around anymore and he left me!"

And I said, "Let's find Dad," because I didn't know what else to say.

But she stopped walking and stomped her foot and shouted, "No no no! I loved him! I loved him and he went away! I'll never love anyone again!"

Even at twelve, I remember thinking, *That's pretty dramatic for a ten-year-old*.

Before I could calm her down, Dad found us and was like, "Why did you make her cry?"

And he scooped Sarah up even though she was too big to be carried, and I followed after them trying to explain what had happened, that I wasn't the one to make her cry, but Dad wasn't listening. He just told us it was time to go.

The next day, when I asked Sarah how she was feeling, she couldn't even remember the little boy's name.

No one looks after Sarah better than me.

That's why I knew better than to tell her about any of Gemma's shit.

No, I told you, Sarah and Gemma didn't have any problems. Did

Jeremy say that? I mean, yeah, they did fight now and then, but it was only, like, normal roommate stuff. Nothing major. Like that time they had the fight about the bathroom.

I wasn't there when it started, so I can't say how it started. But it was sometime after Gemma gave Sarah that gift card—the one to Giorgio's? I was on my way back from Redner's and I found another of those stupid green lighters. I stomped on it with the heel of my shoe until it broke and the lighter fluid leaked all over the pavement. And then I hurried back to the apartment as fast I could.

Anyway, before I even opened the door, I could hear Sarah screaming at Gemma, and my first thought was that Sarah had found out about Ian—that he had threatened Sarah or tried to hurt her like he'd done with me. So I rushed into the apartment, and I saw Sarah had Gemma pinned against the hall wall and was shoving this damp towel in Gemma's face. Gemma wasn't saying or doing anything. She was just standing there while Sarah yelled.

And before I could say anything, Sarah turned to me and said, "Tell her!"

All I did was go out for Pringles. I had no clue what was going on. And the way Sarah was acting, it didn't seem to be about Ian, but I decided to play dumb.

So I said, "Tell her what?"

And Sarah said, "Tell her about the towels."

And I was like, "What about the towels?"

And Sarah just looked at me like I insulted her firstborn—she wasn't pregnant yet, FYI—but she looked so mad that I took a step back.

And she said, "Tell her to buy her own towels and to stop using mine and to stop leaving them wet and dirty on the bathroom floor." She was shaking a towel as she was saying this.

And I thought, *Thank god, this is only about towels?*

Then Gemma said, "I said I was sorry. I'm going to get my own towels. I just haven't gotten around to it yet. And I'll stop leaving them on the floor. Sorry."

And to me that seemed to cover it, but Sarah looked at me like she was waiting for me to make some comment or something. So I said, "She says she's sorry. She'll get her own towels."

Sarah looked like I'd slapped her in the face.

"I come home from that shitty job," she said, "and I smell like rotting vegetables and hand sanitizer and I've sweated through that horrible uniform and all I want is to get a nice hot shower and take one of my fluffy warm towels off the heated towel rack, and instead I go in the bathroom and my nice fluffy towel is all wet and cold and lying in a dirty heap on the floor! Because this—" She pointed at Gemma but she didn't finish whatever she was going to say. She just stood there, waiting for me to respond— they both were—and what was I supposed to say? *Well, maybe you should've gone to college and lived in a dorm and learned to cope with other people touching your things instead of being a spoiled princess at Mom and Dad's?*

Of course, I didn't say that. But I didn't know what else to say, so I said, "She said she was sorry."

Sarah stormed up to me so fast I thought she was going to hit me, but she just reached around me for the linen closet. As she was getting a fresh towel, she whispered, "So you've fallen for her act, too." Then she slammed the closet door, went into the bathroom, and slammed that door. Thirty seconds later, the water started running.

I finally set my grocery bag in the kitchen, then went back to the hall to pick up the wet towel. Gemma was still there.

So I said, "Sorry."

"It's okay," she said. "I should say sorry. I'm the one that's been using your body wash. I heard you yelling at Sarah about it."

"Well, to be fair, she's probably using it, too," I said.

She said, "It can't always be easy, living with your sister."

And I said, "She's fine. Usually. It's just, she hates this job and—"

Gemma said, "Well, there's not much you can do about it, is there? Sisters get mad for no reason. They yell at you about towels and food and boyfriends. They say you stole their shower gel or lied to your mom or killed the dog."

And I was like, "What?"

But then Gemma went to her room without saying anything else, and I was left alone for the rest of the night. Didn't think too much more about the dog comment until what happened a few months later.

Anyway, Sarah can get worked up about little stuff like that. Like, unlike me and field hockey and sports, Sarah's never had anything she's really passionate about. Except maybe her appearance. So I guess she puts all her energy into getting upset about stuff that doesn't matter.

Oh, and boys. She gets really obsessed with boys.

I can honestly say I wasn't shocked when I found out she was pregnant. I'd been expecting that for years. What shocked me was that she'd been seeing a steady boyfriend and I didn't even find out about it until they broke up.

The breakup? It must've been, god, about a month or so before Gemma went missing? Gemma and I had just got back to the apartment, and Sarah was already home. As soon as we walked through the door, I could tell Sarah was upset about something. I don't know if Gemma noticed. She just said goodnight and went down to her room and shut the door, so me and Sarah were alone. I got a Coke from the fridge and asked Sarah if she wanted one, and she said, in this really pouty voice, "No."

I didn't know what her problem was, so I was just like, "Rough night?"

And she snapped, "Where have you two been?"

And I said, "Out."

And she said, "Again?"

And then I could see the tears on her face, how her mascara was all runny. Mom always tells her to buy the waterproof kind, but she never listens. So I brought her a Coke anyway 'cause she usually does want one even when she says no, but when I held it out to her, she slapped my hand away.

"I said I didn't want one," she said.

I thought about chucking the bottle at her head, but I put it on the coffee table instead.

I asked, "What's gotten into you?"

And she said, "Like you care."

And I was thinking, god help me, she's in one of those moods again. Normally, I can be really patient with her, but I was so tired. I just wanted to drink my Coke and go to bed, but instead I had to sit up with her and deal with whatever her drama of the week was.

So I was like, "Of course I care, Sarah. I always care." And I thought about sitting next to her on the sofa, but she was giving off major "don't come near me" vibes, so I sat in the armchair and waited to see what she was gonna say next.

She said, "He broke up with me."

And my first thought was "Who?" But I didn't say that because it would make it sound like I didn't care, so instead I said, "I'm so sorry, Sarah. That's a shame."

And while the words were right, I knew that I said them all wrong because I sounded exactly like Mom. So now I was thinking, *Shit, she's going to blow up*. And I was right.

Immediately, she was like, "Do you even know who I'm talking about?"

And her face was turning this bright red color, and I could feel mine doing the same. So I sipped my Coke at the same time I said no and some of the soda dribbled down my chin.

And she said, "Shane?"

But I didn't recognize the name, and she could tell by the look on my face, and she said, "The guy I've been seeing for the last six months?"

And I had no recollection of that name whatsoever, but I tried to pretend, so I said, "You're still seeing him?"

Sarah looked like she wanted to strangle me. "Yes, I'm—I was—still seeing him! Who do you think I've been going out with all the time?"

But Sarah trades boyfriends like Pokémon cards, so I'd stopped keeping track a long time ago. I may have accidentally said that to her face.

So she said, "No, you've just been spending too much time with your new best friend."

And I was like, "What are you talking about?"

She nodded toward Gemma's door.

I said, "She's not my best friend."

And Sarah said, "Well you're certainly spending more time with her than you are with Zadie."

And I was like, "Zadie's busy. Besides, I thought the two of you wanted me to get out more."

And she looked me up and down and said, "And exactly what are you two doing when you're out?"

Now she was the one that was acting like Mom, so that set me off.

I was like, "How is that any of your business?"

And she said, "'Cause you're tracking mud into the apartment. And there's wax on the coffee table and the counter, and don't think I haven't noticed the salt that's all over the hallway."

I waved her off even though there was still dirt on my clothes and it was coming off my shoes. But I was like, "Well, I clean it up, don't I?"

And she said, "If you spent less time doing that and more time actually talking to me, then maybe you'd know that Shane actually means something to me."

Maybe she was right, but I was also so tired by this point, tired of her shouting and carrying on and always being so dramatic over nothing. So I said, "Well, you couldn't have meant that much to him if he dumped you."

Okay, yeah, it was a really bitchy thing to say.

Sarah grabbed her jacket after that and said, "I'm going to Jeremy's," and she slammed the door so hard, I swear the whole building shook. Gemma must've heard it, but she stayed in her room, and I finished my soda and washed my hands and wiped the mud off the floor.

Yeah, Jeremy's right about that, I guess. Sarah and I did go through a rough patch. It was, like, hard keeping track of all the things she was annoyed with me for. She's always been a bit temperamental. Doesn't like it when she doesn't feel like she's the center of everybody's world, which is why she tends to go through boyfriends so quick. So I thought that's what her problem was. That I was paying more attention to Gemma than I was to her. But I told you, she wasn't antagonistic toward Gemma. It's more like Sarah didn't want me and Gemma to be friends. Like she wanted to drive a wedge between us. Like, there was this one time, a few days after the fight about the towels, when Sarah grabbed my arm and dragged me into her bedroom.

She closed the door and said, "I don't think the money's real."

And because I didn't want to tell her about Ian or Gemma's story or anything, I was just like, "Sarah, of course the money's real. I deposited it at the bank. In person. Myself. The bank wouldn't have taken it if it wasn't real."

But she was like, "Maybe the money she handed us back then was real, but the rest is counterfeit. That's why she can't buy any of her own clothes or—"

I said, "Sarah, you can't go around making accusations like that."

"It's not an accusation. Look." And she took a twenty-dollar bill out of her pocket. "I borrowed one of the markers from work, the one we use to check if money is counterfeit or not and—"

I asked, "Sarah, where did you get this? Did you go into her room?"

Which, yeah, I guess was hypocritical of me to ask.

But I said, "You have to put that back."

And she said, "But look! The marker came up black, and it's supposed to be yellow."

She was practically shoving the money in my face, and I said, "It's none of our business, Sarah. The money she's paid us was real. That's what matters. So put it back. You don't know what you're dealing with."

"And you do?"

"Just put it back. And leave her alone. I'll handle her, all right? Don't worry about it."

I don't know if Sarah ever did put that money back. If there's anyone else she would've told her suspicions to, I guess it would've been Jeremy, but Jeremy knows the money was real. It's the one thing we can agree on.

The money was the reason I thought Jeremy came over last night.

No, actually, he is telling the truth about that. It was probably closer to one in the morning when we first leave the apartment last night.

He had parked his car right outside our building. I sit in the back, but Sarah sits up front with Jeremy. She usually sits in the back with me. So I'm wondering if she's upset with me about something. Whatever it is, she doesn't say anything, but I can't get her attention without Jeremy noticing, so I don't say anything either.

Once he starts driving, I can't shake the feeling that it's wrong to be going out this late at night. Nothing good happens between two and five in the morning. Mom says that all the time.

Anyway, the three of us, we're all on edge. There's a point where I get so nervous I want to tell Jeremy to turn around and take us back to the apartment. I don't know if he would have. But then again, I never asked.

As we start driving, I keep thinking how weird it is that Sarah would say she saw Gemma and then Jeremy would show up and say the same thing. But I don't want to accuse Jeremy of anything while we're riding around in his car.

We go to the Quick Stop first, but there's no sign of Gemma. Sarah walks us right to the spot she says she saw her, and we check the brick wall she says Gemma was scratching, but we don't see anything—no broken fingernails, no blood. So we decide to go to the other Redner's—the big Redner's—where Jeremy says he saw her.

By this point, I'm pretty sure he has to be lying. It just doesn't make any sense. Why would Gemma go to see Sarah and Jeremy and not me? And why would she show up in the parking lot outside a Redner's? We never even went to this Redner's. It's almost like Jeremy is looking for a reason to get us to this exact spot.

Anyway, he parks the car, and of course the parking lot is empty 'cause everything's closed, so it's just us out there. And Jeremy points through the windshield and says, "There. That's where I saw her. Right there."

And I'm like, "Jeremy, where the hell are you pointing?"

And he says, "There. By the streetlight. The one that keeps flickering."

And from where we're parked I can see five different streetlights, but not a damn one is flickering. Maybe Jeremy could see it from where he was sitting up front, but I can't see it from the back. But instead of arguing with him, I say, "Well, she's not here now. You said you saw her move. Did you see which way she went?"

And he says, "She walked that way and turned right. I think. I don't know. I mean, I didn't actually see her walk, but—"

I say, "Well, that's helpful. So did she move or didn't she? Did you even get close enough to see it was her?"

"It was her." He says it like he's never been so sure of anything in his life.

And I don't know what else to say, so I roll my eyes and slump back in the seat, already feeling like this is pointless.

Then, out of the blue, Sarah says, "Garters and Lace."

I'm trying to figure out why she'd bring that up of all things, when she points to the other end of the shopping center and says, "The night she . . . went away, we went to dinner at that Applebee's and then we walked to Garters and Lace. Applebee's then Garters and Lace. Garters and Lace is in that direction. The same direction Jeremy says he saw her go tonight."

Jeremy's nodding along, but I'm like, "So what? She's leading us around the same places we last saw her? Then why'd she show up near our apartment?"

"I don't know," Sarah says. "To get our attention?"

"She apparently got Jeremy's attention. So why would she come find you? And how would she know you'd be walking to the Quick Stop tonight anyway? She slip your crush some cash or something? Why wouldn't she just come to the apartment? Why wouldn't she come see me?"

Sarah and Jeremy exchange a look. And I'm, like, "What? What did I say?"

But Jeremy's looking out the windshield again, in the direction he says he saw her go, like she'll suddenly appear out of thin air.

Neither of them seems to want to say anything else, so I say, "If you think she's headed to Garters and Lace, then let's go to Garters and Lace. I mean, at least they'll be open, right? We can ask around. See if anyone's seen her."

Sarah shudders. From the cold, I think. Because Jeremy turned the car off once we got to Redner's, and he hasn't turned it back on yet. I keep waiting for either of them to say something. They don't.

So I'm like, "Why are we out here then? If we didn't come out here to find her, then what are we doing?"

Sarah looks away from me, out the window. Jeremy doesn't say anything, but he starts the car and off we go. Again.

And that was the first time I really thought they were trying to gaslight me or something.

No, that's stupid! The reason I didn't mention Gemma's ex back in May wasn't because I was "working with him." Who the fuck told you that? Jeremy? No, the reason I didn't mention it was because Gemma and I had handled all that by the time she disappeared. Honestly, it's why I thought she had vanished. Not because Ian had done something to her, but because she didn't need me anymore.

No, when you came to the apartment and settled yourself on the sofa and I made coffee while you and your partner pulled out your notebooks, I was thinking about anything I could tell you that would actually help you find her. And I wanted you to find her because I wanted to know if my theory was right. I wanted to know that she was gone because it was all over.

Do you remember—I sat down in the armchair, waited while you sipped your coffee, and when you asked questions about where I last saw Gemma and what I knew about her, I told you exactly that—what I thought would help. And when you asked if I knew of anyone that might want to hurt her or if there was anyone who she might want to run from, I ate an Oreo. I had put them on the plate next to your coffee, but neither of you had any, so I took one. I knew you must've thought it was because I was hungry, but really it was to buy myself time. Because I didn't know what I was or wasn't going to say until I said it. And when you asked again if there was anyone who wanted to hurt Gemma, I ended up telling you there wasn't—not that I was aware of. But that I hadn't known Gemma for long and she was a fairly private person, so there was probably plenty of stuff I didn't know about her.

Then before you could ask another question, Sarah walked through the door. She'd come home early from work, looking extra tired and lugging two big shopping bags. She was so surprised to see you that she nearly dropped the bags, and she gave me this look like I should have told her you were coming, but I hadn't had time to text her.

So I asked her, "Sarah, do you know anyone who would've wanted to hurt Gemma?"

And her eyes went wide. Like she was thinking, how could I ask her a question like that? Sarah hardly knew Gemma at all. She didn't know anything about all this stuff with Ian, I told you.

You finished your questions shortly after that, but not the coffee. I had to dump it all away. And you never came back for any follow-up questions, so I figured I'd given you enough to work with.

I never mentioned Sarah and Gemma going to Garters and Lace together because I didn't know that they had. I mean, now I do. But I didn't until recently. That's why I didn't tell you about it when you first came around back in May.

No, what I had thought was that Sarah and Gemma went to Applebee's and then to a bar or something because of how late it was when Sarah came home.

When did I find out? I guess it was about a month or two ago. We'd already given up thinking that Gemma was coming back or that you were going to find her. The few things Gemma left behind were still in her room. We still thought of it as Gemma's room, even though the sheets and duvet were ours and most of the clothes were the ones we had given her. It would've been easy to clean it out, but I didn't want to. I thought if I did, she'd come back. Like, as soon as I got rid of everything, there she'd be.

So I left it like it was and convinced our parents that me and Sarah couldn't handle a stranger coming into our lives right then. Honestly, they didn't buy it. But all Sarah had to say was that we needed the room for the nursery. God, as much as they hated being parents, you wouldn't think they'd care about being grandparents, especially with Sarah being unmarried and no father in the picture. But they are over the moon, let me tell you. They want so much to be a part of that baby's life.

Anyway, I don't even remember what prompted Sarah to tell me about going to Garters and Lace. We weren't even talking about Gemma or anything. It was summer, and we were both at home watching the Phillies game, and it was so damn hot that even with the AC on, I was sweating through my T-shirt.

I mentioned something about "sweating bricks" because it was so hot and then Sarah blurted out, "We went to the club."

I didn't know what she was talking about because her pregnancy brain had really started to kick in, and I was used to her saying random stuff that didn't make much sense. So I kept scrolling through the box scores of the other games and said, "What club?"

And she said, "Garters and Lace. Gemma and I went there that night."

Then I looked at her and said, "Why?"

She shrugged and said, "We had dinner. Wanted to go somewhere else. Once we got there, I didn't think it was a good idea. I forgot everyone thought I was a thief. But Gemma convinced me to go, said it would be fun, so we did. I don't know why, but we did."

I knew why. Because Gemma was a good talker. Gemma could convince you to do anything.

"And?" I asked because Sarah had gone quiet.

She looked at me like she expected me to say something, but she was the one that brought it up. When I didn't say anything else, she looked away. Looked almost disappointed.

Then she said, "Nothing. It was stupid."

"Why? Did you think someone would recognize you? What did you think they'd do? I mean, they were only rumors after all, right? And it was probably mostly new people there that night, anyway. You said that place had a high turnover rate."

"Yeah," she said, but not in a very convincing way.

And that was the last time she talked about that night.

See? This is why I never told you and why I didn't want to bring it up now. So no, installing the Eyezy app on Sarah's phone wasn't an overreaction to an "obviously made-up story."

The night I went out to Weis to get frozen enchiladas? No, I didn't trip. I was pushed. And after that I knew I was being followed every time I went out.

It was only partly because of the lighters.

I mean, finding them all the time didn't help. Ever since I started finding them, things just started to feel worse. Like, I started smelling smoke when there wasn't any, and I kept needing to text Zadie to make sure she was okay, and I kept having worse and worse dreams about that dead fucking rat, and all the while I'm getting email after email from my ex-manager and—

I never said I was a perfect person, okay? I'm not proud of everything I've done. But I've never done anything to hurt anyone, okay?

Look, you want to know the truth? Fine. Since you won't let it go, the real reason I'd leave a job every three months or so was because that's how long I could get away with skimming money from the cash register before anyone really noticed.

I don't know why I did it. I didn't really need the money. But I grew up around a bar and other family businesses. I know my way around a cash drawer, and I'm good with numbers. It was easy. So I did it. Not much more to it than that. And since I never got caught, I kept doing it. Until my manager at the Santander figured it out. They were doing some audit that got delayed because of COVID, and my ex-manager realized the numbers didn't all add up and traced it back to me. You want to talk about a real bitch? Instead of turning me in, she decided to blackmail me. She was asking me to pay back triple what I took. Figured she didn't want the higher-ups to know how she'd let this money go missing on her watch and was trying to cover her ass plus get a little extra back for her trouble.

And that's another reason I haven't found another job. 'Cause I don't know if I'd be able to stop myself from doing it again, so why put myself in that position, right? Better if I just stay home where I can't cause any trouble.

But that wasn't why I was being followed. None of my former managers would've known what the green lighters meant. And besides, they were already sending me emails. They didn't need to send me any of the other threats I got.

No, I can't prove it anymore because I don't have my phone, but if I did, I could show you the photos.

It was a couple weeks after I got pushed in front of the car. I hadn't been going out too much and, when I did, I stayed close to the apartment. I didn't go as far as the Weis again. If there was anything I needed that I couldn't get from the Quick Stop, I just asked Sarah to bring it home from work. So this day, I remember it was the start of spring training because Zadie and I had started this tradition in college where, on the day of the first televised spring training games, we'd make our own crab fries and cheese sauce. Not as good as you can get at Chickie & Pete's, but it was close enough. All you need are crinkle fries, Old Bay seasoning, and queso. The queso isn't the same as their cheese sauce but again, close enough. Zadie couldn't take off work to watch the Phillies game with me, but I wanted to keep up with the tradition anyway, so I asked Sarah to get me everything I needed, and she remembered the crinkle fries and we already had the Old Bay but she forgot the queso.

It was getting close to first pitch, and I was warming up the air fryer, and when I saw we didn't have the queso, I thought about skipping it. I mean, I didn't really need it. It was a meaningless game after all. But it felt wrong not to have it. Like I was getting cheated out of something that was special to me. The game was starting at one in the afternoon, so I figured it would be safe enough to go to the Quick Stop and grab a block of cheese I could melt down. Even if it was just sliced American, it would taste better than nothing. So I turned off the air fryer, grabbed my bag, and headed out.

I kept my eyes peeled for anyone I didn't recognize, for any lighters, for any sign that something wasn't right.

Once I got home and locked the door behind me, I started laughing.

I mean, even I knew I was being ridiculous. I turned the air fryer back on, and tossed the cheese into a bowl and popped it in the microwave and, as I'm waiting for it to melt, my phone dings.

It's not a number I recognize. It's not in my contacts list. So I figure it's a scam text. I open it up to check and I see the picture.

It's me.

A picture of me taken less than ten minutes ago when I was walking to the Quick Stop.

And as I'm staring at it, another text comes through from the same number. Another picture. Of me. Taken no more than five minutes ago when I was leaving the Quick Stop. And another one comes through. Me, waiting to cross the street to get back to our building.

I tried to block the number before any more pictures came through, but before I did, I got one more—a picture of Sarah, standing at her cash register at work.

Do you know what you get when you google Ian Baker? 'Cause Baker—that was the name on those bags I found, remember? Never heard of him?

How about the Briar Lane Murders in Dauphin County? You hear of those? I can tell you all about it. I read the news reports so many times, I practically have them memorized.

So there was this woman in her mid-forties and her neighbors got worried when they hadn't seen her in over a week, so they tried getting in touch with her adult son but couldn't reach him, either. They called the police for a welfare check, and that's when they found her body. Neighbors said her behavior had been, quote, "odd." Apparently, she'd become increasingly paranoid, especially in the last few weeks. Didn't come out much, was often glancing out from behind the curtains like she was watching for someone, had put extra locks on the doors. They thought it was this behavior that caused her son to move back in with her a few weeks before her death. The article said that the police didn't suspect robbery as a motive because nothing of note was missing from the house. A family member—not the adult son—reportedly told police that the victim had mentioned recently coming into some money, but according to another article that came out later, there was nothing weird found in her bank statements and stuff.

Police wanted to speak to a young woman who was believed to be living with the victim in the months prior to her death. Unfortunately, the young woman's name was unknown, and police couldn't get a good description of her, which is why they were talking about her to reporters. They wanted to know if anyone could identify who she was. The neighbors believed the girl was either a girlfriend of the son or a tenant renting a room. Some said she moved in before the son came back. Others thought the two moved in at the same time. It was like every neighbor with knowledge of this girl gave a different account, and the police couldn't put together an exact timeline. All they could really establish was that the homeowner's body was discovered in the house. The articles didn't say which room, but they did say no murder weapon was found, although the woman appeared to have been stabbed to death.

And the articles also said that the victim had recently been divorced, and neighbors believed her other child, a daughter, was living with her father—the victim's ex-husband. Apparently, the victim's behavior had become so bizarre in her last months that her daughter insisted on going to live with her dad. But when this guy was questioned, he said that he was estranged from both his former wife and their daughter. He hadn't seen his own kid in over a year and had no idea where she was. The police searched for this daughter, but they never found her or the victim's adult son, the prime suspect in her murder. The son's name was Ian Baker.

So yeah, not only did I suspect that some ex-boyfriend of Gemma's tried to push me in front of car and was stalking me and my sister. This ex-boyfriend was already a fucking murderer.

But he had nothing to do with what happened last night.

Jeremy just wants you to think that.

No, I told you: after we left the Redner's parking lot, we went over to Garters and Lace. It was a little while yet before we'd get to the river.

Anyway, once we get to the club, we sit in the parking lot for forever, or at least it felt like forever, because we couldn't decide what we should do.

Finally, I'm like, "Well, I don't see her. Do you see her anywhere? How about any flickering lights?" Which I say to take a dig at Jeremy.

Then Sarah says, "Maybe she's inside."

And Jeremy looks at me in the rearview mirror and says, "Maybe it wouldn't hurt to check."

I'm like, "You aren't serious about going in there? Aren't they going to think it's weird if the three of us go in and ask about some missing girl?"

And Sarah turns around and says, "Of course it'd be weird if all three of us went in. That's why you'll do it."

I give her this blank stare.

She says, "What? I don't want anyone to recognize me. It's better if you go."

"Why can't Jeremy go?"

"Because they wouldn't tell him anything. A guy goes in asking around about a girl? They'll think he's after her like he's a crazy ex or—"

I ask, "Or a stalker?"

I look at Jeremy. I'm expecting him to complain or something. Say that he's the one that should go in. He normally likes to pretend to take charge, and then we have to shoot him down. But he's not saying anything. He's slunk down in the driver's seat, looking at the other side of the street, but there's nothing there. Just empty pavement bordered by a brick wall.

I say, "Jeremy." And clap my hands to try and get his attention.

He shudders, and I expect him to say *What?* and make me repeat the entire conversation. But instead he says, "Sarah's right. I shouldn't go in. We'll stay here while you go."

I say, "I don't want to go in that place! I've never been there before. I don't know what I'm supposed to say."

Sarah says, "You'll think of something. Come on. Hurry up. It's getting late."

It's not *getting* late. It already *is* late. And I'm trying to say that, but Sarah keeps interrupting me, telling me to hurry up.

And I'm saying, "What am I supposed to ask? What do you want me to say?" But they're not giving me anything. So the last thing I say is, "Don't leave without me."

I slam the door behind me.

So I'm standing there in the parking lot, shivering in my jacket, and the air smells damp even though it hasn't rained. Those pink neon lights light up half the lot and the ugly square building that is Garters and Lace. I think it used to be a Masons hall or something. The other half of the lot is dark. There aren't any businesses on the other side, just a brick wall that blocks a vacant lot and a sidewalk that leads nowhere. Jeremy's car is partially lit by the neon, and I can see Sarah watching me, waiting for me to go in.

I keep my head down as I walk across the parking lot because, to be honest, I'm a little nervous. Because of what happened last time I was there.

I never—*never*—supported Sarah working at a strip club. Are you kidding? Why would you bring that up? Do you have a little sister? God, it makes my skin crawl just thinking about it. Look, it's not like I have a problem with women who do that sort of thing. I mean, we've all got to earn a living, right? But I didn't want *my* sister doing it. Still, what was I supposed to do? She was an adult. It wasn't illegal. She could make her own choices.

All right, so Sarah doesn't know this and I'd appreciate it if you don't tell her when you find her, but Sarah was really blasé about the whole stripper job. She never thought it was a big deal, but I wasn't thrilled about it at all, and Sarah knew that. But what she doesn't know is I'm the one that got her fired.

That's not what I intended. Honest. It's just, well, okay—so I went there to see what sort of place it was. Like, I'd never been in a strip club before. I only knew things from TV and movies and stories from some male friends from college. And none of it was that positive, you know? You heard a lot about drugs—hard drugs, like heroin—and men abusing the girls, so I just wanted to make sure it was safe. So I went one afternoon when there weren't too many people there and I knew Sarah wasn't working. But I didn't say that I was Sarah's sister. I mean, that had been the plan when I got there. Just tell the truth. *Hi, I'm Sarah's sister. I want to make sure she's safe while she's working because our parents don't give a shit.*

But as soon as I walked in—before I could say hello, let alone ask to speak to the manager—the bouncer eyes me up and says, "Interviews are in the back office." I don't know why I didn't say I wasn't there for a job, but I didn't. I nodded and followed the way he was pointing. There was this weird, thumpy club music playing and some older woman swirling around on a pole, and I didn't want to look so I kept my head down, staring at this sticky red carpet, and then I was waiting outside the manager's office with two other girls who were pancaked in makeup and tapping on their phones with these long acrylic nails, and here I was in sweatpants and a hoodie. The next thing I knew I was in the office with the manager, who was a woman, it turned out, which did make me feel better, actually. But instead of telling her the truth, I said my name was Layla—it sounded like a stripper name to me, I don't know—and said I was interested in bartending, not stripping, and I named all these bars I know except the Tavern and gave my usual "looking for meaning after college" speech. I don't remember what she asked me, but I remember answering and her nodding her head. Then she took me on a tour of the place, and we got to the locker room and that was when she got called away and said she would be right back.

So I was standing there alone, and I spotted Sarah's locker. It had her name pasted on it in sparkly letters—purple and pink—and there was a combination lock, the kind you'd normally buy for luggage, not a locker, where you can set your own combination. I guessed her combo because she always uses the same numbers. That's how I could tell you the passcode for her phone. Inside her locker were a few sets of clothes, but underneath them was the teddy bear we used to keep in our shared room at the old house. The bear Dad won for us at that carnival. It went missing when I went to college. I was so upset when we'd lost it. I know how stupid that sounds. It's just a cheap carnival teddy bear. But Dad had won it for us. That made it special. And I thought we'd lost it.

But turns out Sarah must've had it all this time, and not only did she have it, she was keeping it in her locker at a strip club. Like, what the fuck? Was she using it in her act or was she trying to hide it from me or what?

I was so angry, I don't even know what I was thinking or what my goal was. I just grabbed a bunch of random things off the counters and from open lockers and shoved them in Sarah's locker and closed it back up. By the time the manager got back, I was standing there with my hands in my pockets, looking bored. She led me out and told me she'd be in touch.

I hadn't meant for Sarah to get fired. Just in trouble, maybe. I didn't know there'd been a theft problem for a few weeks or that when they found all that stuff in Sarah's locker that they would blame everything on her. She was so angry at the time, and yeah, I felt guilty, but the truth is she got over it and she got the job at Walmart, which might not pay as well but at least I don't have to worry about potential rapists staring at my little sister's boobs all night.

You know the funny part? The manager offered me the bartending job.

So last night, okay? I get to the door, and I say to the bouncer, "Hi, sorry. I'm looking for a girl."

And he says, "Lots of girls here."

I notice he has a little bit of an accent. Like a hint of Russian or Eastern European or something?

I say, "No, I know. I mean a specific one. My roommate. We heard she might've come this way tonight. She's been missing, and the police have done fuck all to find her."

Sorry, but I wanted to get him on my side, you know? And he seemed like the kind of guy that didn't get along well with the police.

Anyway, I say, "Someone called tonight and swore they'd spotted her near here, and it's probably a long shot, but I couldn't just sit around anymore, you know?"

And he says, "You have picture?"

And I say no, but could I go in for five minutes and have a look around? I lie and say it's 'cause she likes a drink and doesn't care where it comes from, so maybe she'd been drinking here at some point. And maybe 'cause it's cold and I'm shivering and look a little bit pathetic, he lets me in.

I stand right inside the door, my shoes sticking to that grimy red carpet. The music's blaring and from the corner of my eye I can see the girls dancing, but I don't look at them or the guys at the tables. It's so dark in there, you can barely make out anyone's face unless they're the girl dancing in the lights. There's no way I could spot Gemma in here. No way anyone could spot her.

And just like that, I realize Sarah and Jeremy don't think she's in here. They just wanted me out of the way.

I try to push through the door, but I have to wait because a group of bachelor party morons is swaggering in. Meanwhile, my brain is like, *They both say they saw her. But you didn't. Is there any proof they saw her? What are they doing right now? What are they talking about? What's really going on?*

I finally make it back out to the parking lot, and Sarah and Jeremy aren't in the car. Before I can think about what that might mean, I see them. They're across the street next to the new brick wall there, looking around at the sidewalk like they've dropped something. The streetlight's shining down on them, and I think of Gemma's story when she told me about the woman waiting for her outside the bar underneath the streetlight.

They don't notice I'm back. I have to shout to get their attention. Sarah jumps, but she calms down when she sees it's only me.

I yell out, "What're you doing over there? You see her again or something?"

But Sarah shakes her head no and they come back to the car, and they ask me what I found out. I tell them what is probably the truth. I tell them nobody's seen her.

And Sarah says, "Are you sure? Did you ask?"

And I lie and say, "Of course I asked. She hasn't been there. There's obviously no sign of her. We should go home."

And I truly mean that because I'm done. I don't like how this feels now.

Whatever the two of them are after tonight, I don't think it's over. But if they hadn't wanted me with them, they would've found a way to convince me to stay home in the first place, so they want me out here with them, but I don't know why. I don't *want* to know why. I look at Sarah and hope she can sense how I'm feeling but she won't look at me.

Jeremy says, "We should go to the Tavern."

I'm asking questions as I follow them to the car, trying not to let them know I know they're up to something. Trying to be my normal self and saying things like "Why do we have to go to the Tavern? You never said you went to the Tavern that night. Aunt Joanie never would've let her in."

But neither of them answer me. Jeremy starts the car while Sarah looks out her window, rubbing her hand over her belly. I'm trying to think about how I can convince them to drop me off at the apartment without it looking like I suspect something. But I can't think of anything.

No, I fucking hate secrets. And it was all about secrets with Gemma. I know that now. How she kept things back from me. How she parceled out information at just the right time. I can't say I wasn't the same. I mean, I could have told her I knew her ex-boyfriend was Ian Baker, that I knew about the Briar Lane Murders. I could have told her right up front all the things I knew.

But I didn't.

I thought, I don't know, that it gave me leverage or something. That I could use that knowledge somehow. But I never did. And now I can't stop thinking, what if I'd just told Gemma what I knew? Would that have changed anything that happened later?

What Sarah said, about me and Gemma spending a lot of time together, about us staying out late, not telling her what we were doing—she's not wrong. But I didn't see it as a big deal then. I didn't see how that was hurting her. But I get it now. After seeing the way Sarah and Jeremy were outside Garters and Lace last night, realizing they'd tricked me into going inside so they could have some sort of private conversation—realizing they'd been hiding stuff from me this whole time—it hurt.

It really fucking hurt.

So I get it now. I get how I was making Sarah—and Zadie—feel when Gemma and I were out together. But I hadn't meant for that to happen. I hadn't even wanted to get involved with all of Gemma's bullshit. I just wanted her to move out of the apartment.

No, when Sarah tried to tell me about the money being counterfeit, the reason I didn't listen to her was because I already knew the truth.

I didn't believe Gemma's story about some woman handing her a bag of cash. And I didn't believe the money was cursed and that some unseen force was coming after her. I wasn't as gullible as Gemma liked to believe. A thief knows a thief.

After I found out about the Briar Lane Murders, I figured I had a pretty good idea of what had happened. Every good lie has a whiff of truth, right? So I guessed Ian Baker's mom really must've had that money. She was probably one of those paranoid types who didn't trust storing their money in banks or something, like our Pop-pop. Ian and Gemma started dating, Ian told her about all this money his mom had stored around the house, and they hatched a plan to steal it. Maybe killing his mom wasn't part of the plan. Maybe it was. Either way, it happened, and Bonnie and Clyde went on the run. But Gemma double-crossed him and took the money for herself. Now, she was terrified that he was going to get her. And judging by the dead rat, she was probably right.

I wasn't going to get involved in all that. But I couldn't just kick Gemma out of the apartment, either, because I didn't think she would go. What I needed was for her to decide to leave on her own. I thought, *if she doesn't feel safe here, if she doesn't think she can trust me or Sarah, she'll go.* That's all I intended to happen. And since the only thing she seemed to care about was that money, I figured the money was the best way to go about it.

So I started sneaking into her room while she was out and taking some from the bag each time. I'd be careful not to disrupt her line of salt or touch the circle of candles she'd set up in the middle of the floor. I'd slide the gym bag out from under bed, unzip it just enough to stick my hand in, and pull out a wrap of bills. I didn't want it to look like I was taking too much at one time, so I'd pull some bills out of the wrap and replace some of it with some counterfeits I happened to have—no, I'm not gonna say how I happened to have them—or single dollar bills.

No, I didn't do anything with the money I took. I kept it hidden in my room. What I thought was, Gemma would notice what was happening and confront me about it. My plan was to at first pretend I didn't know anything. Then, eventually, I'd give in and confess, and then we'd both agree it was better if she lived somewhere else. I'd return the money I took and off she'd go, taking her problems with her.

I thought it was going well. Gemma was looking more and more agitated each time we watched television together. I could tell she wanted to ask me something, but she wouldn't. I couldn't make her bring it up because in order for this to work, she needed to be the one to approach me. So I'd sit there watching *Judge Judy*, eyeing her as people argued over money disputes, and I'd think, *Come on, just ask*. But she never did.

It wasn't until it was too late that I realized my plan had backfired.

I was home alone all day that day. Sarah had left for work at the usual time, and Gemma went out early and was gone for hours. No one came over. I didn't even go downstairs to check the mail. I went in and out of my bedroom. I sat on the sofa and watched TV. I grabbed food from the kitchen. No one could've entered or exited the apartment without me knowing.

At around five in the evening, I went into my room to grab my iPad, and when I opened my bedroom door, I smelled it before I even saw it. Burnt flesh and gasoline.

At the center of my bed was a dead pigeon. Someone had set it on fire. The fire hadn't completely consumed it, but over fifty percent of its body was charred—its flesh this mix of black and red. Its remaining feathers had melted onto its skin. What was left of its wings was stretched out like a cross. A green lighter had been shoved into its beak.

I didn't know what to do at first. I just stood there, staring at it. Smelling the gasoline that someone had poured over it.

Finally, I realized I had to get it out of there before Sarah got home. She still didn't know anything about Ian, and I didn't want her to. I went to grab the edge of my comforter and the pigeon moved. I don't know how it was still alive, but it was. I grabbed the edges of the comforter and bundled it up, and I could feel it writhing inside, so I squeezed the comforter until I couldn't feel it moving anymore, and I carried it out into the hall and got a trash bag from the kitchen and shoved it all inside and ran it down to the dumpster. And when I got back to the apartment, I sprayed my bedroom with Febreze, but I couldn't stay there. I fell asleep on the couch that night. And kept sleeping there every night after that for about a week.

From then on, it was like everything was closing in on me. Mom and Dad were emailing and asking if we'd found a roommate yet, because I hadn't told them about Gemma, plus Jeremy was coming over all the time, and on top of that, my ex-supervisor from Staples was now emailing me asking if I knew anything about what happened to the money in one of their accounts and that they knew my manager from the Santander and something similar had happened with one of their accounts or something, which meant that fucking bitch from the Santander was talking and if she reached out to Staples, she might reach out to other places I'd worked, and Zadie was complaining about her boyfriend all the time and venting to me about work, but when I wanted to vent to her about Sarah or whatever, suddenly she didn't have time and I was like whatever! Leave me alone. Everyone just leave me alone. Once I could go into my room without thinking I smelled a burning bird, I just started staying in there, watching murder shows on my laptop, listening to Gemma whisper things in her room at night. I didn't even feel like watching baseball because now baseball reminded me of those photos Ian took of me. I decided it would be fine if I just stayed in my room. Nothing could happen if I was in my room. I couldn't do anything if I was in my room.

But then I smashed that guy's head at Starbucks, and Gemma did me a favor and I didn't have a choice.

No, I didn't actually smash a guy's head into a wall. I barely touched him, really.

Okay, so the thing is, I hadn't been to Starbucks in forever, even though I used to love going there. Zadie and I went together all the time in college. Their iced lemon loaf is, like, one of the greatest gifts ever given to the world. Nothing tasted better after a really hard run. And I loved picturing the look on Coach Barton's face if he knew we were ruining our healthy diets. But I hadn't been to a Starbucks since I left college.

Anyway, this one day, I'd just had lunch with Zadie. She finally had the day off, so we could hang out for a few hours, and it was only lunch at McDonald's but it was such a good afternoon. Like, the best afternoon I'd had in a long time. I'd been worried about going out, but I hadn't seen Zadie in so long I had to see her. I needed to see her. She told me a little about her work at the hospital, and I told her a little about how life with Gemma was going—they still hadn't met—and Sarah's job at Walmart. She asked me why I kept looking over my shoulder, and I would say I thought I heard something.

I thought about telling her about Ian, about everything Gemma told me, but I didn't. For the same reason I didn't tell Sarah, I guess. I thought . . . I thought I was protecting her by not saying anything. Unlike Sarah, Zadie knew I was holding something back, but she didn't press me on it then. We just started talking about the old days, swapping stories about those two years we lived together. Just, relaxing. Enjoying being friends. Without any sort of cloud hanging over us. So when we finally did leave, I was walking home, and I ended up walking past a Starbucks and I thought, Why not? The talk with Zadie had made me feel better about everything that happened in college. I was like, she's right, I can't let those memories stop me from doing stuff I like.

But after I went in, my heart started beating a little faster. I thought it was muscle memory. Like, I used to come here right after a run, so my body's thinking that I just went on a run. It was late afternoon, and there was a line, and as it inched forward, my palms started to sweat. I wiped them on my jeans, but my heart kept pumping. And when there was only one more person in front of me, I swore I was being watched. I looked behind me, but every other person in line was on their phone. I looked around the rest of the café, but everyone was either talking to one another or on their laptops or reading a book. Then I thought I smelled smoke, so I turned around to look out the big plate-glass windows onto the street.

Someone was standing there, on the opposite side of the street, in the shadows.

"You're next."

I jumped, like straight up in the air. But it was only the person behind me. They pointed toward the cash register and said again, "You're next."

And I realized the barista was waiting for me to give my order, but those words—*you're next*—kept ringing in my head. I wiped my palms on my jeans again and stammered that I wanted an iced lemon loaf, shook my head yes or no to the rest of his questions. When I took my money out of my pocket, it was all warm and damp, and I dropped it on the counter by accident instead of handing it to him. As he was getting my lemon loaf, I kept glancing out the windows, and that person was still there, and the smell of smoke, of burning, was getting stronger. I was almost choking on it.

I don't know how many times the barista said "Excuse me" before I realized he had my order. The little paper bag was barely in my hand before I was rushing out of the café. I ran right across the street—didn't even check for cars—and I tackled this guy. Shoved him right into the wall. The pastry bag was crumbled in my fist, like this. And I was shouting at him, saying, "Leave her alone! You leave her alone! Leave Zadie alone!" And this guy wasn't saying anything, just looked really confused, and I realized what I said, so I said, "Gemma! Leave Gemma alone."

When I was finally out of breath, this guy shoved me away and said, "Who the fuck is Gemma? Who the fuck are you?"

He was nobody. Just a guy, having a smoke. He had a lit cigarette in his hand. I don't know how I didn't get burned. He was even wearing a shirt with the logo of the store that was right next to where he was standing.

I didn't say sorry. I couldn't talk. I just ran. I ran all the way back to the apartment and up the stairs because I didn't want to stop, not even for the elevator. The apartment was empty, and I ran into my room and closed the door behind me, and my chest was burning and I sat on the bed. Somehow the Starbucks bag was still in my hand. The lemon loaf was all smashed up. I ate it anyway, but it didn't sit right in my stomach, and a minute later I was over the toilet, throwing it up.

I had almost hurt that guy. I hadn't. But I almost had. I never wanted to hurt anyone. I didn't come out of my room the rest of the night, but I was still too shaken up to go bed. Sarah didn't ask what was wrong. Sarah didn't care.

But when it was just past midnight, someone knocked lightly on my door. It was Gemma. She handed me a stack of cash and said, "This should get her off your back."

And the next morning, after I left the money in an envelope for my ex-manager at the Santander and got back home, Gemma told me how I could repay the favor.

Gemma didn't want dinners or a job or anything like that. That's what Sarah could never understand. All Gemma ever wanted was to get back what her ex had stolen from her. That was her only focus. It was like she had tunnel vision.

"When I get it back," she said once. "Then I can figure out how to get rid of it all properly. Then I'll be able to stop looking over my shoulder for her."

"You mean him?" I said.

And she said, "Right. Yes. Him. But I don't have much time."

But she never asked for my help until after she gave me that money.

That same night, I was in the living room watching reruns of *Evil*

Lives Here after getting back from my ex-manager's house, but I kept going over the window to check for anyone who shouldn't be there. I had a collection of those lighters by now, in my desk drawer. There'd been another that morning outside our gate. Sarah had gone out with friends after her shift, or so she said. I texted her to let me know where and who with, and she sent back a GIF of someone giving the finger. So I tracked her phone using that app, and she was just at the coffee shop across from her Walmart.

I hadn't seen Gemma much that day. But then I heard what sounded like muffled banging and shouting coming from inside her bedroom. Before if I could see if she was okay, her door opened, and I heard a soft shaking sound that I knew was her lining her doorsill with more salt. She came into the front room holding the container of salt in one hand and something wrapped in a plastic bag in the other. It was yellow. I couldn't see where it was from because the lettering was all bunched. There might've been more than one thing in it too. It was hard to tell, but the whole thing was about this big—too big for a pocket but something you could slip into a backpack without a second thought.

She kept it cradled close to her stomach, almost like she was holding an injured bird, and I was afraid there was another dead creature in there. She didn't say anything at first, then she took a deep breath and said, "You owe me a favor."

She held out the bag. "Get rid of this for me. I don't think we should leave it in our building."

At first I didn't want to. I didn't want to leave the apartment at all, not after those stupid lighters and the pigeon and Starbucks and how I had almost hurt that man.

But she said, "This is how you pay me back. And you have to pay me back."

I took the bag from her.

It didn't seem like a big deal.

When I got back home, Gemma asked me if I had looked inside it. I told her no. She must've known I lied, but she never said anything.

After she had handed me the plastic bag, I put it in my messenger bag—that brown one with the red strap—and caught a bus to the river like she told me to. It's the best place to get rid of something, isn't it? The water can wash anything away.

It was late, but not so late, just starting to get dark. Not unusual for a person to be walking near the river at dusk on a warm night. I kept looking around, thinking Ian could be lurking behind a tree or following me on the path. I looked for green lighters. I would close my eyes and tried to sense if someone was watching me. Thought I smelled smoke. But there was nothing.

I honestly hadn't planned to look in the bag. My plan was to chuck the whole thing in the water and go home. I found a good, quiet spot where the Schuylkill looked deep and took what Gemma had handed me out of my messenger bag. Whatever was inside the plastic was hard. Part of it felt square. The other part longer, thinner. I really was just going to toss it all in.

But without thinking, I started unwrapping the plastic bag. I pulled out the square thing first. It was an old leather wallet. The leather was all stretched out and worn through in parts, like it had been stuffed full of cards and things but had been emptied out. There was nothing inside it. Nothing except the corner of a photograph. There was one slot for a picture, and it was like someone had pulled it out but the corner got stuck and was torn from the rest and left there. I dug it out with my fingers. All it showed was someone's hip, their arm, bent at the elbow, with a small dog, or maybe a big cat, in the crook of the elbow. In the background, you could see green grass and the red edge of a building. I couldn't tell if it was a house or what. I slipped the piece of the picture into the card holder on the back of my phone case. I threw the rest of the wallet into the river.

The other thing inside the bag was a handle for something, but I didn't know what because had it broken off from whatever it was a handle for. Could've been a spatula or a serving spoon or fork. Maybe not even a kitchen utensil. It was dirty, though, like it had been used for gardening or something.

I dropped that into the river, too. The plastic bag wouldn't have sunk, so I stuffed it in a trash can on my way back to the bus stop.

Why would I think it was wrong? It was just trash. It's not like I got rid of a weapon or something.

No, I don't think it was a knife handle.

No, I didn't do it because I owed Gemma anything, the way she said. I did it because I help my friends. It's what I do. Ask Zadie. Ask Sarah. I even tried to help when Gemma went missing. I made some flyers and posted them in the Tavern and on some streetlights, the library, some bus stops. I didn't have a picture of Gemma, so they weren't the best, but I put down a description of her. And that description doesn't match the picture of this girl, this Gemma Horne you keep showing me. No, I don't have any of the actual flyers anymore. Aunt Joanie took them down after a few weeks. It was sort of nice of her to put them up in the first place, considering how she felt about Gemma. But I guess Aunt Joanie can be nice every once in a while. Don't tell her I said that. To be honest, though, if I could, I'd cut off my dad's side of the family completely. Never speak to them again.

Gemma asked me once if I got on with my family. I said sometimes but not always 'cause they're always so up in your business they might as well live up your asshole. I told her they're always around 'cause everyone lives nearby *and* they're all nosy as fuck. Greedy, too. Always asking Dad for money or to "help them out." Personally, I think Dad helped out enough considering everything we did for Jeremy, especially after Uncle Mitchell died. I mean it's not like anyone else was rushing in to help Aunt Mel. It's not like Pop-pop was dropping Jeremy off at anyone else's house every other day.

I told her, when they're not asking Dad for help they're busy passing judgment on everyone else in the family. Asking, "Why aren't you in college anymore? Why's your sister living with you? Parents still paying for that fancy apartment, are they? Your mom doing all right in all that fresh air?" You can't say one word without them passing it on to someone else, and they keep passing it on to someone else until your own words circle back and slap you in the face.

I told Gemma, it wasn't surprising they owned a bar—the Brickhouse Tavern, although we always just call it the Tavern. Maybe that was why they put the responsibility of Jeremy on my dad. Because my dad didn't want to take on any of the responsibilities of the Tavern when Pop-pop retired. I told Gemma, I know people think it's cool when you tell them your family own a bar, but it's not. It's years of free child labor—scrubbing floors and counters and having people call you sweetie and darling while you eat overcooked burgers and fries.

All of our friends would end up at the Tavern at least once, so it was inevitable that Gemma would, too. But she wasn't really welcomed back after she got in that fight with Aunt Joanie.

If this other girl—this Gemma Horne who's also missing—has ever been to the Tavern, I wouldn't know. You'd have to ask Aunt Joanie. She remembers most of the faces that come through that door. And no, I told you, running a bar isn't fun. Only people who have never run a bar think it would be. They think your life is like your own personal *It's Always Sunny in Philadelphia* or something. That you just serve drinks all day and chat with the regulars and flirt with strangers. It's not like that at all. I mean, you might do those things, but they're only a single percent of everything that goes into actually running a bar. Up early for deliveries, up late to close up. Handling staff and menus and budgets. Always budgets. Especially when you're a small family business. There isn't some big corporation that can bail you out if profits dip. And you never get a vacation. Rarely a day off.

I told Gemma, if I had to run the Tavern, I would honestly probably kill myself. I've seen what it's like. I've seen what happened to Aunt Joanie. She's Dad's oldest sister but looks more like a grandmother than my grandmother does. She's been bitter ever since before I was born because Pop-pop wouldn't let her marry some minor league baseball player or something when she was seventeen. But that's a story for another day. Point is, my Aunt Joanie's not a very nice woman, and she's a very fat woman and she never wanted to run the Tavern in the first place. You wouldn't think it, looking at her now, but check out pictures of her from her teens and twenties. She was pretty good-looking, I'm telling you. And she smiled then. No wonder that baseball player wanted to run off with her. But flip through photos of her as the years pass? You can watch her smile fade, her hair get dull, her body fill out and then expand and expand and expand.

When I was little, people asked me what I wanted to do when I grew up, and my first thought was always, "Anything but the Tavern." But I know the family have been talking about it—me taking over. Wouldn't surprise me if Dad put the thought in Aunt Joanie's head.

Has Jeremy told you about going to the Tavern yet? Have you talked to Aunt Joanie? We went straight there from Garters and Lace. It was our last stop before the river. You should really ask Jeremy about it because it was once we got to the Tavern that he really started being weird.

No, I don't remember what time it is when we get there. I just know it's late. We park across the street from the main entrance. There aren't any clubs in that area, you know. Just shops and office buildings. So once Jeremy turns the car off, it's dead quiet. Like the night ate up all the sounds from the air. Sarah's knee is bouncing up and down, and Jeremy keeps staring at his hands on the steering wheel.

I'm like, "What're we doing here?"

But neither of them says anything. It feels like they have something to say but they won't say it around me. I don't know what they're up to, but Sarah's scared out of her mind and Jeremy looks like he's about to shit a brick.

That's when I start thinking, what if Gemma put them up to this? What if I did something to upset her and now she's using them to get to me? It wouldn't be the first time she's done something like that. So I decide to ask them. Get it all out in the open, you know?

But as soon as I open my mouth to speak, Sarah says, "We're here because what if Aunt Joanie saw something?"

Jeremy flashes her this look and Sarah clams up. I'm thinking, there's no way Aunt Joanie saw anything tonight. It's the middle of the night. She has to get up early the next morning for deliveries, and now you want to wake her up? This is just another excuse to get me out of the car, and I'm about to say as much when a light clicks on in a window above the bar. There's an apartment above the bar that the family used to rent out, but now Aunt Joanie and her husband live there. It's cheaper, and they don't have to worry about any renters calling the housing office and complaining about the lack of a fire exit. I can't see anyone, but Sarah starts pushing me out the door.

"Go ask her," she's saying.

And I'm like, "Ask her what?"

"If she's seen Gemma."

I can just picture Aunt Joanie going off on me for showing up in the middle of the night to ask her about a girl she never liked. Plus, I don't want to leave Sarah and Jeremy alone again.

But Sarah keeps saying, "Go on. Before she goes back to sleep. She likes you best."

And I keep saying, "There's no way she saw anything. She's too busy working."

Jeremy's not saying a word. He's just sitting, face forward, gripping the steering wheel like he's ready to speed off, even though the engine isn't running. And I have this image that as soon as I get out, he's going to take off with Sarah and they're going to leave me alone with Aunt Joanie. Which wouldn't be earth-shattering for me, but I don't know what Sarah and Jeremy are planning on doing after they'd leave me. So I don't want to get out, and I don't think I would have if the streetlight hadn't caught the tears on Sarah's face. She's obviously more stressed than I'd thought, and I don't know what else to do, so I get out of the car.

Like I said, Aunt Joanie and my uncle live in the upstairs apartment. While the entrance to the Tavern is on the front of the street, the apartment entrance is around the side, facing the alley.

I raise my hand to the buzzer, but before I press it, the door opens and there's Aunt Joanie in her dressing gown, no makeup. She looks more normal without makeup. More human. But her frown is the same.

"What're you doing here?" she asks, and then she sees Jeremy's car in the street and she shakes her head and says, "Come on in. Shut the door behind you."

Instead of taking me upstairs, she leads me through the back hallway that links to the Tavern's kitchen. One of the lights is already on. Aunt Joanie has her back to me, and she's fussing with a saucepan on the range.

"You're lucky I came down to make some hot chocolate. Otherwise, I would've left you standing there."

"I know," I say. Their apartment has a kitchen, but she'll come downstairs to make something if our uncle's asleep.

"Trouble sleeping?" I ask.

She grunts something that might be "Always." A few seconds pass, and then a little more clearly she says, "Not seen you around here in a while."

I say, "I've been busy. Job hunting." Then I add, "Thinking about maybe going back to college."

I expect her to say something snippy about that, like she always does. But instead she just says, "Good for you."

Like, without any sarcasm or anything. It's the most shocking thing that's happened to me all night. Anyway, she keeps stirring the milk and then pours in some cocoa powder, so while she's talking, she's never really looking at me. And then the next thing she says is "It must've been a shock, losing your friend Gemma like that."

I'm wondering, how do you know I'm here to ask about Gemma? But I say, "A bit. I mean, I think it's the not knowing more than the fact she's gone."

Aunt Joanie looks at me then, a sideways glance, then back at her hot chocolate.

"You didn't like her, did you?" I ask. 'Cause it's one of those questions you can ask at two in the morning and know you'll get an honest answer.

She says, "No, I didn't." And then she adds, "Did you?"

That's the first time I really think about it. And since Aunt Joanie gave me an honest answer, but more so because she wasn't rude when I said I was thinking of going back to college, I feel like I owe her an honest one in return.

So I say, "I thought I did. Now . . ." I pick at a scratch on the metal prep table. "Now, I honestly don't know."

Next time I look up, Aunt Joanie's looking at me, and it's an odd look. One I've only ever seen her have when she's talking about her old baseball player boyfriend. And she says, "You really don't know what happened to her, do you?"

"No," I say.

There's a pause, a long one.

She goes back to stirring her cocoa. It must be nearly done by now. I can smell the chocolate from across the room, but she keeps stirring. And I realize, she hasn't asked me what I'm doing here this late, hasn't asked what Jeremy and Sarah are doing in the car. She doesn't seem like she wants to ask. So I go ahead and tell her.

I say, "That's why I'm here, actually. Some people said they've seen her tonight."

"Where?" she asks. But not *who*. Not *which people*.

"Different places. Around the city."

"Those people should go to the police."

"Police won't believe them. There isn't any proof. So we thought we'd drive around. Have a look."

"Whose idea was it to have a look around here?" she asks.

"Jeremy's," I say.

She stops stirring.

I say, "I just want to go home and go to bed. But he insisted we come here. He and Sarah think you might've seen something."

The milk smells like it's about to burn.

"Seen something when?" she asks.

"I don't know," I say. "Tonight, I guess."

She switches off the range and takes the pan off the burner.

"You won't find any sign of her around here. I never saw anything." She rummages on a shelf for a mug, isn't looking at me. Then she says something quietly. I don't hear her at first over the clanking of the mugs. So she says it again.

"The river."

She pauses.

"Try the river," she says. "All sorts of people turn up there. All sorts of things. Especially this time of night."

Then she starts pouring the hot cocoa into a mug.

That seems to be the end of it, so I thank her and head toward the hallway. Then she calls my name. I look back and wait for her to say something else, like be careful or good luck job hunting. Anything really. I mean, the look in her eyes, it looks like she has something to say. But she doesn't. Not even goodnight. So I say it for both of us.

As soon as I get in the car, Jeremy and Sarah are all over me with questions, so I just cut them off and say, "She says she hasn't seen anything."

I hold off on the next bit, like I don't want to say it. But they know I have something more, and they wait.

So I say, "She says we should check the river."

Neither of them says anything. Jeremy just turns the car on, and Sarah slumps back in her seat and we're driving. Toward the river. Like that's where we were always supposed to go.

I told you it was their idea to go there, but I guess really it was Aunt Joanie's.

No, Jeremy's making too big a deal out of that fight. Is that all he's talking about next door, or wherever it is you've put him? No, I don't know exactly what started the fight between Aunt Joanie and Gemma, but it honestly wasn't anything. And Jeremy wasn't even there when it happened. Like with most things, he just wants to insert himself into a story that doesn't involve him.

No, it didn't happen the first night Gemma went to the Tavern. She'd been there a few times already, but that night was the last time she was there as far as I know. Nothing really interesting happened on those other visits. The first time, we just introduced Gemma to everyone. Aunt Joanie and the other family were there, and Aunt Joanie got this smirk on her face, like Sarah and I were finally learning a lesson or something by having to take in a roommate. But it didn't bother me. I've gone my whole life with Aunt Joanie smirking at me or frowning at me or making some snide comment about me or Sarah, so I'm used to it. And that look was nothing compared to the look I got when she found out I was dropping out of college.

So anyway, we'd been there a few times, usually sat at the corner table all the regulars know is reserved for family. The night of the fight it was just me and Gemma. Sarah had stopped speaking to me, and it was after Zadie and I . . . Well, anyway, it was just me and Gemma. If Jeremy was lurking around somewhere, I don't remember seeing him. It had been a long day, and I was exhausted and nursing a Yuengling. Gemma kept whispering to me across the table, even though she didn't have to whisper because it was a Friday night and the bar was busy.

To be honest, I just wanted to have a beer in peace and talk to Gemma later, but I didn't know how to tell her to shut up without yelling at her to shut up, and I didn't want to yell. But my head was still hurting. The headache I'd had for hours hadn't gotten better at all, and the beer wasn't helping.

"We're almost finished. You've helped me so much already," Gemma was saying, and she was trying to be nice by saying it, which is another reason I didn't want to yell at her even though I wanted her to stop. And right when I was thinking maybe I should go and get some fresh air, this shadow came across the table.

It was Aunt Joanie, and she had her mildly annoyed face on, but at first I only thought she was there to deliver the nachos we ordered. She set the plate down and said, "You shorted the bar."

And I was like, "What?" 'Cause I really didn't know what she was talking about. My mind wasn't on the food at all. So she said it again.

"You shorted the bar."

And I said, "No I didn't."

"You still owe $3.72 for the nachos."

And I said, "Not with the family discount."

And she said, "The family discount is for family." And she looked at Gemma.

And I said, "The nachos are for both of us."

And she said, "And one of you isn't family. $3.72. I'll start your tab." And she walked back to the bar. My brain was in a fog. I couldn't believe what just happened, and I was picking at the cuts on my knuckles, wondering if there was a shard of glass stuck in there, too tired to figure out what to do or say.

Then Gemma said, "It's all right. You've done enough tonight. I'll take care of it." And she got up and went to the bar.

I thought she meant she'd take care of the $3.72, so I dug into the nachos because I knew Stevie was in the kitchen that night—he's not family, just staff, and he always adds extra guac and sour cream for me—and I thought some food would do me good because I couldn't actually remember the last time I ate. But I only managed two chips before I heard this, well, this *screech*. And I looked over at the bar and Aunt Joanie was literally climbing over the top of the counter—I have no idea how—and then she was going at Gemma and got one good slap in before two of the other staff managed to separate them. The customers were looking at each other in shock, and Gemma was holding her face where Aunt Joanie slapped her. Aunt Joanie had this look on her face, and out of all of Aunt Joanie's looks, it wasn't one I'd ever seen before. She started spitting, "Get out! Get out!"

And she looked right at me. And, well, despite everything that happened, I was reaching for another nacho. She screamed right at me, "Get out!"

I shoved the nacho in my mouth, and Gemma and I were out the door.

Outside, I was still mourning the loss of the nachos while also trying to process what the hell had just happened. Gemma lowered her hand, and I could see the red mark on her cheek but also the smile on her lips. In her other hand, she had strands of hair that I realized were Aunt Joanie's. And I was like, "What did you say to her?"

And she said, "Nothing she didn't already know."

Then she whispered some words that sounded like Latin, blew the strands of hair off her fingers, and laughed while they drifted away.

Oh, believe me, I would love to blame all of this on Ian Baker. That's what you think I'm doing, isn't it? I mean, this guy killed his own mother, probably. You would expect me to say he's the reason our Gemma went missing and that maybe he did something to this Gemma Horne, too. And now maybe he's come for Sarah. Maybe he's coming for me.

But I can't say that.

Because I know what happened to Ian Baker.

At least, I have this theory.

See, the day Gemma sat in the armchair and told me about the money, she left out a few key pieces of information. First, there was the whole Briar Lane Murders thing, which I found out on my own and never told Gemma that I knew about.

But there was something else she left out. Something I didn't find out about until after the burnt pigeon and Starbucks and getting rid of the yellow plastic bag.

This thing Jeremy doesn't even know about Ian.

I was in my room, sitting up in bed, looking at that scrap of photograph I'd taken from what I assumed was Ian Baker's wallet. Still couldn't make anything of it. Couldn't even tell if the elbow belonged to a man or a woman. When Gemma knocked on my door, I quick shoved the photo back into the case on my phone. I don't know why. I just didn't want Gemma to know I had it. I guess I should have taken that as a sign.

Anyway, she opened my door and asked if I wanted to go walking with her. I didn't say anything. Just put on my shoes and grabbed a coat and followed her out the door. She didn't have to say anything. I knew we were looking for Ian. She didn't want to talk, but I could tell she was thinking.

We walked for about ten minutes when finally she said, "There is only one true way to get rid of the money, which is to pass it on. Like

Ian's mother passed it on to me. But you can't pass it on to anyone. In the dreams, it shows you who you have to give the money to, and it only gives you so much time to do it."

I didn't know what to say to that. I mean, it sounded fucking insane.

So I said, "Okay, step one: find Ian. Step two: get back the money he stole. Step three: find the person in your dreams. Step four: pass the money on to them. Problem solved. So we need to find Ian, but in the meantime, what about this other person? The one you're supposed to give the money to?"

She hesitated, and then she said, "I've already started."

And I said, "Started what?"

And she said, "Giving them the money."

And I was like, "Well, who is it?"

And Gemma looked at me.

And she said, "The money must go to someone it says needs to be punished."

My hands started shaking, so I stuffed them in my pockets, because I knew what she was going to say. It felt like I'd been waiting forever for her to say it. Like these last few years, like ever since what happened at college, all I've been waiting for was this. Was her.

I'd told Gemma a lot about my life, I knew that. But I hadn't told her everything. I never told her why I left college. *Never.*

But she told me.

She told me what happened at college.

She told me *exactly* why I left.

And she couldn't have known that. There is no fucking way. Because no one knows that. No one except Zadie. And she and Zadie hadn't met yet. And Zadie doesn't even know all of the details. Besides, Zadie wouldn't have told Gemma because Zadie and I had promised each other we'd never tell anyone. Ever.

After Gemma told me, she kept talking, saying things like, "I don't want to give it to you. I like you. You've been kind to me. I don't want anything bad to happen to you. So I thought if I just gave you a little at a time—for the rent, the Roku, to pay back your ex-manager—instead of all at once, that it wouldn't be so bad. But I haven't slept. I haven't slept in weeks because the dreams won't let me sleep. And I can see it's affecting you, too. How you're always angry at Sarah. How you assaulted that man outside Starbucks. And I know you've been sleeping on the couch instead of in your room. So it's not working. And I'm so sorry. I don't know what else to do. I think it's time for us to work together."

And in my head, I was like, her story is insane. It can't be true. There's no way it can be true. But if it's not true, then *how else did she know?*

We came to a stop in the middle of the sidewalk. I mean, right in the middle. People gave us dirty looks because they had to walk around us. I thought we'd go into a café, get a window seat, people-watch. And I was so unsettled by everything that I never thought to ask her the question I should have asked if all this was true, which was: *Why were* you *given the money? What are* you *being punished for?*

Instead, I was watching all these people giving me looks and was like, "Gemma, we should go into that restaurant or—"

And she said, "No. We'll wait and see if he comes through here."

Where was here? What was she staring at?

A solid, brick wall.

So I said, "Should I keep an eye on the rest of the street? It's not like he's gonna come out of the wall."

And I was still trying to wrap my head around everything else she just told me about the money and college and how she couldn't know any of that, when she said, "Of course he can. He is dead, after all."

So that's why Jeremy never had to worry about "protecting" her.

That's why I never told you that she had an ex-boyfriend who was stalking her.

Because she didn't.

Ian Baker was already fucking dead.

VERSION 3

Zadie's still here, isn't she? Can I see her? Why can't I talk to her? She's my best friend. Please.

Yeah, Sarah and I are friends, of course we are. But if we weren't sisters? I don't know. We're so different. But me and Zadie? We've been friends since the moment we met. 'Cause of the Phillies.

You'll think this is really specific, but the years 2008 to 2011 were probably the best years of my life. And it's because of the Phillies.

Even before I started playing field hockey, I loved watching sports. And I've always loved baseball. I mean, we have the Reading Phillies right here, and they've been the Phillies Double-A affiliate since 1967, so not just my whole life but practically my Mom and Dad's, too. Nana and Pop-pop used to be season ticket holders, and they talk about how they saw Mike Schmidt and Larry Bowa play there. Dad remembers seeing Scott Rolen. I was only eleven in 2008, but I remember the couple of years before when Carlos Ruiz first came up to Reading and Nana and Pop-pop told me to watch him. That he would be something special.

So 2008 was huge for me. Like, first of all, winning the World Series was the first Philly championship of my lifetime. But also the team was made up of all these guys I'd seen play right here—Jimmy Rollins and Ryan Howard. Cole Hamels. Carlos Ruiz. Ryan Madson. They felt like family, even though I'd never met them, you know? So those years where they were always at the top of the division and always getting in the post-season, it was just awesome.

Anyway, flash forward a few years. I'm starting college, and I decided to move myself into the dorms. I mean, Albright is right here anyway, plus my parents and I were arguing about one thing or another at the time—Mom was on the verge of another breakdown—and I was just like, I can do it on my own, and if I have to make a few trips back and forth to the house to get everything, then that's what I'll do. I didn't have a car, so I tried to carry as much as I could in one trip. I mean, I was in shape then, so why not? So I had this big old hiking pack filled with clothes strapped to my back, gym bags across my chest, reusable shopping bags dangling from my arms. The driver almost didn't let me on the bus.

"College student?" he asked.

And I could barely pant out, "Yes."

He just nodded.

So I got to the dorm, did the check-in, and the person said, "Looks like your roommate is already here."

I was disappointed because I wanted to get there first, claim my space, you know? But at that point, I was also exhausted and wanted to set all this shit down. It got even worse because there was only one elevator and there was this huge line with all these other new students and their stuff and their parents, and I was like, I'm not waiting. So I headed for the stairs. My room was on the fourth floor, and at one point I swore I was going to die. I had to take this long break on the fourth floor landing. I could barely feel my arms, my back was killing me, sweat dripping off every inch of skin, and I was thinking, *Great, I've broken myself before I've even stepped on the field.*

Then as I was sitting there, I heard baseball. Like someone was streaming a game and had the volume turned way up. So I got back to my feet—bags and all—and I followed the sound and realized it was coming from the room I'd been assigned. The door was open halfway, so I nudged it all the way in, and there was this girl unpacking her clothes—she'd taken the right side of the room, which was perfect because I always prefer the left—and before she even noticed me I said, "Is that the Mets game?"

It was streaming on her laptop.

She looked up, and I saw her taking me in and I was thinking, *God I must look like a homeless person*, and she said, "Yeah, the first game of the makeup double-header for yesterday's rainout. Sorry, it's loud. I can turn it off if—"

And I said, "Are you a Mets fan?"

And she said, "My dad is, but I'm just watching it because there aren't any other afternoon games today. My mom's from South Jersey originally, so I side with her—the Phillies. Are you into baseball?"

I set my bags down and grabbed my '08 World Champs poster that I was gonna hang above my bed. She looked at it, then pulled a poster out of her suitcase and unrolled it. It was the same exact one.

We laughed, and she held out her hand. "Zadie."

We shook and then she looked at all my bags and said, "Did you carry all that here yourself?"

I nodded and said, "And up the stairs."

She immediately helped me set the rest of my things down. We talked for a few minutes while I caught my breath, and at one point she said, "I guess you'll want to clean up before going to the Freshman Welcome Party tonight."

And I said, "Actually, I'm not really that into parties. I was probably gonna stay in. Eat some snacks. Or go to the R-Phils game tonight. They only have a few more home games this season."

And her face lit up, and she said, "The stadium is nearby, right? I wanted to go to a game before the season ended. I hate going out late unless it's for a baseball game."

God's honest truth, we've been best friends since that exact moment.

So can I please see Zadie? Just for a few minutes. I want to make sure she's okay. I don't have anything else to say about what happened at the river. I don't. Why are you so obsessed about that? I know I didn't actually see Gemma. I know it was just my mind playing tricks on me. And yeah, okay, I was a little mad at Sarah and Jeremy for lying to me, but I know it wasn't Sarah's fault. I know it was Jeremy who put her up to it. She wouldn't have kept any secrets if it weren't for him.

What happened to my sister? I left Jeremy alone with Sarah and he showed up here at the police station by himself, and you have the fucking nerve to ask *me* what happened to my sister? When he must've been the last person to see her?

Fine, maybe we did all have a fight, but it wasn't anything major.

But you want my version of it?

Fine.

Last night, after we leave the bar and head toward the river, I keep trying to get Sarah's attention. I want to talk to her alone when we get there. But she keeps looking out the window. Whenever we pass under a streetlight, I can see tears on her cheek. None of us is saying anything. Usually, you get the three of us together, you can't pay us to shut up. It's been that way since we were kids. But now it's like we're afraid that if someone speaks, something will snap because, after going to the Tavern, there's a tension that wasn't there before.

We've been driving for a few minutes when Sarah suddenly sits up and looks out the window. I think she's seen Gemma again, so I'm looking but I don't see anything but dried grass and empty beer bottles. Sarah tells Jeremy to stop the car, so he pulls onto the shoulder and keeps the engine running while Sarah points toward the river and says, "This is it. This is where I saw her."

Now I'm confused, so I say, "But you said you saw her near the Quick Stop."

And she shrinks back, like she realizes she's said something she shouldn't have.

So I ask, "Sarah, have you seen her before tonight?"

And she nods her head yes.

So I ask, "How many times?"

She's chewing on her thumbnail, and I want to slap her hand away but I don't. I sit on my hands and count to ten in my head like Dad taught me. Sarah knows what I'm doing, so instead of answering right away, she waits until I have my temper under control. Jeremy's waiting, too, with this look on his face like he thinks we've been keeping this big secret from him. Or like he's pretending to think we've been keeping a big secret from him.

Sarah doesn't look at either of us when she speaks. She looks at the floor of the car, like the answer's written down there in the empty McDonald's wrappers.

"Sarah," I say. "How often have you seen her?"

"A few times," she says.

I take a deep breath, and I ask, "A few times how often? A few times a week? A month?"

Sarah goes quiet again, but I can't take more silence. So I reach forward between the seats and grab her shoulder. I admit that. But I never hit her. No. I only grab her shoulder, like this.

And I ask her again, "When's the first time you saw her, Sarah?"

And she says, "About three or four months ago."

And I say, "You started seeing her three or four months ago?"

I feel my face getting all hot and it's hard to breathe and I'm afraid of what I might do, so I get out of the car.

Yes, I get out of the car first. Like I told you before. And Sarah and Jeremy stay inside, alone, so I don't know what they say to each other. I can hear them arguing, but I can't make out what they're saying. I'm pacing the side of the road and counting to ten, over and over. Because I'm angry. I'm angry that Gemma went missing. I'm angry that my sister lied to me. I'm angry at being dragged out of the apartment in the middle of the night. Sarah could've told me what was happening. She should've told me before. Why did she spring this on me now? And, like outside Garters and Lace, I feel like she and Jeremy are in on this together—whatever *this* is—even though I don't want to believe it. I don't want to believe my sister would be trying to, I don't know, conspire against me or something.

So I tell myself it has to be Gemma, again. She must really be back. And when I convince myself that's true, I'm thinking, fuck, how long has she been back in town and what is she planning? And why would she be coming after me? Because this must be some sort of plan to get to me. But I did everything she asked. Why won't she leave me alone?

No, I wasn't screaming. Jeremy's a liar. If I'd been screaming, someone else would've heard me, even all the way out there.

No, when Sarah gets out of the car, that's when she has the bloody lip. Her lip wasn't bleeding until *after* I got out of the car. I never laid a finger on her. I never hit her.

As soon as Sarah looks at me, I say, "Why didn't you tell me? Why didn't you tell me she was back?"

Her eyes flicker between me and Jeremy like she's some sort of trapped animal, and she's holding one hand against her belly. In her big winter coat, you'd think she was just fat.

She looks down and she says, "She's not . . . I wasn't sure what I was seeing. Not at first. It was just a glimpse when I was walking home or walking to the store. Then she started getting nearer. Close enough that I could make out her clothes. See she was wearing my old T-shirt. But she'd never move. I never saw her move. She'd just stand there with her back to me and I'd look away, and then she'd be gone. But tonight . . ."

Sarah closes her eyes tight.

"Tonight, she was there near the Quick Stop, with her back to me, like always, and she was so close I could read the tour dates on the back of the shirt. I looked away and thought she'd disappear. But she didn't. When I looked again, she was still there. And this time, for the first time, I saw her move. She started scratching the brick wall until her fingers were bloody, like I told you. And then she started to turn. But I didn't want to see her face. I couldn't. So I ran. I ran all the way back to the apartment. I should've told you sooner. I know that."

Sarah's words sort of hang there in the air. I wait for Jeremy to say something. To tell me his story about seeing Gemma all over town for months, but he doesn't say anything. He's waiting for me to say something. They both are. And I keep thinking, how long has Gemma been planning this? If she's been back in town for even just three months, that's plenty of time for her to set something in motion. And I've been sitting on my ass doing fuck all.

So I say, "We have the detectives' number. Let's tell them what you saw. Let's tell them she's back."

And Jeremy, he's the one that says, "We can't."

Before I can ask why not, he says, "If it's her . . . she can't really be here. Not as something you can put handcuffs on."

It takes me a second to get what he means by that.

What he's trying to imply.

Jeremy thinks she's dead. Or at least *wants* me to believe he thinks she's dead.

Then I start thinking, how did he know to show up at our apartment tonight at just the right time? To say he thought he saw Gemma right after Sarah says she saw her? What a wonderful coincidence, right? And then I start thinking about how he's been acting these last few months. How he practically interrogated me and Sarah about that night, about the money. About where it is. About what we did with it. And that's when I realize what this is all about.

Gemma doesn't just want the money back. If she did, she could get it on her own. She knows where it is. It's right where the two of us left it. So what if this isn't about the money at all? What if it's about me and Sarah? What if, instead, what she wants is to tie up loose ends? And she's using Jeremy to do it?

And then I'm thinking, what if she had been doing shit with Jeremy back when she lived with us? Cozying up to him? Making him think she loved him? Getting him to love her? So she could use him to get to us? It wouldn't be the first time she's used a man like that. And now, Jeremy's dragged us all the way out to the river, where there's no one around and nowhere to go?

All this is going through my head while he's standing there, waiting to see how I react. And I know I have to play my cards right.

So Jeremy's right about what I said next. But what he doesn't know is that I was only pretending.

I know what he wants me to think, so I put my hands on my hips and stare up at the sky and I say, "So what you're saying is she's dead and a ghost. Is that it? You've both seen a ghost. Okay, so what's the big deal? Ghosts can't hurt you. Sarah, the one you saw in Grandma and Grandpa's basement scared the shit out of you, but it never hurt you, did it?"

Sarah looks at the ground.

"Sarah?"

She shakes her head no.

"Okay, good. So we're not talking poltergeists or demonic possession or anything, right? Just a single harmless ghost."

"But—" Sarah says.

"But nothing," I say. "If it is a ghost, you know what it's trying to do? It's trying to do what Gemma always did. Trying to guilt you into doing something stupid. So don't let it. What's done is done. Right?"

So, yes, Jeremy is right about that, but I only said it because I was trying to pretend that I believed him. My plan was to keep pretending to go along with this until I could get away and then reach out to you as soon as I could. Which is what I did.

And yes, I do say a few more things but that's because I'm not sure he's convinced yet. So I add, "She was nothing. Useless. A freeloader. A floater. Street trash. She made us think we were doing something nice for her, that we were helping somebody out, and all that time she was laughing at us behind our backs. Whatever happened to her, she deserved it. Every fucking bit of it."

But again, I don't believe it. I only had to make *Jeremy* believe I meant it.

Then I finish with, "You want to lay this ghost to rest? Then let's put her to rest."

I don't know where the shovel came from. It must've still been in Jeremy's car from when Gemma and I used it. And no, I don't know what I was planning on doing with it. What good would a shovel be against a ghost? But yeah, I am the one that carries it as we make our way down to the river, so yes, my fingerprints will be on it. But I only carry it because Sarah needs both her hands to keep her balance. And Jeremy went ahead of us before I had the chance to hand it to him. Just stormed off, like he knew exactly where he was going.

He led the way. Then Sarah. And I brought up the rear.

So that's what really happened before I lost them. Okay? We had a fight because Sarah had lied to me about how many times she'd seen Gemma, but what I was really upset about was that Gemma was trying to trick me again. And I wasn't going to let that happen.

My plan was to get Sarah away from Jeremy and get us both back to the car so we could leave him there.

I don't know what they, I mean Jeremy, was going to show me. I honestly don't know if he was going to show me anything at all or wanted to lure me to a specific spot. I was trying to figure out what to do, how I could talk to Sarah on her own, but then I tripped, like I told you. And they went on without me—or Jeremy made Sarah go on without me—and I was out there alone.

They left *me*. They abandoned me. And because of everything they've just said, everything Jeremy said, I've got it into my head that they're—that he's—purposely hiding from me. That he's going to leave me out here or worse. He and Sarah have already been excluding me for months with their secret phone calls and secret looks. This must be the plan now that I figured out the truth—he's trying to freak me out so I'll tell him where the money is.

And that makes me even angrier. Makes me want to take that shovel and slam it over and over onto the frozen ground until something breaks. Until the ground is smashed to pieces or the handle of the shovel shatters in my hands and the pain shoots up my arms. Because I am so fucking tired of people lying to me.

And that's what I do.

I slam the shovel against the ground, over and over and over, so hard it hurts. And then I realize I've also smashed up my phone. It must have fallen out of my pocket, and I smashed it without realizing it. So I did break my phone, yes. That's what happened. I hit it with the shovel. But it was an accident. I never hit Jeremy. Or Sarah.

Even after I see what I did to my phone, I'm lifting the shovel above my head one more time because, fuck it, I'm still angry, and that's when I see the person in the headlights.

I told you: at first I thought it was Sarah. I mean, it has to be Sarah, right? It was just her, me, and Jeremy out here, and it's definitely not Jeremy, and this person's wearing Sarah's clothes.

It takes me a second to work it all out. Like, I'm standing there with the shovel over my head while my brain ticks everything over.

But it can't be Gemma, right? It can't be. Would she really risk showing herself to me?

So I'm like, fuck it. If it is her, I'm going to confront her. And I storm up the embankment, shovel in hand, but by the time I get there, she's gone. And that's what freaks me out the most because how could anyone disappear like that? I wasn't that far away. I didn't see anyone move. There isn't anywhere to hide.

I look around. I cross the road. I look under the car. Nothing.

No one is there.

The road is empty.

I check inside the car, including the trunk, but there's no one there. Then I get in the driver's seat and lock the doors. I think about waiting for Jeremy and Sarah, but at this point, I'm like, they were planning on leaving *me*, right? At least Jeremy was.

My thinking is that Jeremy had to have planned this with Gemma. Because the only alternative is that Gemma's stories are true, and that's just fucking insane.

No, I don't have any proof that Jeremy was working with Gemma to stage these sightings. Not now.

But I did.

Okay, so what do you do when your roommate tells you she's stalking a dead man? Like, she's either (a) crazy or (b) making shit up. Back then, I thought she was crazy. But now that I've had all this time to think about it, I'm starting to feel I didn't know as much as I thought I did.

Take the rat. At the time, I thought Gemma was super freaked out by it, right? Which was why she dropped the package and ran back to her room. But now I'm wondering if maybe Gemma did that on purpose. Like, she left the package on the counter because she wanted me to open it. Like she wanted me to see what was inside and ask about it. Maybe she even sent it to herself. Because if Gemma wasn't her real name—and I know now that it wasn't—how would someone have known to address a package to the name "Gemma"? Why wouldn't it have her last name on it? What if there was another reason she insisted on checking the mailbox each day?

And what about that pigeon in my room? We're not on the ground floor, but I do have a window that opens all the way and I don't lock it or anything. Someone could have used the fire escape, got in that way. I wouldn't have seen them. I wouldn't have noticed them come in.

And then there was Gemma's accent. Sarah asked me once where I thought Gemma was from, and I said New Jersey because that's what she had told us. But Jeremy said Gemma was from New York because that's what Gemma told him. And I said she didn't have a New York accent, and Sarah said she didn't have a New Jersey accent, either. But I didn't think much about it. Just like I didn't think much about how Gemma said she never watched TV but she knew who Marie Kondo was. Or how she didn't have any trouble navigating the apps on the TV even though she claimed not to know much about technology, or how she once made a very specific Harry Potter reference but had later asked me, "Who's that?" when I made a Dumbledore joke.

I don't know. I guess there are a lot of things I've been thinking about differently since last night. And not just with Gemma. With Jeremy, too. Like, there's this one memory I have from the week after Gemma went missing, when your investigation had just started.

Me and Sarah and Jeremy were at the Tavern, at the family table, having a drink. It had been two or three days since Sarah and I had spoken to you, and Jeremy had just finished his first interview a few hours before. We were sitting there, all very quiet, Jeremy and I nursing our beers. He was staring at some game on the TV but not really watching. I was sitting with my back to the screen because it meant my back was to the bar. So even though I could feel Aunt Joanie's eyes digging into me, at least I couldn't see them. And Sarah was completely disinterested in her Diet Coke, which I knew she wished had some rum or vodka in it.

We each knew what the others were thinking, but no one was talking, so I figured I'd just say it.

"Do you think something bad happened to her?"

Simple question, right? But you would've thought I'd slapped them in the face. Sarah got up and went to the bathroom, and Jeremy glared at me and said, "You shouldn't upset her like that."

I was like, "How did I upset her? All I did was ask a question."

And he said, "She's already been asked enough questions by the police. She doesn't need you asking more."

I said, "It's a fair question."

And he said, "You really think she wants to believe something horrible's happened to Gemma? That she wants pictures of that in her head while she's dealing with the baby and everything else?"

The pregnancy was still a really raw topic. Sarah hadn't decided yet if she was going to keep the baby or not, and she hadn't told the father and wasn't sure she was going to. Then all this happened with Gemma. I know it must've been really stressful for her. But I stood by what I said. It was a fair question, and it was what we were all thinking anyway.

So I said, "I didn't say horrible. I said bad."

And Jeremy leaned back and said, "What's the difference?"

And I was like, "Car crashes are bad. Slips and falls. A terminally ill relative she had to rush home to." I leaned forward. "Horrible is a lot worse than bad."

I didn't say anything about dismemberment or drowning or rape or kidnapping. Jeremy's making all of that up because that's what was in *his* mind. Not mine. And Sarah didn't hear any of it because she didn't come back from the bathroom until the conversation was over. She looked really pale then, so even though I didn't necessarily feel bad about asking the question, I didn't bring it up again.

Even before Gemma went missing, there hardly ever seemed to be a good time to mention her around Sarah. It was like, after I refused to believe Sarah about the money being counterfeit, she didn't want to talk to me about anything anymore. I tried to have a conversation with her about it once. About her behavior. She was getting ready to leave for work, and I don't even remember what started the conversation, but I said something like, "Can you at least pretend to be nice? Gemma's working through some stuff right now, okay?"

And Sarah was like, "Whatever her business is, it has nothing to do with me. And it shouldn't have anything to do with you."

And I said, "Of course it has to do with me. I'm her friend."

And Sarah looked me right in the eye and said, "And Gemma? Is she your friend?"

And I was like, "Yeah, obviously."

Sarah looked right at me and said, "You don't know her as well as you think you do." And before I could say *Neither do you*, she left for work.

I went to the window to watch her go. You can look down on the gate from there. As Sarah was going out, Gemma was coming in, and they both stopped and stared at each other. I don't know if they exchanged words or anything, but Gemma gave this little wave with just her fingers, and Sarah practically bolted. Gemma stood there and watched her go. And I knew there was no getting through to Sarah about this. That I shouldn't try to talk to her about Gemma again.

Jeremy, though, he's the one who really got worse after Gemma disappeared. I thought that after it was clear she wasn't turning up any time soon, he'd come over less. Go back to being his normal self. But that didn't happen. He came over the same amount, if not more. At first I thought it was because he didn't believe us—me and Sarah. It sounds stupid now, but at the time I thought he suspected we were hiding Gemma from him.

Yeah, I told you it sounds stupid. Especially after what I learned last night. But your brain thinks up all sorts of stupid things when you don't know the answer, doesn't it? Like, anything can be a possibility because there's no certain answer that can explain it all away. So when he'd come around and take a peek in her room or look under the sofa or kitchen cupboards, whenever I caught him doing something like that, I thought, is he looking for her? Is he looking for some sign she's been here?

I assumed he was looking for the money. I know that's all he cared about. I never said much about it when he tried to bring it up in conversation. Just repeated what Sarah had suspected months earlier—that it was counterfeit.

I know he tried to get Sarah to tell him, too. 'Cause he kept calling her at weird hours when he didn't think I'd be around. I only found out by accident. See, this one time, Sarah was home when she normally wouldn't be because she'd switched shifts with someone as a favor, and she was in the shower when her phone rang. I always look at her phone when it rings and she's not there, in case it's someone important. In case it's Mom or Dad. I saw Jeremy's name pop up and I let it go. Jeremy calling was no reason to rush her out of the shower. Plus her back was starting to get stiff from the pregnancy and I knew the hot water made her feel better.

Then the phone beeped. I looked and Jeremy had left a voicemail. Who the fuck leaves a voicemail? So then I was thinking, is it something serious? Did his mom finally die? I looked at my phone and waited for it to ring or beep, but it didn't. So it couldn't be a family emergency because he would try to reach me. I unlocked Sarah's phone and went to her recent calls list, and that's when I saw his number over and over and over. Check their phone records, you'll see. He was calling her multiple times a day. Five, six, seven. Sometimes more. Always when she was normally at work or after I usually go to bed. And they weren't missed calls. Most of the time, she answered. You could see how long the calls lasted—three minutes, seven minutes. One time when she must've been on a break it was a half hour. So now I was wondering what was on the voicemail, but that was when she stepped out of the bathroom. I didn't even hear the water shut off. So I quickly put the phone down and didn't mention the call. The next time I checked her phone, she'd deleted the voicemail. I never found out what they were talking about. I just assume he was pestering her about the money the same way he was pestering me.

And then there was this other time, when they both went out without me. It was only a few days ago. Didn't even invite me along to wherever they were going, not that I would've gone anyway because it was Game 2 of the NLDS against the Braves, and there's no way in hell I'd miss a playoff game. When Jeremy brought Sarah back home later that night, I swore they were looking at me funny. They smelled a little like a bonfire, and when I asked about it, Jeremy said they went to a party at the Davy boys' and ended up burning shit in a barrel. Sarah didn't say anything, but after Jeremy left and she got a shower, she offered to make me some midnight nachos—one of our favorite snacks we used to make together, before Gemma—and on top of the nachos, she also baked me lemon bars. When I asked why she was being so nice, she said she wasn't. She was just craving nachos and lemon bars. But Sarah has never craved anything during the pregnancy, I told you. And she's always hated lemon.

I don't know. Maybe pregnancy really did change her taste in food. And maybe they were just talking about other things, like the baby, or moving into the house. Sarah mentioned a few times that it would be easier to raise the baby in a house than a fifth floor apartment, so why not move into Jeremy's house? Which would mean I'd have to get rid of the apartment, which makes me sick to think about. But maybe that's all it was.

Maybe their calls had nothing to do with Gemma.

Sometimes, I put two and two together and get five. I know I do. Like, take Ian Baker. I googled the fuck out of Ian Baker. I'll be honest, I don't actually know if the Ian Baker of the Briar Lane Murders was the Ian my Gemma talked about. I mean, she never told me her ex's full name. She just said her ex's name was Ian, and I found the surname Baker on those bags, and I assumed. But I mean it would be one big fucking coincidence if it was a different Ian Baker, right?

What I did know was that Gemma's Ian was dead. But I couldn't find any Ian Bakers that were dead. Or at least known to be dead. After Gemma told me her Ian was dead, I went looking through all the articles I could find on the Briar Lane Murders, which all pretty much said the same thing. I checked obituaries and missing persons reports. Anything that was available online. Nothing. I even called the police station that's handling the case and pretended I was doing a true-crime podcast about unsolved murders and asked for an update about the Briar Lane Murder case. All I got was a "no comment." Left my number and everything in case they wanted to call me back, but they never did. As far as I could figure out, Ian Baker's whereabouts remained unknown. So he could be alive or dead, I guess.

What did Gemma tell me? You mean about Ian's death? She told me he killed himself, except that it wasn't suicide. She said that each time he took some of the money, he became more depressed, more desperate. That he became violent as a way of trying to cover up for the guilt he felt growing inside him. She said that was what the curse did to those who took what wasn't theirs. I asked her how she knew, but she would just say that she saw it for herself and wasn't that knowledge enough? She said he decided to get back at her for bringing this curse into his life by hiding some of the money so that she wouldn't be able to pass it all on, which would mean she'd be stuck with the curse for the rest of her life. Even though it was his mom that somehow came into the money in the first place, before Gemma ever had it. She said he killed himself so she would never be able to find it. But the curse was powerful and kept him tethered to her, to the money. So really he'd cursed himself twice over by hiding the money, and wasn't that great, she'd said. It sounded like she meant it.

I asked her where the curse came from. I mean, she did say she'd been trying to investigate it. So did she know how it originated? Like, was it some sort of Egyptian curse? Did the money originate from the sale of stolen artifacts? Was it like the Hope Diamond—something stolen from a god or goddess of another culture? Did it have anything to do with traditional English witchcraft? Like, had the money belonged to a powerful witch who'd had it stolen and cursed anyone who came into possession of it?

"A witch," Gemma had said, "Yeah, that sounds about right."

But then she'd laughed and said, "Maybe Ian's mother was the witch."

So I kept pulling on the only thread I had—the Briar Lane Murders.

I found the Facebook profile for the woman whose body was found in the Briar Lane house—Rebecca was her name. I knew it was her because the account was public and her timeline was filled with all of these condolence posts. Stuff like, *RIP Rebecca, I'll miss you, I can't believe this happened to you.* One just said "JUSTICE" in all caps and a lot of people liked that post, but it didn't seem like any of her friends were doing anything about getting her that justice. I've seen other Facebook pages where people have started action groups or victim support groups, but no one set up any of that for Rebecca. And no one had left any new posts on her timeline since about a month after the murder. The one-year anniversary had recently passed and nothing. It was like, after she died, she just faded from everyone's memory. None of the posts seemed to be from family, either, not that I could see. Friends, coworkers, maybe. No boyfriend or ex-husband. Nothing from the daughter.

She didn't have many pictures, either. The ones she'd uploaded were of coffee shops and this cute Westie, but the shops looked like any other café and she never captioned the pictures of the dog. Her profile pic was the only photo that had a person in it, and it was a partial profile—a woman with long, blond hair looking out over a railing at sunset. She wasn't wearing a beret. Her face was in shadow, but she looked sort of sad to me. I must have stared at that photo a lot, trying to figure out what she might have been thinking and who took the picture and if that person still thought of her.

It was when I was scrolling through her friends list that I spotted the name "Ian B." But the account was locked. That stock profile image was all I could see, the one Facebook uses when someone doesn't upload a photo. I sent a friend request but it was never accepted.

Anyway, when Gemma refused to investigate the curse, when she was adamant that the only way to move forward was to get back what Ian had taken, I asked her, "Gemma, how are we going to find where he put the money? It could be anywhere. He could've buried it or something. Stuffed it in a storage locker at a bus station."

But Gemma said, "No. He wasn't like that. He gave it to someone else. I know it. So we just have to find and confront that person."

And I said, "But we still have the problem of asking a ghost a question."

I said it really slowly because I wasn't sure Gemma was understanding. I didn't think she was stupid—she definitely wasn't—but I certainly wasn't seeing this situation the way she was. She got really annoyed by me, like I was the slow one, and went to her room in a huff. She came back a few seconds later with a book that she shoved into my hands. It looked old and bound in leather, with a weird carving etched into the front. The pages were all yellowed, but when I tried to open it, she slammed her hand on top of mine.

She said, "I can trust you, can't I? I can trust you to help me?"

"Help you with what?" I asked.

Then she leaned down real close, so close our noses were practically touching, and I wanted to back away but I couldn't because I was sitting on the sofa. And I held my breath and she slipped the book out of my hands and asked, "What do you know about holding a séance?"

What? No, I don't have a problem with money. Did Jeremy say that? It's not that. I just . . . I get bored. Taking money from work, it didn't really hurt anyone. But I don't know why I did it. Not really. I wouldn't even do anything special with the money. I don't buy things, and I don't go anywhere. I've mostly spent it on food or a few bills. I guess it wasn't about the money. More about the little jolt of adrenaline I'd get when I'd take some and get away with it. I know it's wrong. I told you that's why I've decided not to get a job again since the pandemic. I can't trust that I won't do it again.

I've paid back my Santander manager now. All of it. But back then, when Gemma was still here, I hadn't. And since I hadn't made that first payment in time—it had been due that same day someone left the pigeon in my bedroom—she'd called my bluff and contacted my ex-supervisor at Staples. If I hadn't made the next payment on time, she was going to continue through my resume and contact every place I'd worked before and tell them what I'd done. Tell them to check their accounts. What was I supposed to do? I didn't have enough to pay everyone back, not without Gemma's money. And Gemma said she would give me more if I helped her with her séance. I already thought she was batshit crazy by this point, so if she wanted to spend her so-called "cursed" money to have me help her track down a ghost, why not?

I'm nervous because I'm scared, all right? Not because I'm lying. I told you. I've been scared since I left the river. Sarah's vanished into thin air, and Gemma's been manipulating Jeremy to do something very bad, and I figured if this isn't the type of situation your best friend could help you with, what is? So that's why I drove to Zadie's after I left the river.

I don't remember the drive over there. I really don't. One minute I'm speeding away from the Schuylkill, and the next I'm pulling up outside Zadie's apartment building. There's, like, no parking, but I manage to squeeze Jeremy's Honda Civic into this tiny space. I know I scratch the bumper and I'm not sure how the people in front or behind are going to be able to maneuver out, but it's the middle of the night, so I figure they're probably not going anywhere soon.

I leave the car there and start up the stairs to her apartment. It sort of feels like someone's watching me, but I don't look over my shoulder. Probably just a homeless guy. I keep my head facing front and get my ass up those stairs, this feeling of eyes on me the whole way.

I probably should've texted Zadie first but, like I said, I'd lost my phone and now it's too late anyway. So I'm already there, standing in front of her door, hoping that boyfriend of hers is still working as a night security guard.

Her apartment complex, it's not great, honestly. Everything in the hall is yellow and green, and while not all the bulbs are out or flickering, enough of them are. There's a puddle of water on the floor—there always seems to be a puddle in this one spot even when there's a drought. And there's a smell that's not just me sweating from running up a bunch of stairs—the elevator in her building has been broken for months—and even though it's pushing four a.m. at this point, there's music coming from somewhere. But not from under Zadie's door. Behind her door, it's quiet, and I feel bad for knocking but I need her help.

So I knock but not loudly. I don't want to disturb her neighbors. They're kind of scary. I don't stop knocking until a light comes on—I can see it through the bottom of the door. As she opens the door she says, "Did you forget your keys again?"

And then she sees it's me, and her whole face changes and she says, "What the fuck are you doing here?"

Right, so there's probably something I should tell you. I know Zadie and I showed up here, hand in hand, talking in unison, and she gave me that big hug before you took us to separate rooms, and I know I've talked about how close we are and everything. But the last few months, our relationship has been . . . rough. I mean, all friends go through rough patches, right? That's what makes them stronger when they come out the other side. And that's what Zadie and I are doing—coming out the other side. At least I think we are. Starting tonight. But I don't know if I would've said that a few hours ago.

It was nothing. Nothing major. Just growing apart, you know? She's busy with work, plus her boyfriend works nights so their schedules are all wonky and whatever free time she does have, she wants to spend with him, which I totally get. It's not like I'm Ms. Party-All-the-Time, either. I know I don't want to go out much, that I'd rather do the same old things lately. Gemma asked me about it once. Well, she was asking me about Zadie, in general. This was before the three of us had brunch.

She asked, "What does Zadie do again?"

I said, "She's a psychologist. Wants to open her own practice one day."

And Gemma said, "Wow! That takes a lot of work. No wonder she hasn't been around much."

And I said, "She's been around."

Gemma said, "Really? Then why haven't I met her yet?"

And I said, "Well, she used to come around all the time, but her hours at work are crazy."

Then Gemma asked, "What about that boyfriend of hers? Does she spend much time with him?"

And I said, "Well, yeah. They live together, so . . ."

And Gemma said, "So that's why she doesn't live here? Because I thought she'd be the perfect roommate for you and Sarah. But she picked the boyfriend over you."

"I wouldn't put it like that," I said.

"No, of course not," Gemma said. "Still, you'd think she'd make an effort considering everything you did for her. It just doesn't seem fair to you, that you always have to go out of your way for her. That's not the kind of friend I'd want."

I could see Gemma's point. I mean, from her perspective, I'm sure that's what it looked like, though I hadn't thought about it like that before. But I guess I did start taking longer to respond to Zadie's texts. Finding reasons to turn down meeting for lunch and stuff. And I stopped saying anything when Gemma would make a comment like, "Oh, is that Zadie again?" or "What does she want now?"

But the three of us did have brunch together that once and, well, yeah . . .

If you want to know what Zadie thought of Gemma, you'll have to ask Zadie. I'm sure she'll tell you whatever you want to know. She takes these things very seriously. She's always very serious, actually. But she wasn't always like that. Like this one time in college, she and I got this blow-up doll in the mail. We hadn't ordered it or anything. It just arrived one day—in a box, not like the actual doll sitting in front of the door or anything. The address and room number were ours but not the name, so we figured it was meant for whoever had lived in that room before us. It was her idea to leave it in Coach Barton's office. She'd never do anything like that now, which proves my point. Like, she makes this big fuss about how I've changed since college, but she's changed, too. We're not so different. In fact, we've always felt like we were sisters, even though we look nothing alike. I mean, she and I have way more in common than Sarah and I do.

I guess the biggest difference between us is that she's always wanted a boyfriend. Imagined herself getting married, having kids. That's a foreign language to me, but still I'd help her pick out outfits for dates, tell her that her hair looked nice, wait for her to text me that she needed an escape route or that she was having a good time and I could relax. Made me feel a little like her guard dog, to be honest. But I would always stay up until she got home okay. And she always did.

No, she met her current boyfriend at work, not college. None of the boys she dated in college lasted long. A few dates at most. And this is what I love about Zadie. She wanted a boyfriend, but she wasn't going to settle. She would wait until she found a guy that was equal to her, and she could tell quickly if a guy met that standard or not. Closest she came in college was Brian. I mean Brian probably wasn't *the one*, but he was a lot better than what's-his-name she's living with now. I never bring up Brian, but sometimes I'm like, "You know, you used to have standards." I'm sure you know how well that goes over, so we stop talking about her current boyfriend, move onto something else. But I've always been honest with Zadie. We've always been honest with each other. And that's never going to change. I mean, unlike Sarah, who gets so passive-aggressive about everything, Zadie gets right to the point. The two of us don't have any secrets from one another.

I don't really know how she felt about Gemma, to be honest. I think she started getting jealous of her and didn't want to admit it. I mean, neither of us has very many friends anymore, not like we did in college. And then I started spending more time with Gemma while all Zadie has is that shit boyfriend. So, yeah. I think that made Zadie dislike her. But Zadie always tries to make an effort. Unlike Sarah, she tried to make nice with Gemma. But that only lasted until brunch.

God, brunch. It was a horrible idea, I admit. This was, like, about a month or so before Gemma disappeared. It was after I found out the ex was dead, and Gemma had been talking more and more about séances and stuff, so I wasn't sure if it was a good idea for her to go out in public much. But I hadn't seen Zadie in forever, so when she texted me about meeting for brunch one Sunday and told me to bring Gemma along, I said yes.

I could've lied, I guess. Could've said I asked Gemma but she wasn't interested and then gone alone. Maybe it would've been better if I did. But I didn't. I guess part of the reason was that I was afraid something was gonna happen to Gemma, and I didn't want to leave her out of my sight.

Zadie had picked out this place near the big bus station that was sort of trendy, and the prices were okay. She wanted to sit outside even though it was a little chilly, because the sun was out and the place had those outdoor portable heaters that restaurants really stocked up on during the pandemic. But Gemma and I both said no. Usually, I give in to wherever Gemma, I mean Zadie, wants to sit. But the thought of sitting outside that day, I don't know. It felt like nails on a chalkboard. Just so . . . so exposed, and I knew I wouldn't be able to eat anything. I wanted to be indoors, tucked away, cocooned in a corner surrounded by walls and tables and other people. Even after I found out there wasn't a real Ian following me around, I didn't want to be that exposed. I mean, someone had texted those photos of me to my phone after all.

I didn't say all that to Zadie, though. I just said it was too cold. Zadie tried to joke about it, said we used to go running in weather way colder than this, but then Gemma interrupted and said, "She said she was cold. Let's go inside."

Gemma didn't have to say that. If I said I wanted to eat inside, Zadie would've agreed with me. She always did. It's just she had to make a joke about it first. But Gemma didn't know that. So, yeah. It did get us off to a bad start, but I thought I could save it.

Have you ever had to be the buffer in a group of people? Like, you have people you know from work and friends you know from school, and you all end up in the same place for some reason, like a party? And you're the only thing they have in common, so they're relying on you to make all the conversation? It's awful, and I'm not good at it. I'm usually the awkward one, clinging to my one friend or the food table until I can leave. So I knew I wasn't equipped to handle this situation. I was hoping Zadie would help me out. She's good at that kind of thing. I've seen her do it before. I thought she'd try. That for me, she'd try.

So we were seated indoors, not in the corner but close enough, and I was feeling a little more comfortable, even though no one had said anything since Gemma, in essence, told Zadie to shut up about sitting outdoors. I opened my menu and, sounding exactly like my mother, I said, "This is nice." I pointed out to Zadie that they had eggs Benedict, which she loves, and I knew this wasn't going well because it's never going well when all you have to comment on is the menu. Like, what's going to happen when the menus are taken away? Which happened shortly after that because the waitstaff was super-fast. I ordered first and got the eggs Benedict, which I don't like at all really. I mean it's fine, but I only ordered it to show Zadie I was still on her side no matter how Gemma acted. Then Zadie ordered the pancakes, which she only ever orders when she's carb-loading or angry, and since we weren't going on a run later, it meant she was angry. I don't even remember what Gemma ordered. Scrambled eggs, maybe. Something with eggs.

So our menus were taken away and our water and juice arrived, and we just sat there. Gemma was, like, staring at her fork, and I was trying to will Zadie to say something but she wouldn't. She kept silent, which forced me to talk.

So I cleared my throat and was like, "So, how're things?"

And Zadie said, "Same old, same old."

And I was like, come on, Zadie. Is that all you're going to give me? Like, why are you making me work so hard here? But I hadn't talked to her in a while, and I knew that was on me, so I kept at it.

"How's the new job going?" I asked.

And Zadie shrugged and said, "It's fine."

"It was the one you wanted, right? That doctor's office?"

And she picked up her water and said, "No, I didn't get that. I got the other one. At the other hospital."

"Oh," I said. "But the hospital is pretty good, right? I mean, you'll get a lot of experience, working with patients?"

She was still holding her glass, and she said, "You know I want to go into private practice."

And I said, "Yeah, I know, but . . ."

Then she said, "How about you? How's the job search going?" And she took a sip of water, waited for me to say something.

"It's been . . . going," I said.

Which meant I'd done fuck all. Normally, Zadie would've started in on me. Told me I couldn't spend the rest of my life on the sofa and all of that, and I'd let her because I know she's right. But with Gemma there, she didn't do that. She just let it go, even though I knew she was itching to say more. Maybe it was because of that—she wanted to tear into me but not in front of this stranger—that she turned her attention to Gemma and said, "What about you?"

Gemma startled a bit, like she'd forgotten she was at the table with us. And she didn't say anything, just stared at Zadie like she'd never seen her before.

So Zadie said, "You just moved to Reading, right, Gemma? Did you come here for work?"

All I was thinking was, *Please don't say anything about ghosts.*

Gemma picked up her glass, sort of mimicking Zadie, and said, "No, I'm between jobs at the moment."

"Well, it's been hard since the pandemic," Zadie said, trying to be polite.

And then Gemma said, "Well, actually I haven't bothered to try. I don't really need a job, thanks to unemployment benefits and food stamps and stuff, you know. A job seems like a lot of effort for little gain."

Now I wished she had mentioned ghosts because there is nothing Zadie hates more than people living off benefits. Her family was on food stamps when she was little, and both her parents worked so hard, her mom putting so much pressure on herself to get off them, which they did. Zadie believes in the benefits system, but she also has a very firm belief that it should be for people who truly need it, who have no other option. Not people who want to take advantage of it.

It was almost like Gemma knew that and said exactly the thing that would upset Zadie the most. I tried to flash Zadie a look that said I was sorry, but Zadie wasn't looking at me.

So I said, "I bet you won't be at that hospital long, Zadie. You're going to outperform everyone there, and a private practice will snatch you up. That's what always happens to Zadie. She's a superstar."

It's true, and I believe every word. But I felt like a teacher gushing over her favorite student. I even winced 'cause I was pouring it on so thick. But then our food came, so at least that kept us occupied for a few minutes. Except I wish I had ordered something I genuinely liked, 'cause I was just nibbling my food while Zadie was attacking her pancakes like they personally offended her. Gemma poked her scrambled eggs around the plate but didn't actually eat anything.

Zadie angry-eating is never a good sign, and I didn't know what to say to defuse the situation because everything I said seemed to make it worse. Before I could think of anything, Zadie said, "Did you go to college, Gemma? I know it's not for everyone, but it can help you discover what you're passionate about. Help you decide on a career."

She said all this between bites of pancake, in her professional voice, the one she uses when she's at work or talking to a professor. I knew Gemma wasn't going to like being spoken to like that, so I started eating faster. Nervous eating, not even tasting my food.

And Gemma smiled and said, "You're right. College isn't for everyone." And then she looked at me and said, "It wasn't for you, was it? But you seem to be doing just fine."

I didn't agree with her. I couldn't. Because I knew, at least in Zadie's eyes, that I wasn't doing just fine. Zadie also knew how much I missed college, how I'd like to go back and finish my degree. I knew Zadie was waiting for me to say that. To say anything that would contradict Gemma.

Instead, I grunted and shoved another forkful of eggs Benedict into my mouth.

Then Gemma said, "I hear you have a boyfriend?" All pleasant as could be.

I could see Zadie thought this was a trap. So I jumped in and said, "Yeah. Tim. He's really nice."

I was thinking, how can Zadie not think I'm on her side now? I remembered her boyfriend's name and didn't immediately bad-mouth him. I saw Zadie relax, just a little. And I thought, *thank god, I finally said something right*.

But then, Gemma said, "Oh! I thought his name was Brian."

Zadie froze.

"But," Gemma said, "no. Of course you're right. Brian was Zadie's boyfriend in college. Isn't that right?"

And Zadie glared at me. Full-on glared, and I could tell she was scared and she was angry and she absolutely wanted to flip out on me, but she wouldn't because we were in a public place. I was so nervous. I was sweating and it was really hot and stuffy inside, and I was thinking we should have sat outside after all.

Zadie, her voice completely neutral, asked, "You told her about Brian?"

I hadn't, but I didn't know how I could explain that to Zadie. I had no way to explain how Gemma knew. So I lied and said, "I think I mentioned him in passing, when I was first telling Gemma about you."

And Zadie was still. Very, very still. And she said, "Why would you bring up Brian?"

And Gemma cut in and said, very casually, "Oh, she told me all about her time at college. God, I don't know why you'd want to go back." And she laughed.

I felt like I was gonna throw up. I didn't know what to say to Zadie because this wasn't a conversation we should be having in public. And Zadie just set down her fork and folded her napkin and said, "I have to go. I forgot I have an appointment."

Her voice was so robotic. I watched her walk away, and I wanted to run after her but it was like I was glued to the chair. I couldn't move at all.

Gemma said, "She didn't leave any money for the bill. How rude."

Then she got up and sat in Zadie's seat. And said, "Well then, I guess she won't mind if you finish this."

And she pushed Zadie's plate toward me. I ate the rest of the pancakes. And Gemma's eggs.

I didn't realize how much time had passed between brunch and the next time I saw Zadie. I just sort of lost track of time. I guess that was why Zadie showed up this one day to surprise me. It was maybe a week before Gemma went missing? Gemma and I were about to go out when someone knocked. The building has a gate you're supposed to only be able to open with a key, but it's been broken since forever, so anyone can come and go as they please.

I said, "If that's Jeremy again, I swear to god . . ."

But I opened the door, and it was Zadie. She looked really serious, so I got worried that something happened to her mom. Then she smiled, and because I know Zadie, I knew it was her fake smile.

Before I could even say hi, Gemma said, "We were just heading out."

And Zadie said, "Oh good! Then I'm glad I caught you."

And I said, "Why didn't you text?"

I didn't mean to be rude. I just meant that Zadie prefers to text. So I was thinking, Zadie, why didn't you just text me? Why did you bother to come all the way across town? It's such a hassle for you because you don't have a car. But I could tell from the way I said it, that was not how it came across.

Her smile dropped, and she said, "What? Are you busy?"

And I was about to say no, when Gemma said, "Yes. I said we're going out."

And Zadie said, "Great. I'll come with you."

And Gemma said, "You can't." And then Gemma was pushing past me to get to the door, saying, "Come on. We have to go."

But this was Zadie. This was my best friend. I wasn't going to just brush her off. But Gemma had this angry look in her eye, and she was clenching and unclenching her fist like she did when she got anxious, and I was getting anxious watching her.

So I said, "Zadie, can we talk later? Gemma and I really have to go."

And Zadie said, "Really?"

And I was like, "Yeah, really."

And Gemma's arms were crossed, but so were Zadie's. So I told Gemma to head downstairs. I said I'd be right down, and neither Gemma or Zadie liked that answer, but Gemma headed off without another word. Zadie waited until the elevator doors closed on her and then she said, "Well, can I come in?"

I told her again, "I'm heading out."

And she looked at me point blank and said, "Why?"

Obviously, I couldn't explain why. It could've put her in danger.

So when I didn't answer, Zadie said, "What's going on?"

I said, "Nothing's going on."

And she said that I shouldn't lie to her, that she's my best friend and she loves me and she's only trying to help, and most of what she said I honestly didn't hear because all I was thinking was that I had to get downstairs, Gemma was waiting for me. It was like I could actually feel her waiting, feel how impatient she was getting, and I knew I had to go, but Zadie was still talking and blocking the doorway. When I took a step forward, she moved to block me, and she was still talking, but it was just words at that point. All that mattered at that moment was that I get downstairs, and Zadie was stopping that from happening.

Finally, Zadie was like, "Are you going to tell me?"

I was thinking, *what? What haven't I told her?* So I said, "Am I going to tell you what?"

She cocked her head to the side, gave me that eyebrow raise like she always does when she thinks I'm going to say something stupid, and she said, "Are we really going to play this game?"

I honestly didn't know what she was talking about. I wasn't playing any games. I was genuinely confused.

She stared at me and said, "Just tell me how long you've been using and what."

It took me a few seconds to figure out what she was implying. When I did, I was like, "You mean drugs? You think I'm on drugs?" And I laughed.

Then she started counting things off on her fingers: "You've lost weight. I can tell you're not sleeping. Your hygiene . . . let's just say every time I see you, you could use a shower. Your face is breaking out again. You're always 'busy,' but you never tell me what you're doing. Sarah says you've been going out with Gemma at odd hours."

"You've been talking to Sarah about me?" I asked, but she ignored me.

"You're all twitchy," she said.

I shouted at her. "Of course I'm twitchy! I always get twitchy when I'm angry. And I'm angry you think I'm on drugs! You know I'm not into that. The only time I've ever tried drugs was with you, when we smoked marijuana that one time after I quit field hockey and I hated it. You know how much I hated it."

Then Zadie crossed her arms and said, "All right. If it's not drugs then what is it? What has Gemma got you doing?"

"Gemma hasn't got me doing anything," I said, which I suppose was a lie, but I didn't know how to explain everything that had been going on to Zadie.

"So where are you two going?"

"Nowhere," I said. "Just out."

And Zadie said, "To do what?"

And I said, "It's none of your business."

And I meant that. Not because I wanted to shut Zadie out. I just didn't want this . . . this darkness Gemma introduced me to . . . to touch Zadie. I could already see it affecting Sarah, and that was bad enough. I wanted Zadie to stay far away from all of this. I figured I could explain it all later if she'd only just let me leave. But she wasn't. She was just standing there in my way, while Gemma was waiting downstairs, getting more impatient.

So I said again, "I have to go."

And Zadie stepped in front of the door and said, "Not until you tell me the truth."

And I said, "I did tell you the truth."

But she didn't move. And I needed to leave. I had to leave.

So I barreled into her. My shoulder smacked her in the jaw and she fell back into the doorway, and then I pushed her again and she fell into the hallway.

And I remember her face. I remember her looking at me like she couldn't believe it *was* me. That *I* was doing this. And I couldn't believe it either. I should've apologized, and I should've helped her up, but I didn't. I just left her there on the ground.

I left her and went to find Gemma.

It wasn't the worst thing I did for Gemma, but it's something I regretted even as it happened, and I'll regret it for the rest of my life. Because I know now that Zadie was right. I wasn't myself then.

But at that moment, I looked down at her in the hallway, and I closed the door to my apartment, and I walked away without saying another word.

I didn't see or talk to Zadie again until last night.

So no, I wasn't surprised by her reaction last night. I mean, what else is she supposed to say when I show up at her apartment like that?

And what does she do next? She doesn't slam the door in my face, like I was expecting. She grabs my arm and pulls me inside the apartment. But she's barely shut the door before she's yelling at me.

"What are you doing here?"

She's wearing the same old bathrobe she's had since college, and there's a fading bruise on her cheek. I keep staring at it until she says for the third time, "I said, what are you doing here?"

Yeah, she's angry.

But what matters is that I know, when it comes down to it, that Zadie will always be there for me when I need her, even if she's not happy to see me.

So I say, "Sarah's missing."

And I see her relax just a little. Zadie's always had a soft spot for Sarah. She says, "What? When?"

And I say, "Just now. We were at the river."

And I tell her everything I've just told you. Almost everything. I don't mention the part where I think I've seen Gemma, too. Because right then, standing in Zadie's apartment, it was like whatever spell seemed to come over me at the river has vanished. Everything seems normal again. Stressful, but normal. So I tell Zadie about how Sarah says she's been seeing Gemma, but I don't tell her that Sarah thinks it's a ghost or about scratching the bricks or the bloody fingernails. What I say is enough, though. The anger completely leaves her face.

"Sarah's been having these hallucinations for how long?" she asks, and I know I was right about how much I told her.

Zadie's a very logical person. It's why she went into psychology. She doesn't believe in ghosts or fairy tales or curses. She doesn't even believe in luck. Before games, most of us would have these pregame rituals, things we would do for good luck, but not Zadie. She'd roll her eyes at us every time.

So as we're talking, I go into her kitchen to make coffee—I'm the one who woke her, I should be making the coffee, right?—but to be honest, it's a distraction from my anger 'cause from what Sarah had said, this had been going on with her for a while and I hadn't noticed. I hadn't fucking noticed.

But I don't want to get any more upset in front of Zadie. So as I'm filling the kettle I say, "Months, apparently."

"And you had no idea?" Zadie asks.

I say, "I thought she was, I don't know, more spacey than usual. She's been crying a lot, but I chalked it up to the pregnancy." I start the coffee-maker and lean on the kitchen counter. For some reason I expect it to be sticky, but it's clean. Not a speck. "I mean, I never thought she was seeing things that weren't there. Not until tonight. To be honest, I'm not even sure if she has been hallucinating or if Jeremy maybe . . . if he and Gemma planned this together or—"

She says, "You always told me Jeremy and Gemma weren't a thing."

And I say, "They weren't! But I wouldn't put it past her to use him for something like this."

And Zadie says, "Assuming she's alive."

I'm thinking, am I the only one who thinks Gemma is still alive?

Then Zadie says, "Or do you think Sarah was making it all up?"

And I'm like, "For what?"

Because I don't want to admit that I think it's possible my sister would lie to me about something like this. Besides, the more I think about it, the more I'm convinced she didn't. Sarah's not an actress, and she's a terrible liar. She was genuinely frightened tonight.

And that's what I tell Zadie.

"So if she was that upset, you don't think she might have—" Zadie stops herself. "I mean, in the river," she says.

I straighten up. "No. Never. I only lost sight of her for, like, thirty seconds, Zadie. There's no way."

I grab us two mugs from the cupboard.

No, I wasn't stalling, okay? I was exhausted. Zadie looked exhausted, too. Like I said, we needed something to keep us awake. And Zadie wasn't even dressed yet. We couldn't just run out into the street with her in her bathrobe.

I don't know how long we stayed at her apartment. As long as we needed to, I guess. I lost track of time last night.

Why didn't I call the police from Zadie's phone? Because I remembered what happened when Gemma went missing. "Has it been forty-eight hours?" That's exactly what the officer said to me when I first called about Gemma.

I was in the kitchen and Sarah was next to me, pacing and chewing on a hangnail on her thumb. I'd been on hold a long time and the phone was sweating against my ear, and when I finally did get through to an officer and told him my roommate was missing and we didn't know what happened to her, all he said was, "Has it been forty-eight hours?"

I said, "No, it's been about twenty-four."

And he said, "Let us know tomorrow if she's still missing."

And he hung up. I remember, I put the phone down, and Sarah went, "What is it? What did he say?"

I was so angry I could barely repeat it. Because it's stupid, you know that, don't you? Police are always saying the first forty-eight hours are the most important—when there's been a crime, when someone's been murdered or gone missing—and yet we call you and tell you someone's missing, that we don't know where they are, we haven't heard from them, that all their stuff is still here, we're worried, and you're like, "Don't tell us until tomorrow." Especially when it's a young woman.

Oh, she probably just ran away, you say. She's probably with a boyfriend, you say. And even when we deny both, when we say this isn't normal for her, when we say she didn't have a boyfriend, you still don't believe us. You think we might believe those things, but we must be wrong. We don't know everything. And yeah, maybe we don't. But neither do you.

So this was what was going through my head when Sarah asked me to tell her what you'd—what that officer—had said.

Sarah didn't seem upset by it, though. She was like, "Well, if that's what the police say, that's what we should do."

I slapped her hand out of her mouth.

"But we know she didn't just run away," I said, and after I said it, I realized Sarah might not understand what I was talking about because she didn't know everything I did about Ian and the money. She didn't know what Gemma and I had done a few nights before. So I added, "With no note? No message?"

"Does she really seem like a person that's big on goodbyes?"

Sarah almost started chewing on her fingernail again but instead lowered her hands and tucked them into her armpits, like this. And she said, "I saw her arguing once. I saw her arguing with this girl. She always told us she didn't know anyone else in Reading. But maybe—"

"She didn't," I said. "We were the only people she knew. That's why we have to get the police to listen to us."

That's why I called back the next day just like I said I would. But it took you almost a week to reach out to us, to take us seriously.

So, sitting in Zadie's, drinking coffee after my sister goes missing? Why should that seem odd to you? If I would've called, you wouldn't have done anything anyway. And it's not like Zadie and I were just sitting there chatting. We were game planning. I had Jeremy's car, so transportation wasn't an issue. So again, what Jeremy's telling you is wrong. I didn't ditch his car after I left them at the river. I drove it to Zadie's. Check the CCTV outside her building. I know there's a camera there.

Before we left, we needed to figure out where to go. I didn't want to be like Jeremy and Sarah and drive around in circles. I wanted to have a plan. And it wasn't certain that Sarah was still at the river. She had her phone. She had friends. Someone could've picked her up in the time since I left. And I didn't have my phone anymore, so she had no way to reach me. Zadie did try calling and texting her, but Sarah never answered.

So Zadie and I talk about where Sarah might've gone, who she might've gone with, what she might be thinking of doing based on her thinking that she had, in fact, seen a ghost. And we don't call the police because, like I said, we knew they wouldn't do shit, no offense. Sitting there, side by side, was like our field hockey days, when we'd come up with a plan for attacking the opposing team.

I say as much to Zadie, but the way she looks at me, it wipes whatever smile I had right off my face.

And she says, "You shouldn't be happy about this."

Before I can tell her I'm not happy—I'm not happy about Sarah being missing, not happy about anything that's happened over the last few weeks or the last few months, that the only thing I'm happy about is that we're talking again—she gets up off the couch and says, "I'll get changed and then we'll go."

She goes into her bedroom, leaving me alone on her shitty green couch, and it's so quiet I can hear water dripping somewhere and I just think, *What the fuck have I done?* I start pacing. Even though my legs are tired, I can't help it. I can't sit still. So while Zadie gets dressed, I'm wandering around her apartment, and I end up at the window. It looks out onto the street in front of the building. There's not much to see, but the longer I stand there, the more I get the feeling someone is watching me.

The same feeling I've had since I left the river. I don't see anyone. But it's a dark night. There's a lot of black between the streetlights, and more than a handful of them are out. I keep staring into the darkness, keep looking, and then I think I see something. Can't make out a shape, just movement behind a line of parked cars. As I'm trying to follow it, Zadie comes out of her bedroom and says she's ready to go. When I look back at the window, whatever I saw is gone. It was probably a fox. They're everywhere. But I can't shake the feeling I should stay in Zadie's apartment.

She has already grabbed her keys and coat and is telling me we need to leave. And I tell her, "I know where we need to go. I know what I need to check."

You really don't think it's cold in here? God, I can't stop shivering. I do a lot better with the heat than with the cold. I'm not really a beach person, but I like being outside when it's warm. I guess it's what I'm used to. Being out on the field, sweating in the sun. When I was a kid, Mom used to slather me up in sunscreen. She wasn't so concerned with sunburn or cancer. She just didn't want me to get wrinkles. I told Gemma once, Mom and Dad might've retired to Florida, but Mom's not like those toasted ladies you see there. She layers on the sunscreen, wears big floppy hats and loose, flowy caftan things that cover her whole body. Dad looks like he's been cooked twice over in the oven, but Mom's a snow princess who never stepped outdoors except in winter. They don't have a lot in common, Mom and Dad. Guess it's the opposites attract thing. Except for the business. That's how they met. In college, in some business management course. I told Gemma how Mom always boasts that she was the only girl in the class and Dad jokes that's why he got stuck with her. Their business was their first baby. Some people get married, have kids. They got married, started an LLC. They always tell me and Sarah they wanted kids. That they put it off until the business was steady on its feet. But even after we were born, they spent more time in the office instead of with us.

Honestly, I've tried to be a better person than them. I'm not interested in relationships—romantic ones—and I don't want kids. But when I'm an aunt, I'll do anything for that kid, I swear. Like, at first, the thought of being an aunt freaked me out a bit, especially since I was going to be around the baby twenty-four seven. I know I shouldn't have felt freaked out. Sarah must've felt worse than me, since she was the one it was happening to. But then I realized, this could be really cool. Sarah and I could do a much better job than Mom and Dad ever did, you know?

I guess that's what people always think, isn't it? That they'll be better than their parents, and then they somehow end up worse. I mean, look how well I'm doing already. The baby's not even born, and I've already lost its mother. Lost my sister.

Gemma was right. I can't help anyone.

No, I'm not going off-track, okay? I'm telling you everything you wanted to know, aren't I? You're right, I don't care about this Gemma Horne girl. The only missing person I care about is Sarah. She's the only person I want to find.

You can come up with any theory you want. I told you that's what happens when you don't know the full story about something. It looks crazier than the truth. You want to know more? Ask Jeremy. Ask him why he's been pestering Sarah so much these last five months. Harassing her, is more like it. I mean, I told you about the phone calls. What were those all about? Have you asked him yet? Because I have no idea. I only ever overheard one conversation between them, but it wasn't a phone call and it didn't clear anything up.

I don't know exactly when it was. Soon after Gemma went missing, I think, but not like right after. Like when we were just realizing that she wasn't coming back. You had started looking, but we were realizing, for the first time, that maybe we weren't going to get any answers.

Anyway, I was in my room. I spent a lot of time in my room those days. I just ... when I was in the living room, I kept glancing over at Gemma's armchair, I mean *our* armchair, expecting to see her sitting there, but I would look and she wouldn't be there and ... honestly, I was giving myself whiplash. So I took to staying in my room for a few weeks, mostly watching Phillies games or true-crime documentaries on my laptop. I was trying to find the one that had scared Gemma so much, but I never have.

Anyway, Sarah and Jeremy must've known I was in my room. I mean, since I wasn't in the living room, where else would I be? I hadn't been leaving the apartment much at all. Maybe they thought I had my headphones on because they didn't hear any sound from my laptop, but there wasn't any sound because I wasn't watching anything at the time. I was staring at Rebecca Horne's profile picture. So I didn't have my headphones on, but they must've thought I did.

Anyway, I heard Jeremy come in. Sarah was in the kitchen making dinner. I heard their voices but not the words. Just seemed like a general conversation, so I didn't pay much attention. But then their voices dropped to a whisper. It was like, I could hear them fine and then suddenly I couldn't. Instead, of general conversation, it was that sort of angry, almost hissing sound you hear when two people are arguing but they don't want you to hear them. Our parents used to do it sometimes. Especially when Mom wasn't feeling well.

So I set my laptop on the bed, and I went to the door and pressed my ear to it to listen, but I couldn't hear much. Just one question from Jeremy.

"Where is it, Sarah? What did you do with it? We need to get rid of it."

That was it. I didn't hear what Sarah said, if she said anything at all. I stood there, my ear getting sore and hot from being pressed against the door, and listened to the silence.

Then someone knocked. Loud. I jumped back and covered my mouth in case I shouted out, and Sarah said, "Dinner's ready!"

So I closed my laptop and left my bedroom, and it was just Sarah in the kitchen, setting out the plates. I hadn't even heard Jeremy leave.

Rebecca Horne? She was the woman killed in the Briar Lane Murders. Ian

Baker's mother. Ian was from her first marriage. Her second marriage was to a man named Horne.

Yes, I've known that for a while.

Yes, I didn't tell you on purpose.

No, the surname Horne isn't a coincidence.

I told you I wasn't going off-track.

I'm just so tired. I keep expecting Sarah to turn up and explain everything. I mean she will. I know she will. It hasn't even been forty-eight hours. She's probably tried to call me, and, since I've lost my phone . . . I mean, smashed my phone.

It's weird, not having your phone on you, isn't it? It's like you keep checking your pockets and then you have a little panic attack when you realize it isn't there, even though you already knew it wasn't there, you just forgot. And then you think it's buzzing and you check, and of course it wasn't because it's not even there, and then you're like, then what did I just feel? Because you know you felt something.

Zadie told you that I seemed really jumpy when we left, didn't she? I don't think she even wanted to get in the car with me. When we got to where I'd parked it, she looked at me, then at the car, then back at me, like she was deciding if she should turn around and go back inside. But I mean, who wouldn't be a little jumpy, right? After everything? But it was only because of my phone, and the fact that I didn't have it and then kept forgetting I didn't have it and checking for it. Because I kept thinking Sarah might call me. But she couldn't. Because I didn't have my phone.

As I'm driving, Zadie's stealing glances at me, and of course I notice but I don't say anything. Finally, after about ten minutes, she says, "How much farther is it?"

And I say, "I don't know. Not exactly. But I'll know it when I see it."

I think about checking Google Maps on my phone, but my phone's not there and I have a little panic attack and then calm myself down again, remember that I already knew my phone was gone.

And Zadie says, "Can you at least tell me why we're going there? What you're looking for?"

And I say, "I just need to check something."

And then I make a sharp right because I almost missed where I was supposed to turn, and thankfully there were no other cars around or else I might've hit them.

Zadie says, "Do you want me to drive?"

And I say, "You can't drive."

And she says, "Actually, I can." She tells me she finally got her license last month.

I don't want her to drive, I'm fine, but I say, "Good for you." And I mean it 'cause getting her driver's license has been this big thing for her ever since I've known her. And then I realize she didn't tell me. She got her license a month ago and didn't tell me. I don't say anything about that, even though I want to, but Zadie can read my face. She must see it through the dark. She catches glimpses every time we pass under a streetlight.

"You could've told me," I say. And I don't look at her because I need to keep my eyes on the road. I need to keep an eye out for the turnoff. She's looking straight at me. I can see her from the corner of my eye. I can feel her gaze burning into my cheek.

And she says, "You haven't been around."

And I say, "Yes I have."

And she says, "Not really."

I'm not sure what to say next, so I let this pause just sort of hang between us, and finally, because she's waiting for an answer, I say, "I've been busy."

And Zadie sort of snort-laughs at that, the way she always does before she gets super sarcastic. She says, "With what? *Judge Judy? The Simpsons?*"

So I say, "I've texted you."

"Oh, yeah, wow. Texts. Every other month. Little three-letter replies. Too lazy to spell out a whole word now?"

I don't get angry. I just get more tired. Her words, they're one more thing weighing on me. Like, I have to handle yet another person's disappointment in me. First my parents, and Aunt Joanie, and my professors, and my coaches, and Sarah, and now Zadie. Zadie, who was supposed to understand, who was supposed to be on my side, no matter what. I wish they would all fuck off and leave me alone. But instead they weigh me down, and I'm tired of it. I'm so fucking tired of disappointing everyone. I could've said that to her. Maybe it would've been better if I did. But I'm too tired to do anything but use my words as weapons.

So I say, "It's because of you. Because of what I did for you."

And that shuts her up, which is what I wanted, but it hurts her, too. Which, if I'm honest, is also what I wanted, at least in that moment.

We're quiet for a while after. I thought that would be better, but actually it's not, because, in the quiet, I get that phantom phone feeling ten times over, and I keep jerking the steering wheel. I want to do so many things at once. I want to pull over. I want to go home. I want to get to this spot. I want to go to bed.

And then she says, "It's why I keep trying to help you."

I'm like, yeah, because you feel guilty, not because you care. But I don't say that out loud. At least, I don't think I do. But I must've said something, because then Zadie says, "Is that why you liked her? Is that why you were always trying to help her?"

And I say, "To be honest, I helped her because she scared me."

Just then, I see the turnoff.

Do you know how many women were burned at the stake for witchcraft? It was something like twenty-five hundred just in Scotland—not even all of the UK. Well, Scotland did most of the executions by burning. Here in the more civilized American colonies, most of them were hanged. But I always found the burning more interesting. Like, what must that have been like? I mean, I know most of them died from smoke inhalation and not the actual burning part, so like hanging, they choked to death. But how does it feel to be choked by smoke—filling up with carbon dioxide from the inside out—rather than being hanged, where your neck is compressed from the outside in? Because let's face it, how many were actually hanged properly where their necks snapped instantly instead of improperly where their necks didn't snap and they were left to just swing there?

Did you know the last woman to be legally executed for witchcraft in the UK was named Janet Horne? She had a daughter that had something wrong with her hands and feet, so they accused Janet of turning her daughter into a pony so she could ride her to see the Devil. She was stripped naked and tarred, then wheeled through the streets in a barrel before they set her on fire. So maybe *she* didn't die of smoke inhalation. Maybe she died from the actual flames. Her daughter was convicted, too, but somehow escaped and was never heard from again. Who knows what happened to her. Or if she had any descendants. Descendants that might have immigrated to America.

I mean, it's probably just coincidence that the victim of the Briar Lane Murders was a woman named Horne. It's a common enough name. There's probably not a connection since Janet Horne was executed over three hundred years ago in another country. Plus, did you know that the name Janet Horne might not even have been the woman's real name? When I was writing that paper for college, the one I mentioned earlier, I read that the authorities would try to conceal the women's real identities, so they used the name Janet or Jenny Horne as a generic name for a witch. Basically, it means the same as "Jane Doe."

So no, I wasn't lying when I said I didn't know any Gemma Horne because I didn't. I still don't. Not really. But when you said Horne, Rebecca Horne is the first person I thought of.

When I remembered the story of Janet Horne, Gemma's idea of a curse wasn't as far-fetched as it first seemed. Like, the woman Gemma helped kill and stole money from shared a last name with an executed witch from the eighteenth century? Some coincidence, right?

That's not really why I helped her, though. Like I said, Gemma promised to give me some more of the money if I helped her with the séance. Earlier that week, I'd got a call from my former manager at Staples saying he was waiting for my payment and didn't want to press charges, so if I could hurry up and pay back what was missing like I did for my Santander supervisor, then he wouldn't have to contact the police. So, yeah, I figured it was the perfect time to help Gemma with the séance thing.

The night of the séance, Gemma and I got to the church around eight or eight thirty. It was mid-April and raining. Between sunset and the rain, it was hard to see anything clearly. And it was quiet as a tomb, which was fitting since we were at a churchyard. Like, the only sound was my stomach growling. Gemma had said that in order for this to work, we needed to fast, so I hadn't eaten anything since the night before and the only thing I had to drink that day was this weird tea she'd made for us. She said it was kombucha or kale or something. Tasted bitter as fuck. My head was splitting, and all I wanted was to get this over and done with and go get some actual food.

The church we'd picked had been closed for a few years and was surrounded by this big chain-link fence that had barbed wire all across the top. The only gate had this huge padlock on it. I didn't know how we were going to get in, but Gemma pulled wire cutters out of her backpack.

"Come on, around the back," she said.

We walked around to the back of the church, which was the part that faced the cemetery, and Gemma handed me wire cutters.

"We need a space big enough to crawl through."

So I took the cutters and started snipping through the links. The blades were dull, and the links didn't cut easily. It sort of felt like someone was watching us while I was snipping away, but I didn't see anyone out there in the dark. Once I'd cut through a bunch of links, I pushed on the fence to open it up a bit and managed to get it wide enough for us to slip through, but my coat snagged and tore.

Once we were inside the fence, we had to get into the church itself. Now this is one of those old churches in North Heidelberg, with really heavy doors and stained glass windows, and even though it had been closed for a while, the doors appeared solid and all the glass was intact. I thought, *we can't break in, someone's going to notice.* I was going to suggest we check each of the doors and windows, see if we got lucky, but before I could, Gemma handed me a rock.

"Get us inside," she said.

I said, "Gemma, someone's going to hear us."

"Who's out here?" she said. Then she shouted. Just screamed into the air.

I went "Shhh!" and wanted to cover up her mouth, but I had the rock in one hand and the wire cutters in the other.

"Gemma, stop!" I said, but she laughed.

"See? No one's here. You were right. This place is perfect. Now hurry up and get us inside. You don't want to be stuck out here all night, do you?" She shoved me toward the church. I lost my balance and fell, nearly bashing in my own face with the rock.

"Can you please be careful?" I said, and she apologized and helped me up, but the fall made me dizzy, and with my headache and empty stomach, the dizziness didn't go away.

"That window there. That should be big enough for both of us." She pointed and I looked around to make sure no one was there, that no one had come to investigate Gemma's screaming. Then I threw the rock at the window. It made a hole but didn't completely shatter it, so I had to use my arm and break up the rest of the glass. I got cuts all over my jacket. Later I realized I cut up my hand, too. But I didn't feel it at the time. It was like I couldn't feel anything.

Gemma pushed me ahead of her, and I climbed through the window. The floor was a few feet below, and I tried to control my jump down but didn't do a very good job. Landed hard on the broken glass. I was lucky not to get a shard stuck in my palm. I swept the biggest pieces away with my sneaker, then called for Gemma. She was much better at sticking the landing.

It was near pitch black inside, so I used the flashlight on my phone. The shadows looked funny, like they were moving, but nothing was really moving and everything was a bit fuzzy around the edges from my headache and it smelled like dust.

I don't know churches very well. I never spent much time in one. It looked like we'd landed in a hallway or something. I don't know if there's an official word for it. But Gemma seemed to know where to go.

"This way," she said, and she grabbed my arm and started pulling me along.

"You been here before?" I asked.

She said, "One church is the same as another."

The whole place smelled musty, like no one had been in there for a while. I kept hearing things skittering around, which I tried to tell myself were mice even though they sounded big enough to be rats. Or worse. None of it seemed to bother Gemma. She kept pulling me along, and it sounded like the rats or whatever were in the walls following us. Soon we got to the main part. The whatever it's called, where they hold the service? The sanctuary, Gemma called it. There were lots of wooden pews, and Gemma walked me through them and up the aisle toward the altar, where there was room on the floor in front of the first row of pews.

"Here," she said, and she plopped down in the middle of the floor and took my bag off her shoulder and started pulling out candles and a Ouija board. Not like the ones you can buy at the store but an old one, made of wood. Looked homemade.

Gemma lit the candles while I stood there and watched. I kept listening for footsteps. For someone to turn up and chase us away. The candles made me nervous, too, because I thought a security guard or something might see the light. But Gemma was super calm. Like what we were doing was the most natural thing in the world.

"Come on," she said. "Sit down."

I did. Gemma held out her hands.

"Aren't we supposed to put them on the board or something?" I asked.

"The board will help us attract the spirits. We don't need it to communicate with them. They'll be communicating through me. Now give me your hands."

She had laid that big old book open on her knees. I couldn't see what was written in it because it was too dark. Gemma squeezed my hands and started to read. It wasn't English. I don't know what it was. Latin, and something else I didn't recognize. I wanted to ask her what I was supposed to do, but I didn't want to interrupt. And my mouth felt thick, like my tongue was swollen. That plus the smoke from the candles and my head-ache made the dizziness worse.

She kept reading and squeezing my hands tighter, and my stomach was getting queasy, so queasy I thought I was going to vomit. Then Gemma wasn't reading anymore. Her eyes were closed, but she was still talking and her muscles were getting all tight and her face looked like she was in pain and her voice was getting hoarse, getting deeper.

There was a draft and the candles flickered, and I thought I heard someone come into the sanctuary, but I was just imagining things because I looked and didn't see anything moving in the dark, and I didn't hear anything. Then Gemma started swaying a bit, pulling me toward her and then pushing me back. Her speech was getting faster but she wasn't saying anything that made sense. And then just when I thought I was going to vomit all over the Ouija board, she froze and shouted Ian's name three times. Just his first name.

All the candles went out, like that.

We sat there in the darkness.

It was completely silent. Not even a creak. I couldn't even hear us breathing. And it felt like the smoke from the candles went right up my nose, but I couldn't cough. It was like I was frozen, too.

Gemma was still holding my hands tight, but her head and shoulders had slumped forward. I was about to say her name when she whispered a name first. But it wasn't her voice. It was all low and raspy.

When I didn't say anything, she said the name again. But it wasn't my name. It was a family nickname—Peanut. There was only one family member who had ever used it. I hadn't heard it since I was a kid.

So that's when I said, "Uncle Mitchell?"

She breathed in sharply. Then she said, "So . . . cold."

Look, it sounds stupid now. But at the time, I hadn't eaten or drunk anything all day except the tea Gemma said would help "open our chakras," and all it did on an empty stomach was make me jittery and dizzy. My hands were literally shaking. It was dark and we were inside an abandoned church and the candles had gone out, and it was like the shadows and the rats were creeping up around me, and I heard the nickname I hadn't heard since Uncle Mitchell died.

So I said, "Uncle Mitchell? I need your help."

Gemma sat there with her raspy breathing, not looking up, her hair hiding her face. I thought if she looked up, I would see his face. Like, see his face melded over Gemma's. Someone I recognized but not quite, like when I used to mistake Uncle Mitchell for Dad when I was little. I could practically see it underneath her hair, but she wouldn't look all the way up.

I said, "Uncle Mitchell, we need to find someone."

That weird breathing went on for a while. I don't know. Thirty seconds? A minute? And I said Uncle Mitchell's name again. Then he—she—started talking.

"Paper . . . I need . . . paper."

So I pulled out the notebook Gemma had brought with us and handed it to him, I mean her, and she took it like she couldn't see it, like she had to feel around for it, and then she set it down and said, "Pen . . . a pen."

I put the pen in his, in her, hand, and she started writing but not looking at what she was writing. Her head was tilted up like she was looking at the rafters or whatever and the pen started moving faster and faster and she wasn't saying anything but her breaths kept getting heavier and louder. Her hand was, like, swirling over the page. I couldn't see what she was writing but the movement didn't look like words, just like scribbles and circles, and it sounded like the paper was tearing. The tearing sound so loud, it was like a person screeching.

And then she said, "Thief . . . me . . . thief . . . you . . . like me, eh, Peanut. Just like me . . . like me."

And he—she—started laughing and laughing, getting more hysterical and gripping my hand tighter, and I tried to pull away but I couldn't, and I shouted at him—at her—to stop it. I was screaming: "Stop! Stop! Stop!"

Then there was this huge crash.

A tall candlestick holder had fallen and knocked over another one, which knocked over another. Like dominoes tipping over one after the other, all around us.

Gemma started shaking like she was having a seizure, and I heard something moving on the altar. A thumping sound. A banging. Like something trying to get out. I thought I smelled smoke and fire but not from the candles. It was too strong for candle smoke. And it was dark. There weren't any flames that I could see. But that didn't mean they weren't there.

I tried to get up, but Gemma wouldn't let me go. She was shaking and her fingernails were biting into my skin. I started saying her name over and over, tried to pull away. Then she went limp, and I could free myself. I got her to her feet. She wasn't unconscious, but she was super groggy. I led her back the way we came as fast as I could drag her, and I shoved her up through the broken window and then dragged her to the hole in the fence and then to Jeremy's car. I didn't stop driving until the church was out of sight, and then I pulled over hard onto the shoulder and slammed on the brakes.

By that time, I could barely see straight, I was so dizzy.

She asked me suddenly, "Did it work?"

I kept trying to focus my eyes on the road ahead and the trees around us, afraid whatever knocked over the candles in the church had followed us. She asked me again, and then I told her what happened. What I'd heard her say. And then we looked at the notebook. She had it gripped in her hand the whole way. It was an address, but I didn't recognize it.

"Do you know what it is?" I asked.

"Maybe. I'm not sure. I can't . . . my brain's all fuzzy. Let's get something to eat. You know what I feel like? Nachos. Isn't that weird? I never eat nachos. Let's go to your family bar and get nachos."

I said, "Nachos were Uncle Mitchell's favorite."

I filled her in more as we drove back into Reading, told her it was Uncle Mitchell she'd summoned, not Ian.

She nodded and said, "That was nice he came to you to help us."

And I said, "He called me Peanut."

She said, "Yeah?"

And I said, "But that isn't right. He would never call me Peanut. That was his nickname for Sarah."

And she said, "Huh, that's weird. Come on, let's hurry up. I'm starving."

But we never got to eat the nachos because that was the night she and Aunt Joanie got into the fight. Later, when we were on our way home, she whispered to me, "Uncle Mitchell told me a secret about her." She smirked, but she never said any more about it.

No, you're wrong about that. No, Jeremy's lying because he wants you to think I'm crazy. I do not have a history of nervous breakdowns. Never have. Mom has Bipolar II Disorder, but not me. I've never had any problems like that. Sarah might have told you, back when you first interviewed us, that I had this breakdown in college and that's why I dropped out, and it's not that Sarah was lying. It's just, that's what I led her to believe. It was easier to let her think that than to tell her the truth.

I do get panicky sometimes. No one really notices, but it's happened since I was a kid. I was amazing on the field, so I guess no one ever thought to ask what I'd been doing in the bathroom twenty minutes before a game. And it doesn't happen all the time. But sometimes I'll get shaky and sweaty and I'll feel my heart racing. Usually, I can get it to go away on its own. Sometimes it's harder than others. But it's just your run-of-the-mill anxiety.

Zadie was the first person to ever notice. We'd been at college for about two months, and everything had been going well. We were getting to know our other teammates, getting into the rhythm of classes and training. And we were about to have our first game, a scrimmage. We were in the locker room, and I was feeling really good. Then suddenly I wasn't. It was almost like someone reached inside me and flipped a switch. I was having trouble breathing, and Coach Barton, he started yelling that it was time for us to come out, stop "lollygagging" or whatever. But I could barely breathe and I couldn't move, and I was so fucking embarrassed this was happening right in front of my teammates. Like, what were they going to think of me?

But they didn't even notice. They were exiting the locker room like nothing was wrong. And I was relieved, but I hated them, too, 'cause it was like they didn't care enough about me to notice. Then Zadie put her hands on mine and she talked me through some breathing exercises, and a few minutes later, I felt fine again. Coach Barton popped his head into the locker room to yell at us, but Zadie shouted something back about women's issues, and that shut him up.

Zadie's always been able to tell when I'm upset. She notices me. More than my parents ever do. Sometimes even more than Sarah.

Don't get me wrong. Sarah cares about me. She's my sister. We've always been there for each other. But sometimes Sarah gets wrapped up in her own world. She makes it very clear when she needs something from people, but she doesn't always notice when other people need something from her.

Everybody should have a Zadie in their life. Everybody.

And I know I should probably have more than one friend. That it'd probably be healthier or whatever. Do you know how hard it is to make friends? I think things could've been different if Albright hadn't cut the field hockey team. If I'd had a chance to get to know my other teammates better. Play with them longer. We found out the summer before our sophomore year. Something to do with budget cuts. I don't know. I never really bothered to find out. I mean, I was too shocked. This thing I'd been doing since I was ten, nearly half my life, was taken from me, and I didn't know how to deal with that, to be honest.

At first I thought it'd be fine. Zadie and I were still rooming together. We said we'd still get together with our teammates. Figured we could play together in the park for fun. Most of us owned our own equipment. It would be fine.

Well, that's what we talked about doing. We were so enthusiastic about it at the beginning. Like—yeah, we're so going to do this! And then college started back up and we moved into the dorms, and you know how many times all of us got together? For anything? A run? Lunch? Just to hang out? Never. Not once. Zadie and I saw each other all the time because we lived together. Maybe one or two of the other girls would come over to hang out. But that was it.

Yeah, I think things would've been a lot different if the team had stayed together.

But of course Jeremy would use my panic attacks to try and make me look like I'm crazy or need medication or something. But, like, what were you doing last night, Jeremy? And the days before that? The months? What were you doing the morning after the séance?

I remember that when I woke up that morning, I still wasn't feeling well. It was like I had a hangover. But I hadn't been drinking the night before or anything, Just that one beer at the Tavern that I didn't even get to finish, but my head was pounding and my mouth was dry and fuzzy. And my tongue felt like it was swollen. When I came out of my bedroom, I didn't even see Jeremy right away because my eyes were puffy and I was rubbing them. All I wanted was a glass of orange juice, so I staggered into the kitchen and—boom—there he was. I couldn't get to the fridge because he was in the way.

I didn't know what time it was because I hadn't looked at a clock or my phone or anything. But it was daylight, and it was too early for Jeremy to be at our place. That much I knew.

And he said, "Have fun last night?"

And I was like, "What's it to you?" And I shoved past him to get to the fridge.

"Heard you had a bit of a kerfuffle with Aunt Joanie, that's all."

I shook the orange juice carton. It was almost empty, and I twisted off the cap.

"Kerfuffle?" I said. "What are you, eighty?"

I drank the juice straight from the carton.

And he said, "Just hope you weren't too spooked."

And before I could ask, *Spooked by what?* Gemma was standing in the living room, glaring at Jeremy.

"What are you doing here?" she said.

And that cocky expression of his vanished. He actually looked sheepish, the way he did when my mom used to chew him out for tracking mud onto the carpet.

He said, "I just wanted to—"

But Gemma interrupted and said, "You shouldn't be here."

And I kept my mouth shut because Gemma was doing more to get Jeremy to leave than I was.

He held up his hands and said, "Hey, okay, cool." And moved to the door. And then he was like, "See you later?"

Gemma stared at him but didn't say anything. And Jeremy looked at me and that smirk was back, and he said, "Feel better, cuz," and then he was gone.

As soon as he left, Gemma acted like he was never there to begin with. She just came right up to me—orange juice was dribbling down my chin—and shoved the notebook in my hands and said, "Let's look up the address."

My head was still thumping, and I'd wanted to grab some Tylenol, but Gemma pulled me out of the kitchen and it was all I could do not to drop the orange juice carton. She pushed me onto the couch and shoved my computer into my lap and took the orange juice carton out of my hand. And then she was pointing at numbers and letters on the notebook page and I was typing them into Google, even though the glare from the screen was hurting my eyes.

I hit Enter, and the address came up right away. It was for a Holiday Inn. One not far from the bus station.

Gemma said, "That's where she is."

And I said, "Who's *she*?"

But then I saw my messenger bag sitting near the door. And I said, "Where did that come from?"

Gemma followed my gaze and saw the bag and waved it off. "You brought it home last night."

And I was like, "No I didn't. I left it at the church."

And she said, "No, you had it with you when we left. I remember."

But *I* didn't remember. And my bag wasn't where I normally put it, either. I always leave it on the right-hand side of the door when we come in, but it was on the left. Before I could say anything else, Gemma was taking my computer away and pulling me off the sofa and saying, "Come on. Get dressed. We need to go to this Holiday Inn."

I checked my bag later, and inside were the Ouija board and the pen and matches and candles—all the things I could've sworn we left at the church. All the things I didn't remember taking with us when we left.

I guess Jeremy was helping Gemma as far back as then. I just didn't realize it until last night.

No, I did! I did tell Zadie this last night. I really did.

Some of it.

Because I didn't want to worry her. Zadie's always been a worrier. I mean, as long as I've known her, she's always been worried about something. The weather. Her grades. Our next game. But she doesn't get anxious. Like, I've only seen her anxious once. So she worries, but she prepares. It's like, because of her mom, she learned when she was little that bad things can happen but you can prepare for them. You can be ready, or at least ready to react. Mitigate the damage.

So as we were driving out of town last night, I could tell Zadie didn't feel prepared. She didn't know what might be out there. I told her there was nothing. That I just needed to check on something. That she didn't need to worry.

We'd been driving in silence for a while. Things were still real shaky between us, and I knew the only reason she was here at all was because of Sarah.

And finally, after all this silence, she asks, "Is this anywhere near where Sarah and Jeremy went missing?"

And I say no, and she says, "Then what're we doing out here? We should be going to find them, not headed in the opposite direction."

It wasn't like I didn't know she was right. Common sense would say that when searching for a missing person, you start with the place where they were last seen. But I didn't want to go back to the river. I mean, I couldn't. Just the thought of it made me hyperventilate. But I couldn't really explain that to Zadie. I didn't know how to make her understand how scared I was.

So instead, I say, "I told you there's something I have to check."

I didn't know for certain that going to that spot was going to tell me anything. I just had a feeling that there was something Gemma hadn't wanted me to see the last time we were out here.

And Zadie asks, "Does this something have to do with Gemma?"

I say yes and leave it at that. Because it's the truth. Just the truth without all the details.

At this point, we're almost there. It's not like I have a photographic memory or anything, but I remember the way, and it's almost like I can hear Gemma's voice in my head, telling me to turn left, turn right, go straight. But when I look at the passenger seat, it's just Zadie and she's not saying anything.

She starts to ask how much farther when I see it—the tree. The gnarled dead tree perched next to the stone fence. I pull the car up almost exactly to where I had parked it with Gemma that night.

I point. "Gemma and I buried something by that tree. Just before she disappeared."

I'm out of the car before she can say anything. We don't have the shovel. I left it at the river. But the ground can't be that hard, I figure. It wasn't so long ago that Gemma and I dug that hole. It'll still be loose. I don't know if that's true or not, but thinking it makes me feel better. If Zadie's wondering how we're going to dig something up without tools, she doesn't say. In fact, she's standing at the front of the car while I start for the tree, shining the light from her phone on the front bumper. I have to call out her name, and then she follows.

We use her phone as a flashlight as we make our way to the tree. There's woodsmoke in the air, probably from the old farmhouse I know is across the field but can't see. As we get closer, I can tell something's wrong. This is the right place, the right tree. But something feels off. Like the air's been disturbed. Like we're not alone out here.

I can't see anyone in the dark, but it's like I know someone's there watching us. The same way I felt someone watching me outside Zadie's apartment. And I can feel that they've got a smirk on their face, and I want to shout out, *What are you so smug about?*

But as soon as we reach the hole, I know why. Because that's what we find—a hole right in the spot where I'd dug five months ago. I had filled it in, but now the hole is back, and even before Zadie shines the light inside I know what I'll see.

Nothing.

The hole is empty.

What Gemma and I buried, it's gone.

Yes, I'm sure Zadie is saying it was dead quiet. That she only heard our breathing. But I swear, as I stared in that empty hole, I heard someone laughing.

I don't know what happened to this girl. I don't. And I don't know who she is, I really don't. I'm not lying. All I know is what Gemma told me, and I told you, I don't know how true any of that is. After the séance, Gemma only got weirder. Manic, almost. Like my mom can get. I didn't know what to do. For, like, a week after the séance, we waited outside that Holiday Inn, watching, but I didn't know what we were watching for, not then, or who. Gemma wouldn't tell me and I was too scared to ask. Finally, Gemma pointed someone out. It was a Monday. I remember because the Phillies didn't play, and Zadie had been super angry at me for missing the game the day before when they hit four home runs off Colorado. But I hadn't been able to pay attention to the season at all, not with Gemma. There was no time for anything but Gemma then. And that day, after watching this Holiday Inn for what felt like forever, Gemma nodded toward this girl who was leaving the hotel wearing a zipped-up hoodie, hands in her pockets, head down, and said, "That's her. That's the bitch."

Yes, it was this girl here. This Gemma Horne.

Yes, I lied about not having seen her before. But only because I know she didn't have anything to do with Sarah going missing. And I honestly don't know who she is. Not really.

All I know is that seeing this girl in person triggered something in Gemma. I mean, the girl I knew as Gemma. She stopped going out. Stopped talking about Ian and the cursed money. All she'd do was, like, pace the apartment and talk about how this girl wanted to ruin her life. How she and this girl had been like sisters and how she'd betrayed her. I hadn't seen her that upset since the day she broke my Japanese peace lily. I'd try to calm her down, but I never could. It went on for a couple weeks. It's like she didn't know what to do.

I kept telling her, "Gemma, just go talk to her."

But Gemma said, "I can't. I can't let her see me. I can't let her know I'm this close. She'll run again. I know she'll run. And then I'll have to hunt her down all over again."

And then one day, after having this conversation for the umpteenth time, Gemma finally turned to me and said, "I need you to do it."

And I said, "Do what?"

She said, "Go up to her and make her tell you where it is. Where she's hidden it."

And I said, "What do you mean 'make her'? No, Gemma, I won't. I can't. Not even to pay back Staples. I can't."

And then Gemma grabbed my open laptop, shoved it in my face.

My search history was up on the screen.

She said, "You still want to know how Ian died? How his family died?"

I didn't say anything.

Gemma kept staring at me. She didn't even blink. And she said, "They died because they didn't listen to me."

She dropped my laptop onto the sofa.

"It's very important that people listen to me when I tell them to do something."

I still didn't move. Didn't say anything.

She cupped my face in her hands.

"This has to happen. I won't let anything stop me. I'm sure you understand. You're the same way. Just look at everything you do for your sister. Look at what you did for Zadie."

She dug her fingernails into my cheeks.

"You'd do anything for them, wouldn't you? You'd do anything to keep them safe, right?"

She waited, her nails cutting into my skin, and I thought of Sarah and Zadie and the fake ID with my name that I'd found in Gemma's room.

What ID? Oh.

This one day after the séance, when we first started watching the Holiday Inn but before I ever saw Gemma Horne, I went into Gemma's room again. I wanted to find that book she'd used for the séance. Something about that day didn't feel right, and I wanted to know what Gemma had been reading. I told you, I've done a lot of research on the supernatural, and once my head had cleared, the more I thought about it, the more off it felt. Staged. So, when she went to take a shower, I went into her room. I didn't have much time. I looked in her closet and the dresser drawers, and that's when I found it.

In an envelope tucked along the side of one of the drawers, there was a driver's license with our Gemma's picture on it. But it didn't say her name.

It said mine.

It was her picture on a driver's license with my name on it and my date of birth and my address. I stared at it until I heard the water shut off in the bathroom. Then I put it back where I found it.

Because I didn't know what else to do.

So a couple weeks later, when Gemma is cutting my cheeks with her nails and telling me I would do anything to keep Sarah and Zadie safe, I thought of that fake ID, of the burnt pigeon and the pictures someone had taken of me outside of the apartment. I thought of the Briar Lane Murders. And I nodded yes.

And Gemma said, "Then you need to be a good girl and do as I say."

Based on what you've told me, this Gemma Horne disappeared a week later.

But I didn't have anything to do with that.

No, Jeremy's wrong. I would never hurt anyone. I wouldn't do that.

Not again.

VERSION 4

I can still remember Uncle Mitchell's funeral. Being surrounded by a sea of black dresses and suits, lots of hushed chatter, the smell of Pop-pop's cigarettes, and the taste of egg salad sandwiches. There was a whole tray of them, and I kept eating them even though they were supposed to be for all the guests. Haven't had one since. Every time I see one, it takes me back to that day. I don't remember grief, exactly, just this constant feeling of being uncomfortable and not knowing why. It was like, every room I went into, I couldn't find a place where I wasn't in everyone's way. So I ended up in the kitchen because that's where the food kept coming from.

At one point, I was walking into the kitchen for another egg salad sandwich even though I still had a half of one in my hand. I remember I had taken a bite and had a mouth full of soft smushed egg, and I stopped in the doorway because my dad and Aunt Mel were in the kitchen together and I hardly ever saw the two of them alone. Aunt Mel was gripping the sink, and my dad was standing next to her, leaning into the counter beside her, like he was trying to get her to look at him, and Dad was saying something like, "This is what he wanted. He wanted to help you."

Aunt Mel said something like, "It's a terrible thing to want." And then she said something else I couldn't hear, and finally she turned to my dad and said, "—didn't you? He couldn't have done this on his own. You put the idea in his head. You—"

And then she saw me and stopped talking, and my dad turned and he saw me, too. I remember Aunt Mel wiped the tears from her eyes and smiled at me and said, "Did you want another sandwich, sweetheart?"

She grabbed two from the table and pressed them into my hand, and Dad was telling me we should go find Mom, and I was looking past them to the glass door to the backyard, where Jeremy was standing, watching all three of us, and I wondered if he'd heard the same things I heard and if he knew what they meant.

No, it wasn't suicide. Uncle Mitchell died of smoke inhalation caused by a fire in this garage he was renting. It was to store a shipment of electronics he'd purchased with a plan to resell. Problem was the electronics were all British DVD players. British electrical plugs. Could only play British region DVDs. And wherever he got them from, he couldn't return them. I learned later that he'd sunk the rest of their savings into opening this electronics retail store. He thought he could get a whole chain going or something, like sort of a new Best Buy, but all he had was an expensive storefront with a nonrefundable deposit and not a single piece of sellable merchandise.

No, I don't know what he was doing in his garage that night—I was only, like, ten—but I understand an electrical problem was the cause of the fire. Crappy wiring or something. The smoke detectors were working. He just didn't . . . or couldn't . . . get out.

I also found out later that the insurance policy on the garage plus his life insurance paid off his debts. Replenished their savings. But that's what insurance is supposed to do, isn't it? Replace what you lost?

I think Jeremy has always blamed my dad for what happened, and because he blames my dad, he blames me. I think that's why he's doing this. That's why he's sitting in that other room, trying to contradict what I'm telling you. I don't know how he knew I was here, but that's the only reason he came. He probably rushed over here as soon as he heard I was talking to you to "set the record straight."

What do you mean? But no. That can't be right.

But I've been here for hours. How did he get here before me?

No, he didn't come straight from the river. He couldn't have. He's been following me and Zadie.

Hang on. You're saying that you were talking to him for at least two hours before Zadie and I showed up? That he's been with you all this time?

When you said he was here and he was talking, I thought you meant he showed up after me and Zadie. Is that why you've been leaving the room and giving me these "breaks"? Because you want to ask him if what I'm saying is true?

So, since he got here first, his story's the one you believe and you're, just, what? Trying to catch me out in a lie or something?

Then fuck you and fuck Jeremy. I've been trying to help you! But of course you would take his word over mine. Everyone always does. As if he knows shit. I told you from the start he's a liar.

How could he have been here when he was following me and Zadie? No, I didn't see him. But he was there! I know he was.

Because someone was following us, and who else could it have been? I'm just supposed to take your word that it wasn't him?

What about a cut on his head? I don't know anything about a cut on his head. Is that why you keep asking me if I hit him or Sarah? No, I never touched him. He was fine when I last saw him. If he has a cut, he did it to himself, or he got it someplace else. Like from throwing my laptop into a wall.

No, I swear I never hit him, and I never hit Sarah either.

He's just trying to distract you because he knows what I found in his car. Bet he didn't tell you that, did he? What I found after I got in the driver's seat?

I ran back to the car, right? When we were at the river, like I said.

Jeremy and Sarah have left me, I thought I saw Gemma standing in front of the car, so I run up there and I'm looking for her or whoever is pretending to be her, and when I don't see anybody, I get in the car. In the driver's seat.

Remember, I've been riding in the back all night. I couldn't see up front. But now I can, and I notice something crumpled in the footwell on the passenger's side.

I bend down and pick it up. It's a T-shirt. Sarah's T-shirt. I know it's Sarah's 'cause it has the same bleach spot at the bottom from when she tried to get a sriracha stain out and didn't realize bleach would stain. The same shirt Sarah saw on that person near the Quick Stop. The same shirt I swear I just saw on that person in the headlights. Bleach stain and all.

And it's not just a shirt that looks like Sarah's. This is the actual shirt Gemma was wearing when she disappeared.

So what the fuck is it doing in Jeremy's car?

And that's when I drive off.

No, I don't look where I'm going.

Yes, I just take off.

Yes, I go straight to Zadie's.

No, I don't have the shirt anymore because I left it in Jeremy's car, and then the car got stolen. So you'll find it once you find his car.

No, Zadie and I didn't ditch the car somewhere.

What? Jeremy's saying I stole his car, then dumped it after I left him at the river? Why would I do that? That car had the T-shirt in it—the proof that he set this whole thing up. I need that car. You'd believe me if I still had the car, but it was stolen, I told you. Zadie will tell you the same thing!

I'm not lying! The shirt was there. I saw it. I held it in my hands. And I left it in the car because I didn't have a bag or anything to carry it in, and I was going to drive here anyway. But I went to Zadie's first.

And Jeremy knows all of this because I know he's the person who followed me and Zadie from the farm. It had to have been him. He beat us to the farm somehow, and then he beat us back to my apartment. And then he followed us when we left the apartment. It has to be Jeremy. I know it was Jeremy. Someone has been after me since I left the river. Who else could it be? Unless—

No, I'm not lying to you! I'm done lying to you. I swear.

What about Zadie?

No, that wasn't my fault. The first time I saw Zadie in forever was last night, I—

She told you that?

No, I wasn't trying to hide anything. It's just embarrassing. That's why

I didn't say anything. But I wasn't really lying. It's just that it has nothing to do with what happened last night.

No, she's right, I did see her last week. And yes, I hit her. I admit that. I punched Zadie, and that's why she has the black eye. But that doesn't mean I would hit Jeremy or Sarah. If Zadie told you about last week, then I'm sure she told you it was a mutual fight. We were both rolling around on the floor and pulling on each other's hair and she had this really firm grip on me, like she was going to take a huge chunk of it right out of my head. So I cranked my arm back and landed a fist to her face. I had meant to slap her, but I was so tense, I guess my fingers clenched up into a fist. I didn't even know what I was doing.

That's what ended the fight, though. That one punch. She let go of my hair and we separated and I left. I went into my bedroom and didn't come out until I heard Zadie leave the apartment. And then I showed up at her door yesterday. And that's the real reason why she was so angry when she saw me last night.

The fight was stupid. It wasn't even really about anything. I was just angry.

Angry about everything that went on with Gemma. How it's like everyone's abandoned me because of it. It's, like, even though she's gone, every day my life gets more fucked up by what happened when she was here. Aunt Joanie looks at me funny. The rare times my parents do get in touch, they only ever want to talk about the baby. And while Sarah and I are getting along better, she spends most of her time with Jeremy, and they share these looks, like they have their own language, like Sarah and I used to have. Like the two of them know something they don't want me to know. It's like that with everyone, really. Like everyone is looking at me sideways, talking about me behind my back.

I know what everyone's thinking.

They think I did something to Gemma. Or that I know more than I've been telling them, but they won't bring it up in front of me. But I didn't have anything to do with Gemma going missing. You know that. *You* told me that. You said the surveillance video showed that I never left the apartment that night. That only Sarah and Gemma went out, and Sarah came back later, alone. I've told everyone that. I've straight up said, "I am not a suspect."

But they don't believe me. I don't think they *want* to believe me.

Do you know what that's like? Having everyone think you're a murderer or something? It's like . . . like I'm walking around in this bubble and everyone's staying away from me. Or, no, it's like—there was that *Black Mirror* episode, okay? You ever watch *Black Mirror* on Netflix? Anyway, in this one episode, this guy—Jon Hamm, I think?—is a convicted sex offender and gets "blocked" so that other people can't see the real him, just a blurry red silhouette. So he was allowed to be free and in the general public, but the general public could see what a terrible person he was and everyone ducked out of his way. That's what I feel like. Like I've got some mark on me that everyone can see, that I can't get rid of.

So, yeah, sure. I've been angry, and I've wanted to talk to someone about it, but every time I try to bring it up with Sarah, she shuts down, and this is absolutely not a conversation I want to have with Jeremy. So I keep coming back to Zadie. She's the only person I could think of who might talk to me. Who might let me talk this out. And up until last week, we really hadn't spoken in months. That part is true.

I was scared as shit to text her, too. Like, my hand was literally shaking. But I had to do it. Jeremy had just stopped by the apartment again while Sarah was at work. I could tell he hadn't expected to see me because he used his key to let himself in and then he froze in the doorway when he saw me on the sofa.

And I was like, "What the fuck do you want?"

He said, "I got in."

And I said, "Got into what?"

"Her phone. And I found . . ."

"Whose phone?" I said.

But he just stared at me. He almost looked like he was scared to be alone in the same room as me.

And then he said, "I just wanted you to know."

And he left.

I didn't have a fucking clue what he was talking about. But it freaked me out. I'd never seen him look like that before, not since the first time his mom wandered out into traffic and almost got flattened by a tractor trailer.

After he left, my heart was racing. I could feel a panic attack coming on, and I wanted to talk to someone. I needed to. So I texted Zadie. One of those long texts that looks like a novel, the kind that makes you think, "Oh god, this must be serious." Zadie can show it to you. I would except, you know, my phone. Anyway, I said how I was sorry, that the past year had been hard, I told her how Sarah's pregnancy was going, that I was excited to be an aunt, said I had started looking at colleges again, that I was going to go back to school and was going to get my degree this time, something in sports management or sports education. Some profession that would keep me busy. And at the end I asked her if she could come over, if we could talk, that I wanted to talk to her about Gemma, or we didn't have to talk about Gemma but please, could she come over so we could talk.

It was a seriously long message. I didn't proofread it before I sent it, and I was rereading what I sent and seeing all of these typos, which was embarrassing, but feeling embarrassed is better than feeling anxious over what her response was going to be.

Then I saw the three little dots show up, so I knew she was typing, and I was thinking, *Oh god. What's she going to say? If she just says no, does that mean she never wants to speak to me again, or does it just mean she doesn't want to speak to me yet?* And then the three dots disappeared. But I didn't get a message. And then the dots reappeared, and I'm just like, Zadie, what are you typing? And finally, *finally*, her message pops up.

And all she'd written was: *ok*.

I was like, that's it? I texted you a novel, and you're just going to say "ok"?

So I did get angry about that, but then I was like, I have no right to be angry at Zadie at all. So I just texted back, "See you in a few?" and she sent me the thumbs-up emoji.

I quickly cleaned up the apartment—took down the recycling,

straightened the throw pillows and blankets, cleaned off the coffee table and kitchen counter and wiped them down, and then I realized I was still in these dirty old sweatpants. I'd just put on my jeans when I heard a knock on the door.

I was zipping them up as I looked through the peephole to make sure it was her, and it was, so I opened the door wide and smiled and welcomed her, and she came in. But she wasn't smiling, and she didn't take her coat off. Just stood there in the doorway with her hands in her pockets and said she'd just come off a long shift, and then she said, "You wanted to tell me something about Gemma?"

I know I wrote something about Gemma in the text, but it was only one small mention in that entire long text. And even though I did want to talk to her about Gemma, I was angry that Gemma was the first thing she brought up. We could've talked about anything else first—her job, Sarah's pregnancy, tomorrow's Phillies NLDS game versus Atlanta. Anything else I'd mentioned in that text. And she brought up Gemma.

So I said, "Not everything has to be about Gemma. Gemma's gone."

And Zadie said, "Yeah, I guess she is." And she gave me that look I told you about—that look everyone's been giving me the past five months. The one that means, *We know you did something.*

So everything else I wanted to talk to Zadie about flew out of my head because all I could think was: *Zadie's just like everyone else. Zadie doesn't believe me, either.*

And that was when I started shouting. I honestly don't know everything I said. Just that I was sick of Gemma, sick of everything I did being linked to Gemma, that I didn't know what happened to her, that Zadie was supposed to be my friend, she was supposed to be there for me. And that was when she started in with the "I can't support addictive behavior" routine, and that set me off even more because, one, I'm not one of her patients that needs to be analyzed. And two, none of this has anything to do with drugs. She was the one obsessed with drugs because her mom was the addict, not me, and . . . yeah, I said that.

You say anything about anyone's mom, whether it's true or not, there's going to be a fight. It really was a low blow on my part. I mean, there are things that are off-limits, even when you're best friends. So maybe I did say it on purpose. Maybe I provoked her because I wanted someone to hit me. I had all this anger that I wanted to get out, and what better way than a fight? I mean, men do it all the time, right?

So I know I provoked her, but I don't know who put whose hands on who first. I honestly don't. It's all a blur. If I had to say, I think we both went for each other at the same time and ended up on the floor, and I landed the lucky punch and that ended it.

I wouldn't have bothered Zadie for any other reason except Sarah, and Zadie knows that. That shows how much she still cares, doesn't it? It means something that she did all of this for me last night. That she's here with me now. Well, in the room next door or whatever.

Zadie really doesn't know anything, so don't harass her, okay? None of this is her fault. I didn't even tell her any of what happened with Gemma until we were driving back into Reading.

See, after we leave the farm, she's begging me to tell her. About what happened at the river and what happened with Gemma and what had been in that hole, what was missing. And she keeps asking me, begging me, and I just, I can't hold it back anymore.

So there in the car, I tell her. I tell her everything. It seems to take forever, and I'm getting hoarse from talking, but she listens. Doesn't interrupt or contradict me or anything.

And we're just pulling onto 222 when Gemma, I mean Zadie, asks me, "Did you believe her?"

And I say, "Of course not!"

And she says, "Then why did you help her bury it?"

Because I believed the part where somebody was after her, I said. I told Zadie my theory that Gemma had probably stolen that money from someone and her life was in danger. I didn't have to believe her whole story to believe that.

And Zadie says, "Did you tell the police this? When she went missing and they came to talk to you, did you tell them about this?"

I lie then. I don't want her to think worse of me now than she already does. And it's obvious by now that I should have told you, so I say, "Yes, of course I told them!" But that's the only time I lied to Zadie last night.

We're quiet for a few minutes after that. I'm driving down the highway not knowing where to go, what exit I should take, and I realize how bad I need Zadie. I need someone to tell me what to do, and right then, I know I'll do whatever she says. That I can't lose her, and I almost have.

Zadie says, "Let's go back to your apartment. Maybe Sarah and Jeremy made it back home."

So I drive us back to the apartment, and I park the car on the street, like I normally do. The CCTV camera has been out for weeks now. We got a letter about it from the property management company—it stopped working in September and they still haven't fixed it—but I swear I parked the car right there, locked it, and took the keys with me. Like I always do. Zadie gives the car one last look, then we go up to apartment.

It's been hours since Sarah, Jeremy, and I left. I was the last one out, and I know I shut the door tight. But when Zadie and I get there, it's standing open, the front door. Not wide open. Just a crack. Zadie gets excited. She doesn't even have to say it, but she thinks it means Sarah and Jeremy are back.

But I know it means there's someone on the other side of that door waiting for me. I know it. I can feel it. I want to hold Zadie back, but I can't get any words out. She goes through the door and calls out, "Sarah?"

When I don't hear her being attacked or anything, I follow her inside.

Nothing seems out of place. It looks just like Sarah and I left it earlier that night—my open bag of Doritos on the coffee table, Sarah's unfinished soda next to. My fleece Phillies blanket scrunched up on my end of the sofa.

Zadie calls for Sarah again. I try saying Sarah's name, too, but my voice breaks. We don't hear anything, but that doesn't surprise me. I didn't expect to find her here.

It feels like someone has been here, though. I have a sense of a presence. Like, that feeling of when you walk into a room and you can tell someone has just been there, but they're gone now. It reminds me of when Gemma lived with us, how she would often disappear inside her room right after we'd come out of our bedrooms. I almost call out, "Gemma."

All the bedroom doors are shut, like we'd left them. Sarah's shoes aren't by the door and neither is her coat or her purse, so I know she isn't there, but I knock on her door anyway.

Nobody answers. Of course nobody answers. But I open it just to check.

No one's there. Her bed looks like it normally does—unmade, the pillows flattened, the duvet kicked all the way down to the bottom because Sarah always sleeps hot. Yesterday's clothes are on the floor, piled in the corner next to her laundry basket but not in it. The only difference from how it usually looks is the stack of baby things on the opposite wall. An IKEA crib, still in the box, stuffed animals, bags of baby clothes in blue and green and pink and yellow. Boxes of infant diapers. A brand-new baby book from the Hallmark store. All these new things she bought for the baby this week with money she says she got from Mom and Dad.

It's the stuffed Phanatic that gets me.

See, I got this stuffed Phillie Phanatic for the baby after Sarah officially announced she'd be keeping it. I came home with it one day from the R-Phils team store. Took a rare trip out that wasn't for food. I wanted to surprise her when she came home from work. I said other people could get the stuffed teddy bears and dogs and bunnies and all the usual things, but my niece or nephew would always know the Phanatic came from me. I would be the cool aunt who got them the cool toys, and the Phanatic was just the start.

Sarah had hugged me then. I think it was the first time we'd hugged since Gemma moved in. Gemma had been gone a few weeks by then. And it was a real hug, a squeeze-the-life-out-you hug, and I hugged her back just as tight, and that was when I knew everything was going to be okay. We were going to be okay.

And now that Phillie Phanatic is sitting on top of all the other clothes and toys, staring at me like, *What have you done? You promised her everything was going to be fine, and now you've lost her. You lost her.*

I back out of the room and shut the door.

"No sign of her," I say, and I don't see where Zadie is because I'm wiping my eyes. Then I hear her call my name. I turn, and she's standing in front of my bedroom door. She'd opened it to check for Sarah, and now she's standing in the doorway like she's afraid to cross the threshold. I go and stand beside her.

The first thing I notice is that my mattress is overturned. It's been flipped off the bedframe. Then I notice the walls. All of my posters and pictures have been torn down, including my '08 World Champions one. Frames are broken, glass scattered over the carpet. Anything that wasn't framed is torn. The drawers to my dresser are all pulled out, clothes tossed everywhere, mixed in with the broken glass. My laptop, which had been on top of the dresser, looks like it was thrown across the room. There's a dent in the wall just above where it lies in pieces on the floor.

Zadie puts her hand on my arm to stop me, but I go in anyway. Glass crunches under my sneakers. The only thing that isn't broken is a framed picture of me and Sarah that had been on my bedside table. I pick it up. It was a picture of us taken at the Tavern from some random family gathering a few years ago, from before Sarah moved in with me, before our parents fucked off to Florida. We both look really happy in that photo.

While I'm staring at the picture, Zadie waits in the doorway. She's talking, saying we should call the police. That it's time to call the police. But I'm like, no. There's one more place we need to check. As I'm leaving my room, I close my door. I need to shut all that chaos away, but I take the picture with me, and I set it on the kitchen counter so that Sarah is right there. Right in the center of everything.

And Zadie's begging me to go to the police now, and I'm the one that keeps saying no. I admit that. I mean, we got here eventually, but at that moment I'm not ready yet.

"One more place," I say. "Go with me to one more place, and then we'll go to the police."

When we leave the apartment, I triple-check that the door is shut and locked. We didn't check Gemma's bedroom—the nursery, I mean—before we left. Someone could have been hiding in there, but just as I realize we should've checked, I completely forget about it because we're on the street and Jeremy's car is gone. I check my pockets, and I don't have his keys on me. I must have left them in the car even though I thought I took them with me.

I just told you someone fucked up my bedroom, and all you want to hear about is the car? I said I don't know what happened to the car. Jeremy must have taken it. He's the only person other than Sarah who has a key to our apartment, and Jeremy knows where I normally park his car when it's at our place.

I don't care that he was here with you when it happened. It doesn't mean it still wasn't him. If he didn't take it himself, then he got someone to do it for him, like Gemma. Or the Davy boys. I know he's been doing shit with them again. I could tell by the state of his house.

No, Zadie and I didn't do anything to that car! Just like I haven't done anything to Gemma and I didn't do anything to Sarah, even though Jeremy apparently thinks I did.

I don't know why he would say those things. He knows I wasn't the last person to see Gemma alive. He was. And as far as I know, Gemma *is* still alive.

So maybe it's her. Maybe it was her following me tonight and her who took the car. If Jeremy was here, then why couldn't it have been her?

I've told you and told you. There was nothing weird about the night she went missing. She went out and didn't come back. I wasn't worried about it at first because this was the night after the two of us had taken care of everything. Her curse, her ex, all of it. It was finished.

We had got back late, and I crashed. I mean, I was out as soon as my head hit the pillow. Didn't even bother to get under the sheets, and I didn't wake up until the next afternoon. The sun comes right through my bed-room window at that time of day, and I'd left the blinds open, so I started roasting. Woke up all sweaty, and admittedly, I smelled. But it was the best sleep I'd had in forever.

When I first sat up, I couldn't quite remember what happened. I didn't know why I was still in my jeans or why my hands were filthy. I had dirt caked under my nails. And then slowly it started coming back to me. The drive, the digging. And suddenly, I wanted a shower. Needed a shower. I didn't even wait for the water to warm up. It actually felt good to get hit with the cold water first. It's like those clichés in movies, you know, the woman taking a shower to cleanse herself? But I honestly was covered in dirt and smelled like cow shit, so you know ...

While I was in the shower, I kept thinking about Gemma. When I first woke up, I got this really sour taste in my mouth when I thought of her. Like, I didn't even want to look at her because I was afraid I might throw up. I kept picturing her ordering me around, laughing at me. Kept feeling her fingernails pinching my arm as we walked from the hole back to the car. In my mind's eye, her face had morphed into something darker than what it was. Like she was older than she looked, meaner.

But as I stood under the water, the shower washed that away, and where the night before she had sort of scared me, like she'd become some sort of manic creature, now I remembered her as someone who'd been very scared. By the time I got out of the shower, I'd convinced myself that most of what I'd felt the night before was an overreaction from being tired and how late it'd been. I told you I don't like being out late.

I wrapped myself in a big towel, and as I was stepping out of the bathroom, Sarah was coming into the apartment. It was, I don't know, two thirty or three in the afternoon at that point, so I figured she'd been out that morning and was coming back from whatever errand she'd run. But then I saw her clothes were the same as she'd had on the day before, and her hair was pulled back but you could tell it hadn't been brushed.

Things were still pretty chilly between us, so I blurted out without really thinking, "Where were you?"

And she said, "Out. Where were you?"

She said it really accusingly, so I just said, "Out."

I was getting cold standing there in only my towel, so without saying anything else, I went into my room. My comforter was all dirty from me sleeping on top of it in my dirty clothes, but I didn't feel like washing it. I just grabbed some clean sweatpants and a hoodie, and when I came out of my room again, Sarah was in the kitchen making coffee, still in the same clothes. She kept looking at me like she wanted to say something, but then she didn't. I was about to ask her what it was, when Gemma's door opened.

You had asked me back then if Gemma had seemed distressed at all that day. And the truth is, she didn't. That day was honestly the happiest I'd ever seen her. When she walked out of that room, she was, I don't know how to explain it. Lighter? She'd changed clothes and her hair was pulled back out of her face and she was barefoot and she was almost smiling. Looked like someone's yoga instructor. She said, "Good morning," even though it was the afternoon, and went into the kitchen to get her bowl of Cheerios.

Then Sarah—real suddenly, like she wanted to say it quickly before she could take it back—said, "Hey Gemma, do you want to go out tonight?"

At first, Gemma didn't say anything, and I was afraid she was going to laugh in Sarah's face. Then Sarah started talking really fast, and it took me a second to realize she was apologizing. She was saying how she's been stressed at work, and this relationship she's in hadn't ended well, and she's been taking it out on Gemma and so she was wondering if Gemma wanted to go out so maybe they could get to know each other better.

I kept my mouth shut. Sarah was trying to work something out on her own for once, and I didn't want to get in the way.

Gemma thought for a moment. And then she said, "Yes, all right. Let's go out. Do you want to go with us?" she asked me.

They both looked at me—one urging me to say yes, the other no. And I said, no, I didn't want to go out that night. I wanted to get some rest, stay in, watch the Phillies game. I said they should go and have fun. Nobody tried to change my mind.

Not much else happened the rest of the day. Like I told you back then, it was a pretty normal day. Especially considering what Gemma and I had been doing the night before. Gemma stayed in her room for most of it. I sat on the couch with snacks, watching TV and playing games on my iPad. And trying to text Zadie. Well, I *was* texting her. She just wasn't texting back. Sarah was in and out of her room, doing laundry, cleaning, texting.

Then it was night. I was staring at my phone, willing Zadie to text me or call me, and Gemma and Sarah were coming out of their rooms, neither really dressed up, not like I expected. Sarah was in, what do you call them? Skinny jeans? Are those still a thing? And this sky-blue sweater that really made her eyes pop. Hair and makeup done but not overdone. And Gemma was in jeans, too, and Sarah's old concert tee, plus this leather jacket that may or may not have been real leather. Her hair was down and teased a bit, sort of eighties style but in a retro way? Like she could pull it off, but I would've looked like I was going to some lame eighties-themed Halloween party.

And I remember how nervous both of them looked. I couldn't remember the last time the two of them had been alone together in the same room. I thought maybe Sarah might have suggested they go to a club or something to listen to live music so they wouldn't have to talk much, but they weren't dressed for that, and then Sarah told me they were going to Applebee's for dinner and Sarah asked me if I was sure I didn't want to come, and I was thinking she knew I'd never say yes to clubbing so maybe she chose Applebee's because she knows how hard it is for me to say no to their spinach and artichoke dip. And I was getting hungry. But I looked at my phone and remembered my last text to Zadie. How I'd told her that I'd be home all night and she could call me any time or stop over and we could talk, so how could I go out now? I didn't know if Zadie would come over or not. I mean, I was thinking it was pretty unlikely, since she hadn't responded to a single one of my texts. But what if I did go out and then Zadie came over and I wasn't there?

I didn't say that to Gemma and Sarah, though. I just said I was exhausted and wanted to stay in and watch the game and eat a frozen pizza. I couldn't tell if Sarah was relieved or disappointed. After she went out the door, Gemma paused and gave me a wink.

"Everything'll be fine," she said. "It's all sorted out now, isn't it?"

And she went out the door with a smile on her face.

Like I told you before, that was the last I ever saw her.

I spent the night on the sofa watching the Phillies beat the Cubs 12–3, realizing it was already May and this was the first game I'd watched from beginning to end this season. I hadn't even paid much attention to spring training. Then I wondered if Reading was home that weekend and if Zadie might want to go to a game, but that would involve Zadie actually texting me back, which she hadn't, so I ate the whole frozen pizza and ended up falling asleep on the sofa to some old episode of *Homicide Hunter*.

The door opening is what woke me up.

No, I don't know what time it was. I told you before. It was late, middle of the night. I couldn't even make sense of what was on the TV. I sat up, all groggy, and Sarah whispered, "Sorry," and I grunted and turned the TV off and shuffled to bed.

It didn't occur to me until morning that Gemma wasn't with her, so no, I didn't think it was weird that Sarah came home alone. And no, I don't remember if Sarah was wearing the same clothes as when they went out. But I remember neither of them had told me Jeremy was meeting up with them that night. I didn't learn that until the next day, when we couldn't find Gemma.

I've always thought Gemma would come back. To finish what she started, tie up loose ends. Because I know what she's capable of.

No, I only ever saw this Gemma Horne girl twice, and I only ever spoke to her that one time. And she was alive when I left her. She even went back in to work. Ask the Holiday Inn. It was May 12 when I talked to her. And your flyer here says she didn't go missing until May 17.

Zadie can confirm that. It was that same day she came over unannounced. The one I told you about. The day I knocked her down and left her in the hallway. That's why Gemma and I were in such a rush. We had to get to the Holiday Inn before this girl's shift ended.

My whole head was spinning after fighting with Zadie like that. It felt like I needed to vomit but couldn't. And the sun was out, which meant the streets were crowded, and there were so many people I just wanted to run back inside, but Gemma had her hand on my wrist and dragged me along. I didn't have any sunglasses. I wished I did. I was squinting. I barely paid attention to where we were going until we suddenly came to a stop and I bumped into her back.

"We're here," she said. It took my eyes a minute to focus, and when they did, I saw we were standing across the street from the Holiday Inn.

I said, "Okay, so you want me to ask her where—?"

Gemma took my messenger bag off her shoulder and shoved it into my hands and said, "You have to make her tell you where it is."

"I can't make people do anything," I said.

She said, "Of course you can. You made sure the Bartons left Zadie alone, didn't you?"

Gemma patted the messenger bag. "But just in case, there's something inside that'll help you get your point across." She smiled when she said *point*.

Then she left.

I didn't know what else to do, so I stood there, waiting for this girl to appear. Whatever was in the bag didn't weigh much, but the bag seemed to get heavier the longer I stood there. I smoked a cigarette or two but mostly just for something to do. It didn't calm my nerves at all. I kept thinking, what do I do if I don't see her? Gemma would know if I lied or if I failed. And then what would she do to me? She'd made it very clear that I didn't have an option. I was just thinking that maybe I should go inside and wait in there when she came out.

She went around the corner into this alley beside the hotel, and I followed her. Watched her pull out a pack of cigarettes, light one up. She paced a bit, but slow, not like she was nervous or anything, just bored. Not like she was expecting anything. Then I realized I'd been watching her so long she was almost done with her cigarette and would be going back inside. I'd miss my chance. So I crossed the street and dug my hand into the bag at the same time.

She was crushing the butt under her shoe when I shouted, "Excuse me!"

She looked startled then, but she didn't run or anything. Maybe she thought I wanted to bum a cigarette or something. My mouth was dry, making it hard to speak, so I didn't say anything else right away. I just pulled out what was in the bag. It was the biggest knife from Sarah's butcher block.

The girl's face was hard to read at first. She was older than that picture you have here. Ten years, at least. Or else something aged her fast. She had creases around her eyes and mouth. The skin on her neck was a bit saggy. But it was the same girl. And then I saw her eyes had started to water. She was about to cry, and I didn't know if it was because she was sad or angry or what. But she didn't seem scared or try to run, and she didn't try to fight me.

She said, "So she found me."

I wasn't doing anything with the knife, just holding it. I could see it shaking in my hand.

And I said, "You have to give it back."

She looked up at me like she wanted to kill me. Or that's what I thought. Like, it was a brief look, but there was so much hatred in it. Then it slipped away, and she said, "It's my insurance policy."

I said, "It's not yours."

I wanted to sound confident, but my voice—like my hand—was shaking too much for that.

She shoved her hands in her pockets, stared at me. Even with me holding this great big kitchen knife, she didn't seem scared of me.

She said, "She's dug herself deep under your skin, hasn't she?"

I didn't say anything. She pointed at my face.

"I know that look. I used to have that look. She gave it to me."

I said, "Can you just tell me where it is? Please?"

She said, "You know what she is, don't you?"

She took a step forward. I took a step back.

She said, "She's a leech. She ingratiates herself into a family. She gains their trust and then takes everything from them and disappears and leaves them in ruins. And she doesn't just take their money. Although she takes that, too. She takes their love. Their trust in one another. And she breaks them. She breaks them apart into little pieces. And then she laughs about it. You can hear her voice even after she's gone. Laughing in your ear."

By the end of her little speech, she was crying. Angry tears rolling down her cheeks. I was still standing there with the knife raised, blocking the exit from the alley.

I said, "I just need to know where it is. Tell me where it is, and she'll let me go."

She laughed at that. "You really think so? You really think she lets any of us go? No. She's a collector. She collects us."

She took another step forward, but this time I held my ground. Tightened my grip on the knife.

She said, "My greatest dream was to have a sister. An older sister. An older sister who would play princesses with me when I was little. To giggle about boys with. Who would show me how to use makeup and tame my hair. She found that out. I don't know how. But she did. And she became that person for me. And I loved her for it. I dreamed of a loving big sister, and she gave me that dream, just long enough for me to believe it was real. Then she burned it all to the ground. What did you want? What did you dream of?"

I knew the answer right away.

I'd wanted an interesting life. I wanted the same thrill I used to get from field hockey, the thrill I couldn't get through stealing from the cash register or learning about the supernatural, no matter how much I tried. I wanted my life to be like one of those true-crime documentaries I've gotten obsessed with.

But more than that, I wanted someone who needed me. Zadie and Sarah didn't need me anymore. But Gemma—with her crazy ex and her curses and her loneliness—did.

And this girl standing in front of me, unafraid of the knife she could see shaking in my hand, looked me in the eyes and said, "You understand."

She said, "If I give it to her, I lose the only protection I have."

I don't remember exactly what happened next. She came toward me, and I knew I couldn't let her go because I didn't have the information Gemma wanted, and I couldn't go home without it. So I blocked her, and we started fighting. The knife got knocked out of my hand, and she was grabbing at the neck of my sweatshirt, and I was trying to get my hands on her arms to push her away. I remember thinking she was stronger than she looked. I was able to kick my leg out and knocked her feet out from under her, and we both went down. My head hit the ground hard, but hers bounced off the corner of the dumpster and she staggered away from me. The blood coming out of her temple was bright red. It dripped down her face and onto her jacket. She put a hand over the cut, but blood kept coming through her fingers. I rolled onto my knees and picked up the knife and got to my feet. She stood there, her hand pressed to her bleeding head, and waited for what I would do next.

I put the knife back into my bag.

I said, "She'll tell you what happened to your brother. She'll tell you where he is."

It was a total guess on my part. She hadn't mentioned a brother. And Gemma, of course, wasn't going to tell her a thing. But the girl's eyes opened wide.

"She'll . . . what?"

"If you tell me where it is, she'll tell you what happened to Ian."

I held my breath. If I had said the wrong thing—the wrong name—I knew that was it: I'd lost her.

But she said, "She told you about Ian?"

I didn't say anything. I just let her think whatever she wanted.

Then she said, "It's with Roger."

And I said, "Who's Roger?"

But she just shook her head, then winced and prodded the cut again. "She'll know what it means."

And I left. I left her standing there, blood all over her clothes.

I swear I'm telling you the truth.

That is the only time I got close to this Gemma Horne.

I should have figured it out sooner, I know that. I know it's stupid. The "curse." The stories. The séance. Even the fucking rat and pigeon. It was all for me. She made it happen because *I wanted it to happen*. Because I needed something like that to happen. She made it all up so she could use me.

It makes me wonder what Gemma Horne's life was like before Gemma came into it. Like, were her and her family happy? Did she look up to Ian? Did he take her for ice cream when she was little? Did their mom dote on both of them? Did Ian help Gemma when her parents were getting divorced, since he'd been through the same thing? Or did they always resent one another? Did Ian hate his mother for finding a new husband, having a new child? I guess what I'm wondering is, did our Gemma bring her darkness into the family or was that darkness already there and she just used it?

You want to hear my current theory? The girl I knew as Gemma—she's some sort of con artist, right? I mean, that's obvious. She moves in with people, steals from them, then disappears when she gets what she wants. That's what she did with the Baker/Horne family. Started dating Ian, and that's what got her into the house. But something went wrong. Something went bad. Ian ended up killing his mother. Or Gemma convinced him to do it, and then Gemma killed Ian and hid his body somewhere so the police would keep thinking he was still alive and that he was the prime suspect. But Ian's younger sister took something from Gemma and ran before Gemma could kill her, too. Gemma needed to track the sister down to tie up that loose end. And she found her in Reading and moved in with me and Sarah and used me to get to her.

But Gemma's smart. Picking me and Sarah was no accident. No coincidence. Why waste time on her next con while waiting to track down Ian's sister? Why not do both at once? Gemma didn't find us just because we placed an ad for a roommate. Our family's last name is plastered over a few businesses in Reading. It's no secret our parents did well for themselves. She chose us because she figured she could use us to both find Gemma Horne and maybe get some cash off us like she did with the Hornes. Jeremy's always been jealous of our parents' money, so she used that. Convinced him to help her con us so she could get some money—said it would be for the both of them—although she never did get anything. We never gave her—or Jeremy—any money.

That must be what she was doing last night, using Jeremy to finish us off. To tie up her loose ends. That's why he lured me and Sarah out to the river.

So that's why I convinced Zadie to go to Jeremy's house last night. I wanted to see if he was there. Or if Sarah was there. And I wanted him to give me some answers. That's it.

No, I didn't know he was already here at the police station, or so you say.

I go to his house *because* I think he'll be home. Not because I know he won't be.

Zadie uses her Uber account to get us up to his place from my apartment. I'm uncomfortable the whole ride, even though the driver doesn't try to make awkward conversation or anything. Me and Zadie don't talk either. I mean, what is there to say? But the whole time we're on our way, I feel like we're being followed. It gets worse when the guy drops us off. We have him drop us off a few houses away because I don't want Jeremy to see a car pull up to the house, in case he is there, and then Zadie and I walk the rest of the way, and I told you I don't actually see who it is—I thought it was Jeremy then, but maybe it was Gemma—but I *know* someone's behind us because I can hear their footsteps echoing ours. They're not too far behind but far enough so they can duck around a tree or something every time I turn round. Zadie asks me once what I'm doing, but I don't want to worry her, so I don't say anything, and I'm actually relieved when we get to his house.

All the lights are off, but of course that doesn't mean anything. Jeremy doesn't keep too many lights on when he's home anyway. I guess technically the house still belongs to his mom. Dad bought it for her a couple years after Uncle Mitchell died—this nice little cabin-style place up on the mountain, off Skyline Drive, the kind of place Uncle Mitchell always wanted to buy for her, according to Dad. But Aunt Mel hasn't lived there in years. She was never quite right after Uncle Mitchell died. That's why Pop-pop was always bringing Jeremy to our house when we were kids. But then the other year, she really started to get disconnected from, well, everything. Talked like Uncle Mitchell was still alive, like Jeremy was still in elementary school. Couldn't remember what day it was or even month.

At the Tavern, the family started whispering about early-onset Alzheimer's or something, and then Jeremy's mom wasn't living in the house anymore but at this care home in West Lawn, some expensive specialist place. My dad is paying the bill for it, but whatever.

I guess Jeremy doesn't like having the entire house to himself, which is why he's always coming over to ours. Sarah and I don't ever go to his. I mean, rarely. There's just something . . . let's just say neither Jeremy nor his mom have done much to keep it up since Dad bought it for them, and that was about a decade ago now.

I don't bother knocking. I just open the door.

Yes, I have a key, but no, I didn't steal it. Sarah and I have had keys to his place forever. Pop-pop and Nana gave them to us in case of an emergency. They were getting too old to run over there all the time and check on Aunt Mel, before she went into that special home, and asked us to do it. So I was given that key in good faith. But, unlike Jeremy, I've never abused the privilege.

All the lights are off, like I said, and we don't hear anything. But the smell . . . It's not a dead body smell. Nothing like that. Just trash. Rotten food. That sort of thing. We look around the front room, where Jeremy usually hangs out to watch TV, the room his mom would refer to as "the parlor" and that Aunt Mel filled with porcelain cats. The porcelain cats are still there. But no sign of Jeremy.

The kitchen's at the back, and we go there next, drawn by that smell. Zadie turns on the light and, god, it's a mess. Dishes packed high in the sink. All dirty of course, so I can only imagine what the dishwasher looks like. Empty pizza boxes and takeout cartons all over the counter and that round kitchen table they've had for forever. The trash is piled high up in the can—lots of food waste, dirty paper towels, coffee grounds. That's where the worst of the smell's coming from. You might not think that's strange. A single guy, young, whole house to himself, what else do you expect? But Jeremy's always been a clean freak. Ever since we were little, he'd be picking the dirt off his clothes, making sure the dishes were washed and put away. My dad sometimes called him . . . well, something not nice that I won't repeat behind his back. The only time I've seen Jeremy's kitchen like that was when he let the Davy boys stay with him this time when they got kicked out of their place for a few months.

I didn't think the Davy boys had anything to do with this. But after I saw the state of Jeremy's kitchen last night, I don't know. I don't know much about them, to be honest. They were just kids—brothers—that Jeremy went to school with. "Bits of trouble," Aunt Mel used to call them. You know, in a way, it must be nice for her, the way her brain makes her live in the past. Things were better for her in the past. She doesn't have to see what Jeremy's doing now.

I'm wondering if he owes the Davy boys money again. The last time he owed them, they stayed at the house for free as payment. It was filthy, Sarah said, the way they never threw anything away, never washed a dish. How they let food go moldy in the fridge. So maybe it was them staying over. I've heard they know how to make things, like fake IDs. I think it's possible Jeremy could've taken my driver's license and given it to them so they could make a duplicate with Gemma's picture. And maybe he let them stay with him again, as repayment.

While Zadie and I are in the kitchen, we check the backyard. I don't see anyone. But it would be easy for someone to hide at the back of the yard and watch from the darkness. There's some grass and behind that, the tree line that marks the start of the woods. The more I think about it, the more I'm convinced someone's there. I can feel them. Whoever's been following us must have gone around back after we went inside.

Zadie joins me outside and asks if I see anyone, but before I can answer, we hear the scream.

Well, of course Jeremy told you the house was like that because of his mom and not because he's had anything to do with the Davy boys. He would say that, wouldn't he? It makes sense. Sometimes she gets out of the place she's in and finds her way to the old house. The new owners call Jeremy to pick her up, and Jeremy doesn't have the heart to send her back right away. He lets her stay, lets the care place know where she is, until he can't take it anymore and takes her back. Aunt Mel used to pride herself on keeping a clean house, but that's when she was herself. I've seen her take boxes from the trash can and put them in the sink, put the milk carton in the cupboards, that sort of thing. So maybe it was her. Or maybe it was the Davy boys. I thought about going to them—the Davy boys—myself, about Gemma. I thought maybe they could do something.

I thought about it all the way home from the Holiday Inn that day. And when I got home, I thought about it some more because Gemma wasn't back yet. And that was fine. After the séance and Gemma's fight with Aunt Joanie and what just happened in that alley, I needed a break. I was exhausted. For weeks I'd been jumping at shadows. Hearing noises in the dark. I drank coffee by the gallon to stay awake and didn't sleep because I didn't want to have any more dreams.

When I stepped into the quiet apartment that afternoon, I didn't realize how much space Gemma's voice had been taking up inside my head.

I had made up my mind to send the Davy boys a Facebook message when Sarah came home.

I was in the kitchen. I'd just washed the kitchen knife and returned it to the butcher block, and Sarah asked me where Gemma was, and I said, "I don't know. Out, I guess."

Sarah didn't have any other plans that day, and we ended up having a nice dinner together, just talking. Random stuff like sisters do, and I realized I couldn't remember the last time we'd done that. Just the two of us, chilling on the sofa and laughing, like it used to be. For months, Gemma had always been there. Like a shadow. Even when she wasn't in the room, we knew she was there and we'd stifle our laughs, or not say everything that was on our minds, you know, keeping the really personal stuff to ourselves, in case she overheard. It felt nice to be just the two of us again. For a couple hours, I forgot about Gemma and the Horne girl. I forgot about why I wanted to message the Davy boys. Sarah was just starting to tell me about her ex, the guy she'd been dating at Walmart, that he was actually her manager, when the door opened and there was Gemma.

Sarah went quiet, and I said hi, and Gemma said, "Can I talk to you?" And then she looked at Sarah, then back at me, and said, "In private?"

And I wasn't going to make Sarah leave, so I went with Gemma into my bedroom.

She said, "Well?"

I tried to be calm, pretend it was no big deal. So I shrugged and said, "She said it's with Roger."

I expected her to get mad and say she didn't know what that meant or something. But instead she said, "That sneaky bitch. Okay, grab your bag."

And I said, "What? You mean right now? Where are we going?"

She said, "We're going to get Roger. God, why are you being so stupid? Jeremy left his car outside for us. Let's go."

But I didn't move. So she grabbed my messenger bag and shoved it into my hands.

I said, "But Sarah and I were going to watch that new Adam Sandler movie together."

"We're running out of time. You can watch some crappy Adam Sandler shit once this is over. Let's fucking go."

When I went back into the front room and Sarah saw me following Gemma, my bag over my shoulder, god, I felt really shitty. If there was one moment I could change, that would be one. I should've told Gemma . . .

But it doesn't matter now, does it?

I could barely meet Sarah's eye when I told her I had to go help Gemma with something. Sarah crossed her arms and sank into the sofa, the way she always does when she's upset. She started to say something but stopped herself. Wouldn't look at me as I followed Gemma out the door.

Gemma rode next to me, giving me directions, while I drove and tried not to think about the fake license I'd found in her room the other week. What was she going to do with it? Where'd she even get it?

Anyway, every few seconds, Gemma gave me another direction. She wasn't looking at a phone or anything. She had it all in her head, like she'd been here before. Every time I asked her how much longer, she'd just say, "Soon."

All in all, it took about an hour to get there. At that moment, I didn't exactly know where "there" was, there were so many turns and route changes, but finally she had me pull up alongside this row of houses. It was a fairly normal street of matching houses in some small town. Kind of looked like Privet Drive in the Harry Potter movies? Except more American. Nothing extraordinary. Every house the same. It was dusk by this point and the streetlights were on, but nobody was out. You could hear a dog bark occasionally. That was it.

Gemma pointed to a house across the street that looked like all of the others except it was dark and had a For Sale sign out front.

"That one," she said, pointing to the sign.

So I asked, "What about it?"

She didn't answer. She had a way of doing that. Just ignoring your question if she didn't want to answer. Instead of asking again, I said, "It doesn't look like anyone's living there."

And she said, "No it doesn't."

So I said, "So should we go? If this Roger isn't home—"

But Gemma opened her car door and said, "Wait here for me."

I could barely get out a "Wait, what?" before she closed the door. Then she was jogging across the road without even checking for cars. I didn't know what to do, so I stayed put like she told me. At first. I wondered when Gemma had talked to Jeremy and how she was able to get permission to use his car. Then I thought, we're going to have to put gas in it and how much would that cost, and I wondered if I had enough in the bank, and basically anything to keep me from thinking about where I was and what was going on and what Gemma was doing inside that house, because I was starting to feel nervous. Like, it was getting late, and I was parked on this strange street, and this seemed like one of those neighborhoods where everyone would know every car, so I was probably attracting attention already. I tried to tell myself it wouldn't matter because I wasn't doing anything wrong. I was just sitting in a car. But I didn't know what Gemma was doing, and if she was doing something illegal, did that make me an accomplice?

After a few minutes, I couldn't sit still anymore. I got out of the car and went toward the house. I didn't see anyone outside or inside, so I whispered, "Gemma?"

She didn't answer, so I walked around to the back. I figured, where's the harm in that? The backyard was fenced in, but it was a low fence and broken in some places. I could see over it easily, but I didn't see Gemma or anyone else. I whispered her name again, but still nothing.

The backs of the houses bordered what looked like some woods, and I thought maybe Gemma went in there. I mean, there didn't seem to be any sign of her in the house, so she could've, right? But no way was I going back there. It was already dusk, and I'm not much of a nature person to begin with. So I decided, fuck it, I'm going back to the car. As I turned around, something about the place looked familiar, like I'd seen it before even though I'd never been here. I dug the little scrap of photograph out of the stick-on pocket on my phone—the one I found in Gemma's ex's wallet—and held it up, shone the light from my phone on it. It was a small piece, but the red brick in the photo looked like it matched the red brick of the house. Whoever took the picture would've been standing about where I was.

I shoved the picture into my pants pocket and hurried back to the sidewalk. As I stepped out in front of the house, the neighbor was putting her trash out on the street. She startled when she saw me, and I had to think fast. So I smiled and said, "Evening! Just having a look. You know . . ." And I gestured to the "For Sale" sign. I was really glad I put on jeans before we left. It made me look more presentable than sweatpants would've.

But she huffed and said, "Oh, we get all sorts of lookie-loos."

Before I could stop myself, I said, "Sorry, what?"

And she said, "It's bad enough that poor woman died. We don't need people like you coming around here gawking at the place it happened, making your Tikky-Toks or whatever you kids post on social medias. You won't see anything. The police had professionals come in. They cleaned it all up. You'd never know what went on in there."

So I said, "What happened? Honestly, I just came to look before I contact the real estate agent. Someone died in there?"

But she turned her nose up like I was putting her on, which I guess I was, but not for the reasons she thought, and she just said, "As if you didn't know." And headed back into her house.

Earlier, I was just being paranoid, but now I knew this woman really was watching me from behind her curtains, so I casually walked back to the car, trying not to seem nervous. I thought about just leaving. Driving off and leaving Gemma there. But then I saw that Gemma was already in the car.

I got in quick. My bag was at her feet, and I could tell there was something in it. The first thing I said was, "Where were you?"

And she said, "Thanks for distracting that woman so I could get back."

Which wasn't what I was doing, but I didn't say that. And then Gemma said, "Come on. Let's go. We don't want the neighbors asking questions."

So I started the car and we pulled away, and all Gemma said after that were the directions to get us back home. But as we drove away, I saw dirt underneath her fingernails. She caught me looking, so I looked away, and that was when I saw the road sign marking the street we were leaving. I don't have to tell you the name of the road, do I?

When we got home, Sarah was either out or in bed, I don't know which. I knocked on her bedroom door, but if she was in, she didn't answer. I was about to peek in when Gemma called me over to her room. She beckoned me forward with her finger, like this, then she pulled something out of my bag—a wooden box, with the silver engraving of a dog, a Westie, on the lid. She smiled and said, "Meet Roger."

It was the same kind of dog in Rebecca Horne's Facebook pictures. No, it wasn't just the same kind of dog. "Roger" *was* Rebecca Horne's dog. And I remembered what Gemma had said all those months ago.

Sisters get mad for no reason. They yell at you about towels and food and boyfriends. They say you stole their shower gel or lied to your mom or killed the dog.

Last night, in Jeremy's backyard, when I heard the scream, I thought of the look on Gemma's face when she held up that dog's wooden box of remains. How happy she was.

I know Zadie doesn't think it was a scream.

She said, "It's a fox. It's just a fox."

But I knew it wasn't. I know what foxes sound like. That was Sarah. There was not a doubt in my mind. *Sarah's nearby and she screamed and she needs me.* And I must've said that out loud, because Zadie's following me as I'm running into the woods and she's saying, "It was a fox. It's not Sarah. That was a fox."

But I'm not listening to her because I know my sister, and I definitely know the difference between my sister and a fox. That was the same scream she made when she flew off the swings when she was eight and broke her arm. Whoever has been following us has Sarah, and they want me to come get her.

I shout her name. I know she won't be able to answer, but I want her to know I heard her. I need her to know that I heard her. That I know she's nearby. Zadie's caught up to me, and she's starting to say something about going back inside, but I don't listen. I just keep fighting through the underbrush.

We used to explore the woods when we were kids, crawling around in the leaves and dirt, pretending we were animals, weaving our way through the branches and the bushes and the thorns. But I don't weave now. I force my way through. Branches are scratching me, thorns catching me. I'm getting all cut up. And I don't even know where I'm going. I don't know if I'm close or not. I stop and scream Sarah's name again and I listen, but I don't hear her. I close my eyes and listen harder and then it's almost like I can hear Gemma's voice, but I can't make out what she's saying. It's like she's all around me. I want to call out Sarah's name again, but I don't because the longer I stand there and listen, the clearer Gemma's voice gets. A branch breaks behind me. It's Zadie, coming through the brush, and she starts to talk but I shush her. The sound of her stepping on that branch silenced Gemma's voice, and I need to get it back. So I hold out my hand to tell Zadie to stay still. I close my eyes and listen, and Gemma's voice starts to come back, and I can sense every time Zadie is starting to speak again and I wave her off so she doesn't interrupt.

I know that sounds crazy. If I could hear Gemma's voice, then Zadie should be able to hear it, too. So I can't really be hearing anything.

But then how else did I know where to go?

Because the more I listen, the better I can hear which way she wants me to go. Instead of fearing her, of running away, I run toward her.

That's how we get to the little clearing. I thought Sarah would be there, but she isn't. Nobody's there. And I get really angry because, what was the point of running all that way, getting scratched up and everything, and Sarah's not even here?

Then Zadie goes, "What's that?"

And I see the burn barrel in the center of the clearing. It's too dark to see what's inside, to see any sign of what might've been burned, but it doesn't smell fresh. Zadie shines her phone down, and the first thing we both see is the green lighter lying on the ground beside the barrel.

Zadie picks up the lighter and asks me, "Did you do this? Did you set this fire?"

I say no, and she can tell I'm telling the truth. She shines her flashlight into the barrel, and we lean over to see what was burned.

The last time my Gemma mentioned the Horne girl? I guess it was a few days after we drove to the Briar Lane house. She'd spent the entire weekend in her bedroom, only coming out to use the bathroom. And then one night, when Sarah was at work, Gemma came out and grabbed her jacket and left. She didn't say where she was going. I told you, she never did. I thought she might be going to see the Horne girl, but I didn't try to follow her. I didn't want to know what was going to happen. I told Gemma what I'd said to the girl about the brother—that Gemma would tell her what had happened to him in exchange for the information I needed. So Gemma knew the girl would be expecting to see her. Because of what I said, she knew the girl wouldn't run when Gemma came toward her. But I tried not to think about that.

While Gemma was gone, I went into her room. It wasn't hard to find the box she'd found at the house. It was on the floor of the closet.

No, I never said I didn't see what was inside it. I just said Gemma never showed me.

Like I said, it was a wooden box. Not tiny, but small enough I could hold it one hand. And there was a metal plaque on top with engraved letters that said "Roger" and the etching of the Westie. There was dirt in the seams where the box opened and closed and around the edges of the metal plaque. Like it had been buried.

I opened it expecting to see ashes. There weren't any.

I don't know what happened to the remains of Roger the dog, but in his place were ID cards. Driver's licenses, passports, school IDs, workplace IDs. All of them had Gemma's face on them. But all of them had different names. Different addresses. Different dates of birth. There were dozens of them. One toward the top was a Marriott employee ID with the name Gemma Horne. There was another ID I remember, for the Borgata Casino in Atlantic City, with the name Lydia DeLuca and a driver's license with that name and an address in Egg Harbor Township. Both had Gemma's picture. They all had Gemma's picture. I put them back in the box, put the box back where I found it, and went to my room.

I googled Lydia DeLuca and Egg Harbor Township. There was a Lydia DeLuca from Egg Harbor who died in an apartment fire.

This had been Gemma Horne's insurance policy. This was proof our Gemma existed and evidence of where she'd been, the path she'd cut through people's lives. Give this to the police, and they could probably track down her victims. As long as Gemma Horne had this, she was safe. And I'd convinced her to give it up.

I swear I didn't know Gemma Horne disappeared, too, that she was reported missing. Not until you told me. But no. It didn't surprise me.

Gemma's hurt a lot of people, not just Ian Baker and the Hornes. There must have been other people hunting for her. Other people who'd want her hurt or worse. So why do you keep asking me these questions? *What Sarah did that night. What me and Sarah talk about. What Sarah has been like since Gemma disappeared.* How are those going to help you find Sarah? She's out there somewhere. Alone. She needs me, and I've been sitting in this room talking to you, and you're saying this is oh-so-helpful, but what would be helpful is if we were out there looking.

Why do you keep asking about Sarah like she's . . . like she had anything to do with—

Look, everything that's gone on with Sarah since Gemma disappeared, it has nothing to do with Gemma or whatever happened to her. It's because of the pregnancy. It's just the pregnancy. Her mood swings, her nervous tics, all the times I overheard her crying. It's nothing to do with Gemma. It's the pregnancy plus the breakup drama. Every time she breaks up with a guy, she gets like this. It was worse this time, but I figured it had to be 'cause this guy got her pregnant. I mean, that's what you get for messing around with older men, isn't it? More than once I've even heard Jeremy say to her, "It's done. It's over. It happened, and you can't take it back."

Every time I heard him say that, I thought, *Thank god it's not me in there with her.* Because I can't do that anymore. I can't be that person for her. I can't deal with her boyfriends, her breakups. I can't let myself get worked up about it because I've already done that. With Zadie. In college. And I can't. It took so much and—

You don't understand. You don't understand, even though she's my sister, why I don't want, I can't, deal with her. I can't get caught up in that sort of drama again. I don't trust myself not to—

No, I never hurt our Gemma. And I didn't have anything to do with Gemma Horne's disappearance, I swear. Because I made a promise to myself that I wouldn't lose control like that ever again. Never. Not after what happened with Brian Barton.

I told you. He was one of the guys Zadie dated briefly in college, although it wouldn't have been brief if things had gone the way Zadie had wanted. Brian was Coach Barton's son. Assistant Coach Barton. Brian didn't actually go to Albright. He was older than us but not that much older. Already had his degree but not a job, so he was always hanging around his dad at training and games. And I guess he was sort of cute. Could look a bit like Matt Smith if you squinted, David Tennant if you were drunk—Zadie's joke, not mine. I've seen like two episodes of *Doctor Who.* Anyway I immediately pegged him for a loser. Who graduates but then hangs around with their dad and a bunch of college-age girls? Which I suppose is unfair to Brian because he didn't hang around us. He kept his distance. Genuinely helped his dad out with team-related stuff. And he wasn't there all the time, I guess. Just some of the time.

Anyway, I didn't realize he and Zadie got to know each other until the start of our sophomore year, after the team was disbanded. Honestly, I don't think they spoke much at all before that. But Zadie came back to the dorm one day and said she'd bumped into Coach Barton's son at the Sheetz and they had started chatting about how terrible it was that the team was gone, and Zadie said they should go to a bar to drink to its passing, and she had meant, like, the whole team but Brian interpreted it as just him and her and he smiled and said he'd like that, and Zadie, she said she felt so comfortable talking to him, there in the Sheetz without his dad around, that she hadn't even realized how much time had passed, so she didn't correct him and they exchanged numbers and made plans for the next night.

It didn't seem weird to me or anything. I said Brian wasn't that much older than us. Four years? Five at the most. And I never got any creepy vibes from him. Coach Barton wasn't our coach anymore, anyway, not that it would've mattered, but still.

She and Brian didn't see each other every week, not at first, but two or three times a month at least, and they were texting all the time. Then, after winter break, they started seeing each other more. Like, a lot more. I never wanted all of the details. That would've bored the shit out of me, but Zadie was my best friend, so I never shut her down when she wanted to talk about their latest date or what he'd said that day. One day in February, when she got to a stopping point after rambling on about their date the night before, I asked what I always asked, which was a running joke we had.

I asked, "So how long's this one gonna last?"

Zadie's response was always, "Oh, another day or so."

This time she didn't say anything. I had been working on a paper or something, and I looked up, and Zadie was staring into space with this dreamy look in her eye. Finally, she said, "I don't know. Everything feels different with Brian. I don't know. I think . . ."

She didn't finish her sentence. Just let it go and laughed and changed the subject. But I knew what she was going to say. "I think I love him." And I was happy for her. I really was.

But then the *very* next day, Zadie left to meet him for their date. It was supposed to be Thai food and a movie or something. I was still working on this paper when suddenly, she was back way sooner than she was supposed to be. I didn't look up at first. The flu had been going around, so I assumed maybe Brian got sick and had to cancel. And then, when I did look up, I saw her crying. I mean, tears all over her face. Her eyes were already swollen because she'd been crying so much.

I was up out of my chair like that, and I was asking her, "What happened? Did he hurt you? What did he do?"

I was thinking the worst because I had never seen Zadie this upset. And she started shaking her head and said no, Brian didn't do anything. She didn't even see him. He wasn't at the restaurant.

So then I was thinking, he stood her up? But I couldn't imagine Zadie getting this upset over that. Angry, definitely, but she didn't look angry. She looked, well, broken. And I wanted to keep her talking, to help calm her down, get some answers. So I just repeated what she said.

"He wasn't at the restaurant? You didn't see him?" And she shook her head no. So then I was like, "Who *was* at the restaurant?"

I was racking my brain trying to figure out who Zadie might've seen that would get her this upset, and I honestly couldn't think of anyone.

Then she said, "Coach Barton."

I was like, "Coach Barton? Why was he there?"

And then she told me what happened.

The gist of it was, apparently, Brian never told his dad that he was dating anyone. On purpose. He'd kept it a secret. But Coach Barton found out. And as soon as she got to the restaurant, Coach Barton started yelling at her.

He'd gone in place of Brian and called her all sorts of nasty names. Berated her ten times worse than anything he had ever said to us on the field. "Whore" and "slut" and "jezebel" and all those stereotypical slurs men use to make themselves feel better. Then, he started talking about Zadie's mom. How her mom was a drug addict and scum and Zadie's no better and he won't have her kind fucking up his son. And he was saying all of this to her *in the middle of the restaurant*, pointing at her and asking the patrons if they'd want their child dating a drug addict's whore daughter. Zadie was paralyzed, she said. She couldn't yell back at him like she used to during training. She was just frozen. Because he was screaming all of these things at her that she'd secretly thought herself. That she'd never be good enough for anyone. That she wasn't good enough to be loved. Ever. Which is what her mom would say to her when she was high. Her deepest fear, and Coach Barton was shouting it in her face in the middle of a crowded Thai restaurant. Zadie loved Thai food. She hasn't eaten it since.

Finally, she ran. She didn't know what else to do, she said, so she ran and didn't stop until she made it back to our room.

I sat with her all night and let her cry and talked about whatever she wanted and watched whatever she wanted, and I thought, *I'll help her through this. I'll help her get over this, and everything is going to be fine.* It was bad, but she'd be fine.

It took a week for me to realize she wasn't fine.

Coach Barton and I had our issues. I've never denied that. He may have only been the assistant coach, but he had our head coach's ear. So I know it was Barton's fault I ended up a backup my first—and what turned out to be only—year. I was a starter. I was always a starter. But when Barton saw me panicking in the locker room with Zadie trying to comfort me, I was knocked down to backup. I don't know why he didn't like me. I never did anything to him. But everything I seemed to do or say rubbed him the wrong way.

So yeah, when Zadie told me she had bumped into Brian Barton and then they started dating? I wasn't that happy about it. But I know as well as anyone that kids aren't their parents, and Brian did seem to be making Zadie happy, so I stayed out of it. But after what Coach Barton did to her in that restaurant? Humiliated her like that? I've never hated a person more in my entire life. If Zadie had gotten over it, if she'd bounced back like with most things, that would've been the end of it. I would've let it go.

But she didn't.

She stopped showering. Wouldn't eat. Started missing class. Didn't turn in assignments. Even then, I thought she'd be fine. I thought she'd come out of it.

Then I got back to our room late one night. I had been at this study session. I closed the door and said hi and set my bag on the floor, and I thought Zadie was just lying on her bed. But then I smelled the vomit. Zadie was passed out and she was all pale and clammy. Without thinking, I grabbed her and got her down to the showers, and I put her in a stall and soaked her with water. I didn't know if it should be cold or warm, but it was cold to start with and I called her name and I started tapping her face and she started to come around. Then someone came into the showers, but I shoved them out and said "Showers are closed" and blocked the door with the trash can and went back to Zadie, who was looking around to see where she was but not really trying to sit up or anything. I crouched beside her in the shower, the water was still running, getting both of us soaked. We sat for a while, and finally I said, "He's not worth it. I promise he's not worth it."

She was quiet for a little while longer. Then she said, "I wasn't trying to . . . I just wanted to know what it was like not to feel. I wanted to know why my mom likes not feeling."

What could I say to that?

After a while, she felt like she could stand, so I turned off the water and helped her back to our room—dripping wet the whole way because I hadn't brought any towels or anything. We locked ourselves in our room and got into dry clothes and piled the wet ones—mine and hers—together in the corner. I kept asking her if we should go to the hospital, and she kept saying no. She looked a lot less pale but still just as sad. Eventually, she slept, but I stayed awake the whole night, just in case.

Do you know what it's like, watching someone you love, someone who's a sister to you in all but blood, what it's like to watch them for hours knowing how much pain they're in? The worst kind of pain they've felt in their entire life? And you can't do anything but watch them and feel the hurt they feel? And no matter how much you suffer, it's only a fraction of what they're going through, and you think, *Oh, my god, if it hurts this much for me, what must it be like for them?* You want nothing more than to take that pain away, and knowing you can't only makes it worse. It makes you angry. Every ounce of hurt you feel gets channeled into anger. Not all at once. Just a little bit at a time. Like little grains of sand falling in an hourglass until half of you is filled with anger and the other half feels empty.

I didn't go to class. I told our friends we'd both come down with the flu and asked if they could leave food at our door. We were always together, so of course they believed me. I didn't want to leave Zadie's side. I couldn't. I made excuses to my professors, and I didn't worry about my assignments because I already knew then it wasn't going to matter. I wouldn't be coming back. Zadie slept a lot, and ate a little of the food our friends brought us. I ate a lot. I thought if she saw me eating, it would encourage her to do the same, or something. And we kept going like that until finally I felt safe enough to leave her.

That night, I waited until she was asleep, and then I left. It felt like I was someone else. Or like, someone else had taken over my body, like the anger had become its own person. I don't know if I had control or not. I always knew what I was doing. I saw myself doing it. I let myself go through with the actions. I just didn't feel myself doing it. Any of it. Almost like when I watched a recording of one of my games. I saw myself on the screen, I remembered doing those actions during the game, but at that moment, just watching, I couldn't feel any of it.

So that night I watched as my body—my anger—burned that fucker's house to the ground.

Of course, Coach Barton was the first one out. Selfish piece of shit. He just stood there like the cowardly little fucker he is and eventually Brian made it out with his mom, and they were looking for their dog, but I was holding their dog because obviously I had made sure their dog wouldn't get hurt. As they watched the fire take everything from them, their dog yipped and somehow Coach Barton heard it over the sound of the flames and the sirens. He turned around and saw me standing there holding their dog. He didn't say anything. Just stood there and gaped like a fish. In the light from the fire, I saw how nervous he was. I put a finger to my lips. I'm not sure if he saw me, to be honest. I think he did, but it was dark and the smoke and the distraction of the fire, it probably obscured my face. So I'm not sure if he knew it was me. He never talked about me to the police or anything. He never tried to seek me out. Or maybe he did see it was me and he was too scared to say anything. Men like him usually turn out to be cowards.

I tied their dog's leash around a tree so he wouldn't run off, and then I walked back to the dorm. Dropped the green lighter I'd used into a trash can on my way back.

I had already changed clothes by the time Zadie woke up.

She was asleep the whole time. She had no idea. It wasn't her idea. It was mine, and I did it alone. I'm sure she would've tried to stop me if she'd known, which is why I didn't tell her beforehand.

I've replayed that night in my head a lot. Sometimes, I remember things differently. Sometimes, I remember being in Coach Barton's bedroom, standing over him in the darkness with a gas can and willing myself not to douse him. Sometimes, I remember going to Jeremy's after and changing clothes there. Sometimes, I remember Jeremy helping me spread gas over the backyard and in the doorways. Sometimes, I think it was Jeremy who held the dog while the fire blazed and Jeremy who had to pull me away from watching the flames. And that Jeremy warned Coach Barton not to say anything to anyone. But I think I just dreamed those moments. I don't think they were real.

Who told Coach Barton that Zadie and Brian were dating?

I have no idea.

So now you know why, when Zadie first saw the burn barrel last night, she thought it was me. But it wasn't. I hadn't been in those woods since I was a kid. Someone else set that fire.

I lean over the barrel, and it feels like someone's watching. It's dark, so Zadie shines the light from her phone over my shoulder and onto the ashes.

I pick up a stick and start poking around the ashes, and I stir up this piece of fabric. I pluck it out, and I can see part of the Adidas logo.

Zadie starts calling my name, saying it's time to go, we need to go.

But I'm staring at this scrap, telling her, "This is Gemma's bag. It's Gemma's. This is the bag I buried. We buried it. What the fuck is it doing burned up behind Jeremy's house?"

And she's saying, "Leave it for the police. Let's go to the police and tell them what happened. Let's tell the police everything that's happened tonight."

Only Gemma and I knew where that bag was. And until last night, when I drove Zadie out to that farm, I hadn't told anyone. But Gemma must've said something. It confirms what I've suspected since the river—that Gemma is alive and she helped Jeremy plan these sightings. Gemma concocted this bizarre story and got Jeremy to convince Sarah it was true.

You never found any evidence of what happened to Gemma, right? And Jeremy was supposedly the last person to see her, right? So what Jeremy and Sarah told me at the river really was a lie. Gemma is alive. And she must be close.

So I tell Zadie, "We need to finish searching the house."

That fucking bag.

Burying that bag was the last thing Gemma asked me to help her with. It was the last time we were alone together.

I should've stopped helping Gemma before then, but I didn't. I didn't have anyone else then.

Zadie was the one person I thought would always be there for me. And she is. She wouldn't have come with me last night if she wasn't. But at the time, I didn't know if she'd ever speak to me again. It felt like the only person I had left was Gemma. Zadie wasn't talking to me and neither was Sarah, really, and my parents were down in Florida pretending they didn't have kids because it was "better for Mom's mental health."

But Gemma was there. Gemma would talk to me and Gemma would listen. So it was Gemma I talked to and Gemma I would listen to. When she told me we had to borrow Jeremy's car again, that there was a place we had to drive to and that we had to take the money with us, I didn't feel like I had a choice.

I didn't feel safe driving. I was so tired I was practically seeing things, and my hands were jittery and shaking. I was afraid I'd accidentally jerk the car off the side of the road or something. But Gemma told me it would be fine. It was late, hardly anyone would be on the road. There was nothing to worry about.

The bag in the back seat made me nervous. It looked like a normal gym bag and it was zipped shut, but there was something about it now. Whenever I glanced at the back seat, it wasn't just a bag. It was this bulky, heavy thing. The stains were more like bruises. The money poking at the fabric from inside made weird lumps that looked like swollen tumors. I could swear it was going to groan or something, like it hurt. Like it could feel pain.

Which of course it couldn't. It was just a bag. And all that was inside was some money. That's what I assumed.

I could feel it the whole time we drove. Like it was breathing down the back of my neck.

I hadn't looked at the clock before we left, but it was two in the morning when she told me to stop. I remember because I looked at the clock then, and it said 2:00, on the dot.

We were on a narrow road in the countryside somewhere, and when I opened the door, I could smell cows or sheep, although I didn't hear any animal noises.

"What are we doing here, Gemma?" I asked, but she didn't answer. She went into the back seat for the bag, then picked something up off the floor of the car, which I hadn't realized was there. A shovel.

"This way," she said. The bag seemed heavier now. It took the two of us to carry it into the field that was near where we'd parked.

"Now that I have everything I need, we can end this," she said. "This will protect us both."

I didn't say anything. I just let her speak.

"I can't hold on to the money any longer, and I can't give it to you."

It was so dark, and Gemma said we needed to leave our phones at home, so we didn't have anything as a flashlight. But I never asked her how she knew where we were going. Gemma always knew, and I knew better than to ask.

"We're giving it to the earth," she said.

She didn't say anything more until we stopped walking. My eyes had adjusted a bit to the dark by then, and I could tell we were next to an old stone wall, underneath a tree. The bag thudded against the ground when we set it down.

"We're going to bury the money here," she said. "We'll bury it and let the earth have it, and then neither of us will have to worry about it anymore. This field is barren, no one will dig here. No one will plow. No one will find it. That's why it's perfect. It can't kill what's already dead."

She pointed to a spot, and I started digging. The ground was full of rocks and roots from the dead tree. My shoulders were aching, and I was getting blisters on my hands. I thought Gemma would offer to take turns, but she didn't and I didn't ask. It was like I couldn't say anything. Like I wasn't in control of my own body.

Finally, she told me the hole was deep enough. I crawled out and crouched down by the bag to unzip it. I figured if she wanted the money to decompose, it would be better if we tossed it into the dirt, but Gemma grabbed my hand.

"Don't!" she said. "Just take the whole thing."

So I sighed and dragged the bag over. It was really heavy, maybe too heavy. But my arms were tired from shoveling, so it was hard to tell. I pushed the bag in. Then she had me cover it up with the dirt. When I finished and stood up, she put her hands on my shoulders.

"Promise me," she said, "if anything happens to me, you won't come back here. You won't open the bag. This has to end here. Promise me."

And I did.

She cupped my face in her hands and looked me in the eye and said, "You've been such a good friend."

Then she took something from her pocket and pressed it into my hand.

"I don't think I'll need this now," she said. Then she smiled and walked back to the car.

When I got near the car, I could see from the headlights what she'd put in my hand. It was the fake driver's license with my name on it. Gemma's picture had been scratched out. You could see the hair, but the face was completely gone.

I put it in my pocket, and then I drove us back home while she told me the way.

No, I don't have it anymore. I threw it away.

But I kept my promise. I never went back there until last night. I never looked in the bag. I never saw the money again. But somehow the bag ended up in a firepit behind Jeremy's house.

I don't own an Apple AirTag. I never go anywhere. Why would I need one?

No, I didn't find one in the ashes. That's what Jeremy is saying? Gemma put an AirTag in the bag and that's how he knew where to find it once he was able to unlock her phone? That he only wanted to find the bag because he was trying to protect Sarah? That he was trying to protect *me?*

Fuck no. The only way Jeremy knew to find the bag is because Gemma must have told him. I don't believe any story about an AirTag. And Gemma didn't have a phone. I never saw one. How many times do I have to tell you that? Even if she did, why would Jeremy have it?

The only thing in that bag was the money. I know it. That's it. Whatever else Jeremy is saying is a fucking lie.

Go look through the barrel yourself. The fire couldn't have been that hot if there were still pieces of the bag left. Not hot enough to burn an AirTag. Definitely not hot enough to burn anything else.

No, Zadie and I didn't take the bag. We leave what's left of it where it is and go back inside. At this point, we don't think Jeremy's in the house, but we haven't checked upstairs, and we don't feel like we can leave until we know. Jeremy's house has three rooms upstairs—two bedrooms and a bathroom. I go up first, Zadie behind me. There's a light in the hall at the top, and with my feet still on the top step, I reach out and flick the switch.

There's no one in the hall, and both bedroom doors are closed. The bathroom door, which is right in front of me, is only half-open and dark. We check there first. I push the door in the rest of the way, thinking maybe I should have a weapon or something, then switch on the light.

There's a damp, moldy smell, some dirty, crusty towels on the floor, toothpaste staining the sink, beard hair from Jeremy's razor, but nothing out of the ordinary. Nothing that says he'd been there recently. So, no, there isn't anything to indicate he'd showered and changed before coming to see you. At least not there.

We leave the bathroom light on and stand in the hall. Zadie's waiting for me to say what we should do. The bedroom to the left was Aunt Mel's. The bedroom to the right is Jeremy's. I figure, out of habit, if he came home exhausted, he would've just gone to his bedroom. You know, muscle memory. So that's where we go next. I press my ear against the door. Listen. I don't hear anything. I look at Zadie, she nods, and I slowly open the door.

It creaks.

We stand in the doorway. The backlighting from the hallway would've made it difficult for Jeremy, for anyone, to see our faces. But there's no one in there. Jeremy's bed is neatly made. Everything is clean in Jeremy's room. Like, it's the complete opposite of the rest of the house. Everything super neat and tidy, the way Jeremy normally likes it.

We leave the light on and head back to the final door—the master bedroom. If he's here, that's the only other place he could be. His house doesn't have a basement, and the attic is just a small crawl space.

We walk down the hall together. I listen. Nothing. I open the door.

The rooms are at the opposite ends of the hall and mirror one another. I've always found it a bit disorienting. How similar they are to one another—mirror images. So when we open the door, it's like looking into a mirror of Jeremy's room, a mirror into a different dimension. There are things everywhere, like they've just been tossed inside because he didn't know where else to put them. Not trash, really. Clothes and bags and candles. And then everything starts to look familiar.

Zadie finds a plastic bag of greenish-white powder, opens it, and takes a sniff. "Is this . . . I think this is mescaline."

In the far corner, near the head of the bed, I notice a beat-up reusable grocery store bag. I look inside. The name Baker is written on the inside edge.

"This was Gemma's," I say.

And Zadie says, "Maybe he borrowed it?"

I start looking around the room for more. I see the Ouija board and the candles we used at the church. And Gemma's book—the old one with the fancy cover that she used for the séance. I pick it up and open it. But it's just a massive car manual with yellowed pages. The cover is fake. I set it down.

"She was here," I say. "He was lying. She's been here all along. That's why her stuff is here. It's not 'cause he and Sarah were trying to hide it from the police. Everything Sarah said at the river, she was making it all up. Gemma's alive."

And Zadie asks, "What did Sarah say at the river? What was Sarah making up? Tell me what happened tonight. Tell me the truth."

And I'm about to answer when I notice some clothes I haven't seen in a while. Skinny jeans and a sky-blue sweater.

Yes, Sarah's clothes from the night she and Gemma went out and Gemma didn't come back.

Yes, there's blood on them.

There's blood all over them.

That's what you've been waiting for me to say, isn't it?

But it's not what you think.

VERSION 5

I don't know if it means anything that Gemma gave me that fake driver's license back. Maybe she did something like that to everyone. Made them feel they were special to her but then later ... If someone had that box, they could trace back her victims to the start.

But that box disappeared just like she did.

No. I swear, what Jeremy's telling you is a lie. Zadie and I didn't ditch his car somewhere. Why would we do that? We had no reason to get rid of his car. It's not evidence of anything. And he's wrong about my bedroom. I didn't trash my own room. I went straight from the river to Zadie's. I didn't have time to stop at the apartment in between. I don't remember doing that.

Zadie must've got her times wrong. Or I had my times wrong. Why would I do that to my own room? I honestly don't remember it. Why would I be so angry I'd do that?

No, Gemma has to be alive. She must have faked her disappearance with Jeremy's help. She took him to the farm to get the money back. She manipulated all of this to tie up one more loose end—me.

Sarah's clothes? I don't know. Maybe Gemma convinced her to help, too. Maybe Gemma used Sarah's baby as blackmail or something.

Please, you have to understand. None of this was Sarah's idea. It couldn't have been. And Jeremy hasn't been trying to protect her or me. He's lying. He's the one responsible for everything. Him and Gemma.

No, what Sarah said at the river, when we were fighting, that's not what she meant. She didn't know what she was saying. She was confused. Sarah's not like that. She's not. She's . . .

No, I didn't kill the Horne girl. I told you I never even looked in that bag before Gemma and I buried it. I had no idea what was inside. There couldn't have been a body.

If Jeremy had found that bag himself and opened it and saw a body, he wouldn't have gotten rid of it. He would have called the police—you. All he found was the money. And he only found the bag because Gemma helped him. She's here, and she's manipulating everything.

No, I didn't hit Sarah!

I've only been trying to protect her.

From you.

From what she thinks she did.

I told you, ever since Jeremy showed up at the apartment last night, he and Sarah were giving each other these weird little glances and talking in hushed angry whispers when they thought I couldn't hear. And it got worse as the night went on. They kept getting angrier with each other.

I saw how they were trying to argue without me seeing. I knew they were keeping something from me. I didn't bring it up because I didn't care, not until we got to the river. Because it was all right driving around to different places in town looking for Gemma's "ghost," but after this supposed sighting led us to the middle of nowhere, in the middle of the night, and they weren't telling me why, I had enough. I'd had enough with Gemma, and I wasn't going to go through that again.

By the time we get to the river, I'm yelling at both of them. I'm telling them this is stupid, I don't want to be here. I want to go home. I want to go to bed. I'm exhausted. Don't they understand? I'm so fucking tired.

But they aren't listening to me. They're just arguing with each other, Jeremy saying they should tell me, and Sarah telling him to shut up. There is so much shouting in the car. As soon as Jeremy stops—before it's even in park—I jump out.

It's so much quieter out there. I can still hear them, but it's so much quieter. When they do get out, it's like they've come to some sort of decision. And Sarah's lip is already bleeding.

I did *not* hit her. I didn't. I never touched her.

They're standing there, staring at me, but I don't want to hear what they have to say. I just want it to stay quiet. I keep saying, "I don't care. I don't want to know. I don't care why we're here. I don't want to know."

It's Jeremy who says, "Gemma's here."

And I throw out my arms, wide, like this, and I say, "Where? We've been hunting for her all night. So where is she? I don't see her."

And that's when Jeremy opens the trunk and pulls out the shovel. The same one Gemma and I used at the farm.

And Jeremy says, "Her body. Her body is here. I'll show you where it's buried."

I don't move. I look at Sarah, and I say, "Sarah, this is ridiculous."

But she doesn't say anything. She's hugging herself, her belly sticking out from under her arms. She doesn't even want to look at me. And I say, "Sarah, what's he talking about?"

When Sarah starts talking, this dribble of snot starts coming down her nose. She looks cold, but I know that's not why she's shaking.

Sarah says, "She was so mean. She was so mean to everyone. She was so mean to you. Especially you. Didn't you see it? You had to see it."

I don't like the way she's talking. I don't like how her voice sounds. But she keeps talking.

She says, "There was something wrong with her. She kept telling me these awful things. Kept threatening me. Saying she was going to tell Shane's wife about me. She bought me that gift card for Giorgio's to mock me. Because she'd seen me and Shane eating there. Knew he liked to take me there because it was a quiet spot where no one would see. But worse than that . . . she . . . she kept making up these awful stories about you."

I think of the money, the rat. I think, *Did Gemma tell Sarah everything?*

Sarah says, "She made up this story about how you got me fired from the club, how you stole money from all those places you worked and how she's helped you pay it back in exchange for favors. She made up the most ridiculous story about why you left college. Like you would've ever done that to anyone, let alone your coach."

My heart stops. Full-on stops. I can't breathe.

I want her to stop talking. But I don't hit her.

I did not hit my sister.

All I do is shout, "Stop it!" again, and again, and again. And when my voice stops, it's quiet. The quietest it's been since Sarah came home and said she saw a ghost.

In that quiet, Sarah says, "She was a terrible person. Look what she made you do."

And I say, "She didn't make me do anything."

And Jeremy says, "I saw what was in the bag. We both did."

But I don't listen to him. Not really. I'm only looking at Sarah.

She's crying now, and she says, "I didn't mean for it to happen."

She says, "I just wanted her to leave. I thought if we were out in public, at a public place, she wouldn't cause a scene. So we went to Applebee's, and I told her she could get whatever she wanted, I was buying. I wanted to be nice about it. And she seemed like she was in a good mood. Almost too good. Like the way Mom gets when her meds aren't quite working. We didn't say much at first, and when our food came out, that's when I told her.

"I said, 'Gemma, I think it's time for you to move out.' And she laughed like I was joking and said, 'You think?' I said it again. I said, 'It is time for you to move out.' And she stared at me and there was . . . there was nothing in her eyes. They were just . . . dead. Like she didn't have a soul. And she said, 'You're very serious tonight, Sarah.' And I said, 'Yes, I am.' And then she didn't say anything else until she ate another chicken wing."

I want her to stop, but Sarah keeps going. She says, "I remember sitting there, waiting for her answer—a real answer—and she was just calmly chewing away and it made me sick. She wiped her mouth and she said, 'What if I don't want to go? What if I like playing with your sister? She's such an obedient little puppy.' That was exactly what she said. Talked about you like you were some sort of stupid dog. And it made me so angry. I wanted to take my Diet Coke and throw it in her face, but I didn't. I said, 'I know most of the money was counterfeit. I know you've been stalking this red-haired girl.' And she just smirked and said, 'Oh, little Sarah. You really don't know anything at all.' And she stood up and said, 'Let me remind you why I won't be doing anything you say. Come on.'"

And Sarah says, "She patted her leg like I was some little dog that was supposed to follow. Like she could treat me the way she's been treating you. I threw some money down on the table, and I followed her. I walked behind her the whole time. She never turned around. All I could see was the back of her head. It wasn't until we got there that I realized we were going to Garters and Lace. We didn't go in. We just stood across the street. And she kept her back to me, and she said, 'If you try to get me to leave before I'm ready, I'll tell everyone how you really got that job at Walmart. I'll tell everyone how you really met the manager, and what you've really been doing when you say you're picking up extra shifts. I'll tell everyone, including your sister. Including your manager's wife. I'll even tell that poor barren lady that you're carrying her husband's baby. Maybe they'll take the little bastard off your hands. What would your sister say to that? You shouldn't put so much stock in people who call you their sister, Sarah. Sisters will always let you down.'"

And Sarah says, "She wouldn't even look at me as she spoke. But I knew she was smiling. I could hear it in her voice. And she started saying something else, was trying to tell me what I was going to do for her, but I wasn't listening. They were redoing part of the retaining wall there, across from Garters and Lace, and there was a pile of bricks. I picked one up. I didn't think. I wasn't thinking. I picked one up, and I hit her in the back of the head. And she stumbled, and for the first time, she looked genuinely surprised. And she felt the back of her head and looked at the blood on her fingers, and she said, 'How about that?' Her speech was slurred, and I could have stopped. But I didn't. I hit in her in the face. Twice. And then she fell down. And I kept hitting her in the face. And I hit her, and I hit her, and I hit her until . . . until she didn't have a face."

And Sarah says, "Then I realized what happened. I realized what I'd done. There was so much blood. On my hands. On my clothes. I didn't know what to do, so I called Jeremy. I told him there'd been an accident. And Jeremy drove over and . . . and we put Gemma in the car, and we were both panicking, so we drove to the Tavern because we knew it'd be quiet there this time of night. And Jeremy went in to get those heavy-duty trash bags, and we put Gemma inside one, and I thought I heard Aunt Joanie on the stairs but we didn't see anyone, so we carried the bag out to the car and then Jeremy dropped me off at his house so I could change while he went to the river, and once I changed, I got an Uber home. I had the brick in my purse. I don't even remember putting it there. But I found it the next morning. It was covered in blood, and there were bits of . . . bone stuck to it. I hid it in my room because I didn't know what else to do with it."

This is what Sarah says to me at the river.

I look at Jeremy. He's nodding.

And then he says, "I told her we needed to get rid of it. And anything else of Gemma's. She was using me, too. I didn't realize it until Sarah told me everything that had been going on. So we took all her stuff and we've stored it at my place, but we could never find that bag. We had her phone and I got the Davy boys to help me unlock it. Then I saw she had an AirTag that was named with just a dollar sign. I figured that was where she'd hid the bag with the money. I told Sarah we'd put the brick with the bag. Take the money out and replace it with the brick. But when we got there, when we dug up the bag . . . There wasn't money inside it anymore. We know you helped her with the bag, so we didn't want you to know we'd found it. We didn't want you to know we knew what she made you do. I thought I could protect you, like I've protected Sarah."

I try to say *I didn't do anything* but I can't get the words out. They think I'm a monster and they're okay with it. But I'm not a monster. I didn't do anything.

And then Sarah says, "I know you helped Gemma bury that bag because I saw you when you came back that night. I know what was really in the bag. But it's okay. It doesn't matter to us. We won't tell anyone. We got rid of it. Because we love you. We just want to protect you."

Sarah says, "But I want to check. I need to check that she's still here.

Because I've been . . . I really have been seeing her everywhere. And I don't . . . I just need to check that she's still here. Then we'll go home. Then we can go home."

And they stand there, waiting for me to answer.

But you have to understand, none of it makes sense. I can't . . . process any of this. Sarah would never. She couldn't. She's my little sister. All I can think is, I already knew who the father of Sarah's baby was. I knew she was seeing a married guy. Gemma couldn't have hurt Sarah by telling me that. She's my sister. I love her no matter what.

And it's because I love her so much that I can't believe anything she just said is true. It has to be a lie. Maybe she convinced herself that was what happened, but it wasn't what really happened. That's not how it happened. It can't be.

Jeremy must have done this. He's been mad at us ever since his dad died, and this is how he's getting back at us. He's not trying to protect me, or Sarah. He doesn't give a shit about family. He just wants to hurt us. He's still working with Gemma. This is all some part of her plan to get to me. And now Sarah's been dragged into it, too.

So the two of them are standing there watching me, waiting for me to say something. They want to show me Gemma's body and, if they do, that'll mean what Sarah said was true, but it can't be. There must be another reason they want to take me down to the river.

That's when I grab the shovel from Jeremy.

I yank it out of his hands, and I start running. I don't believe Sarah. I don't. Gemma must be out there. She has to be because Sarah couldn't have done what she said she did, and she couldn't think I was capable of doing what she thought, so I had to find Gemma, because if I found Gemma, it would prove she was still alive.

I leave the two of them behind, and when I turn back, I can't see them because of the dip of the embankment. I don't know where I'm going. I just know I need to find Gemma.

I don't know how long I was running for or how far I got. But I still have the shovel in my hands. I trip and fall and when I get back up, I look around and realize I can't see the car or Jeremy or Sarah. But I don't call out, because I don't want to see them. I don't.

I didn't hit Sarah. I didn't hurt Gemma Horne. I didn't hurt anyone. I took the shovel from Jeremy because I wanted to get rid of it. But I never hit him with it, and I never hit Sarah. I don't know how he got that bruise and cut on his forehead, but it wasn't from a shovel. I took the shovel from him and ran. That was it.

He's a liar. I told you that from the start. And you know he's a liar because you say he told you I hit Sarah, that he saw me do it, and I would never. Never. She's my sister. I love her. She's all I have. I'm going to be an aunt, and I'm going to help her raise the baby so she doesn't have to do it on her own, and if that means I have to take over the Tavern, then I'll take over the Tavern. That's how much I love her. Jeremy's a liar. I never hit Sarah.

I didn't hit her.

I grabbed the shovel from him, and I ran away, down to the river. That's when I saw . . . I swear, I thought I saw Gemma. And it freaked me the fuck out because she was just standing there in the headlights, with her back to me, like Sarah had described her.

So I dropped the shovel and ran to the car, because if Gemma was here, there was only one reason. She wanted me dead. She manipulated Jeremy and Sarah just like she'd manipulated me and Ian Baker and Gemma Horne, and now she was going to kill me. So I went after Gemma.

But I would never hurt Sarah.

I didn't hurt her.

I didn't hit her!

I got in the car and locked myself in, and the car was still running. I found Gemma's shirt in the footwell, like I said, and I bet it'll be in the car if you find it. I told you the car was stolen after I parked it at my apartment. Zadie and I didn't ditch it. Why would we do that? I told you. There's no reason for us to do that. The car would only help prove what really happened.

So I was freaked out and in the car, and Sarah said all these confusing things and I'm tired and cold and angry but mostly scared, and I just want to get away. I'm not thinking about leaving anyone behind. I'm thinking about getting away. I need to get away. As fast as I can.

When I put the car in gear, I see Gemma again. In the road, her back to me, wearing Sarah's clothes.

Gemma was always wearing our clothes because she didn't have any of her own.

Gemma is standing right there, and I know she wants to kill me.

So I drive. I close my eyes and drive.

I drive straight into the thing in the road.

And when I open them again, there isn't anything standing in the road anymore. It's gone.

You're trying to manipulate me, just like Gemma did. Trying to get me to believe something that isn't true. That's why you're showing me this picture. But I won't be tricked again.

You say this is a picture of Sarah. That this is Sarah in the road. That this is Sarah's body and Sarah is dead, and Jeremy says he saw me hit Sarah with his car, and Zadie helped me get rid of the car, and we went to his house to plant evidence. But it's all lies. He's lying. You're lying. Yeah, that's what Sarah was wearing, but look, you can't see this girl's face. She's turned away from the camera and you can't see her face, so how do I know that's Sarah? That could be anybody. You're making this up. It's all a fucking lie.

I never hit Sarah. I would never hurt her. I couldn't.

I didn't hit anything! I didn't. Because there was nothing there to hit! Nobody was in the road. I was imagining things.

Sarah's out there somewhere, so can we please go find her? Please?

She's out there all alone and she's looking for me, and she needs me and something bad's going to happen to her if we don't find her. I need to find her. Please.

Please.

This isn't Sarah. This can't be Sarah.

But something bad will happen to Sarah if I don't find her. I know it.

Something bad will happen, and it'll be all Gemma's fault.

ACKNOWLEDGMENTS

I've been very fortunate to have had pretty good roommates. There was a time during a study abroad semester in college when things got a little iffy, but . . . Anyway, thank you to everyone who has been my roommate at one point in time or another, especially Jannicke Bevan de Lange and Cathrine K. de Lange. (I was the weirdo who moved in with two sisters, although our experience living together was nothing like the one in this book. I mean, at least from my perspective.) If you have the opportunity to move to another country to live with your best friend whom you met on the internet, I highly recommend it.

Thank you also to Cal Barksdale, Jesse McHugh, and the team at Arcade Crimewise for bringing Gemma to life (even if no one should really have a Gemma in their lives). Thanks, also, to my agent Sandra Sawicka and everyone at Marjacq. And to Sarah L. Blair for reading a very early draft of this and letting me know it didn't suck.

Thank you to Hyun Davidson for sharing fancy cocktails, The X-Files, and knowing how to use GrubHub. (I promise your husband's name will end up in the next book—you know what I mean.) Thank you to my family—Mom, Cherie, and Lindsey—for again allowing me to steal some small tidbits from our lives and use them for creative purposes. (Just wait until you see the next book.) And another big thank you to Mom for my love of the Phillies and taking me to games at Veterans Stadium the very first summer of my life. (Anyone who brought an infant to the Vet deserves props.) Thank you to the Phillies for 1980 and 2008 (and every other season, too). Thank you to the Reading Phillies and FirstEnergy Stadium, my second home during the summer, which has been part of my family since my grandpa help build the stadium's original brick walls.

Thank you to my dogs Gizmo, Watson, and Milton, the ultimate writing buddies. And finally thank you to my Harry, named for Harry Kalas, who taught the other three boys everything they know, who was with me at the start of this book but not at the finish. Love you, buddy.